69 Day Run

A Sea Story About Winning the Cold War

How America's Heroes Triumphed in our Longest Conflict

and

Why it Matters More Than Ever Today

Edward L. Bartlett Jr.

69 Day Run
A Sea Story About Winning the Cold War
*How America's Heroes Triumphed in our Longest Conflict
and Why it Matters More Than Ever Today*

Published by Focsle LLP, Annapolis, Maryland

ISBN: 979-8-9860857-6-0 (Hardcover)
ISBN: 979-8-9860857-7-7 (Paperback)
ISBN: 979-8-9860857-8-4 (eBook)

Library of Congress Control Number: 2023923538

This book is, in part or in whole, a work of fiction, except as discussed immediately below. Certain facts included in this book are incorporated, in keeping with the longstanding nautical tradition of *Sea Stories*, to provide a foundation upon which this fictional characters and story have been crafted by the author. The author is solely responsible for, and regrets, any inadvertent factual errors or omissions. Except for the inclusion of the book's fictional characters and the events directly related to these fictional characters, Chapters 2, 14, 16, 28 and 29 are non-fiction and are based upon the author's research and decades of experience in the submarine business. Further information is provided in the "Fact vs. Fiction; the Fictional Characters" section at the end of the book.

Photo and Other Exhibit Credits and Disclaimers

- The two tables included in Chapter 2 were developed by the author using data from official US Navy websites, principally the Naval Vessel Register at www.nvr.navy.mil. The analysis was conducted by the author, who accepts responsibility for any transposition or other analytical errors. The conclusions developed and presented related to these tables are solely the author's own.

- The noted and attributed discussions concerning the loss of USS THRESHER (SSN 593) and USS SCORPION (SSN 589) were sourced at/copied from the Wikipedia website (www.wikipedia.org). (https://en.wikipedia.org/wiki/USS_Thresher_(SSN-593)) and (https://en.wikipedia.org/wiki/USS_Scorpion_(SSN-589))

- Cover Photo, and GATO photos which are not specifically attributed are readily and freely available at multiple public internet sites. This includes official US Navy-originated photos.

- All photos and other graphical/visual items which are not specifically attributed are readily and freely available at multiple public internet sites. This includes official US Navy-originated photos.

- GATO swim call and departure program – author's private collection.

- Images of the Author, Admiral Frank Bowman, USN(Ret), Mr. John Alden and CDR Richard Severinghaus, USN(Ret) provided by the subjects of the image.

- GATO commissioning announcement, commissioning ship leadership plaque, christening and commissioning photos provided by General Dynamics Electric Boat.

- Within the book there are several images with specific website attributions. These images are freely available at the attributed websites.

- The concept of a "black inky abyss" was shared with the author many years ago by Mary. *Thank you for this and for your contribution to other less specifically identifiable elements of this story.*

- The appearance of any and all US Navy or DoD photos, visual information or other material in this book does not imply or constitute US Navy or DoD endorsement of this book or any related information included herein.

- The views expressed in this publication are those of the author and do not necessarily reflect the official policy or position of the Department of Defense or the U.S. Government.

- This book received a pre-publication review by the Defense Office of Prepublication and Security Review to verify that it contains no classified information. This book was approved for publication on that basis in Department of Defense, Defense Office of Prepublication and Security Review letter Ref: 23-SB-0176 dated October 31, 2023. The public release clearance of this publication by the Department of Defense does not imply Department of Defense endorsement of factual accuracy of the material.

Dedication

This book is dedicated first to my immediate family. In particular, this book is dedicated to my wife Lisa and to my 5 children. From youngest to oldest they are my daughters Abigail and Jennifer and my sons John, Christopher, and Edward (Ted).

This book is also dedicated to the brave men and women who have sailed America's nuclear-powered submarines in both peace and in war. Without the fanfare of other similarly risky endeavors such as the space program, the submarine force has silently soldiered on in success – delivering for America 24-7-365 in ways that _Blind Man's Bluff_ never comes close to describing. Most particularly and specifically, though, this book is dedicated to the 229 men who have lost their lives in the four horrific nuclear submarine accidents discussed in this book. From 1963 at the dawn of the nuclear submarine age through the chaotic days of program growth and shakeout in the late 1960's and on until 2021, these four accidents serve to remind all submariners just what they are doing and risking every single day – and should serve to remind all Americans of the sacrifices made by all submariners.

Now on eternal patrol, may they rest in peace and enjoy the Grace of God.

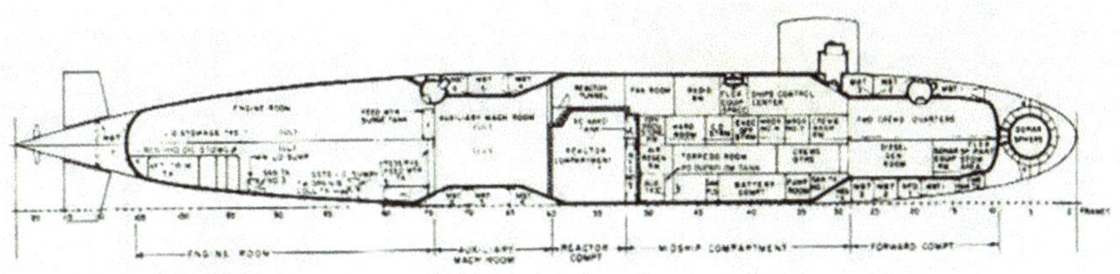

THRESHER Class Submarine USS GATO (SSN 615)
– The Black Cat –

Author's Note

This book covers a period when the Submarine Force was an exclusively male domain. Much has changed in the more than 35 years since the deployment memorialized here in *Sea Story* format, including welcoming women to the Submarine Force. The author joins submariners, both active and former, in celebrating this progress.

As this book was completed, the Navy's first female submarine Executive Officer had just reported for duty. On the surface, the first woman in command of an aircraft carrier has completed her first deployment in command.

Despite the many changes over the more than 35 years since this deployment, however, fundamental underlying principles remain both immutable and key to current and future success. To best express these fundamental underlying principles, and to give the reader the most authentic possible experience and true sense of history, the author has chosen to simply let the story speak for itself, with no cultural or other "updating." It is 1985, the Cold War is at its peak. This is exactly the way it was. . .

Buckle up and enjoy the trip onboard the mighty mighty warship GATO – for I certainly did. ELB

*"World War 2 Medal of Honor recipient Vice Admiral Lawson P. "Red"
Ramage, USN and his wife Barbara A. Ramage as she prepares and
then christens USS GATO (SSN 615) at launch from General Dynamics
Electric Boat in Groton, CT on May 14, 1964. The final ship of the
THRESHER Class to be commissioned, GATO was launched 13 months
after USS THRESHER (SSN 593) was lost, with 129 souls onboard, on
April 10, 1963 during sea trials following shipyard maintenance."*

Imagine, for a Moment . . .

You are dancing on a razor-sharp knife edge for days, weeks, even months at a time, with no breaks. On either side of this razor-sharp knife edge is a black, inky abyss. On one side the abyss offers certain, instantaneous death. On the other side the abyss offers certain mission failure, with consequences that include unacceptable damage to everything that you love in life, on up to – *in the limit* – the end of the world (Armageddon, in <u>literal</u> terms).

Does this sound like anything that you want to run right out and sign up for?

Well, when an American military member "steps into the breach" and goes to the front lines of a battle this is precisely what they are doing – and have done since the opening Battles of Lexington and Concord during the American Revolution. This is not a trivial matter, asking our youth to take up these burdens of Freedom for the rest of us. Yet, as our heroic youth have always done, our heroic youth will continue to do this with dignity and pride.

This, my friends, is what you are "thanking" a veteran for when you thank them for their service. You are thanking them for heroically dancing on the knife-edge, for staring down at that black inky abyss on either side, and for persevering and succeeding. This is no small matter; respect it; never ever trivialize it.

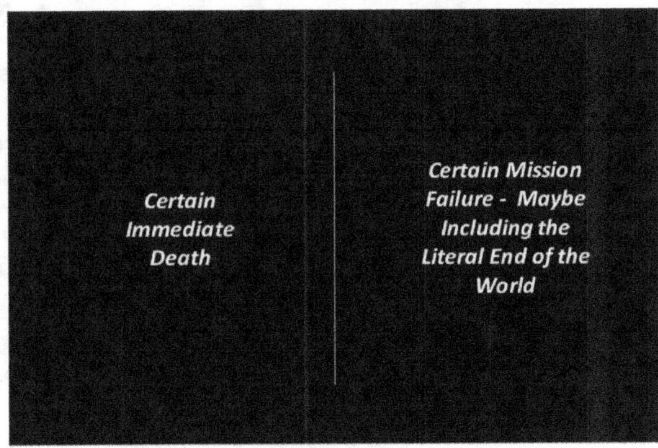

Consequences:
Dancing on a Razor-Sharp Knife Edge

On Sea Stories

Sea Stories are a very special form of literature, uniquely melding fictional hyperbole into a fact-filled basic story to create a fantastical, but plausible yarn. Sea Stories, both oral and written, are a long, storied nautical tradition.

For now, realize that **<u>69 Day Run</u>** *is of this genre, told by someone who enjoyed the privilege of being part of it all.*

In the fall of 1985 the United States nuclear-powered attack submarine USS GATO (SSN 615) did, in fact, exist. Further, GATO did, in fact, conduct an extended training exercise in the Western Atlantic region to evaluate the capability of an American nuclear-powered attack submarine to conduct independent operations for an extended period of time.

The rest of it?

Well, this story is a true NO SHITTER.

What, you say?

Well, I say, NO SHIT man, this is exactly how it happened! ! !

USS GATO (SSN 615)
Swim Call in the Bermuda Triangle
August 1985

The Essential Element

The Lone Sailor Statue
US Navy Memorial, Washington, D.C.
http://lonesailorshipstore.stores.yahoo.net/lonesailor.html

Sailors, Officer and Enlisted:
The ESSENTIAL ELEMENT of any ship.

594 Tough

The "Wild Animals" of the Submarine Force

USS GUARDFISH (SSN 612)

Thresher Class – Classic *Wild Animals*. "The sailors who served aboard them, either loved them or hated them for this trait, but the fact that they endured as frontline, first rate fast attack boats right up through their retirement, gives real meaning to the phrase "594 Tough." This phrase symbolizes both a respect for and/or hatred of a class of submarines, that like a wild animal, if not tamed, could bite the men who sailed in them, just as easily as their Soviet prey; indeed, as one crew paid the ultimate sacrifice. Still, these ships were the *Apex Predators* of their day. . .

Nevertheless, the phrase also symbolizes the type of men who went to sea in these boats and carried out hard assignments that very few in the US Military could handle. So, whether referring to the submarine or the sailor, they were and forever will remain 594 Tough." *(From a social media post, November 2022)*

"The fact is that, because they existed so close to the limits of physics – always operating with so very little margin for anything less than perfection from either their crew or their equipment

– *'unusual events,'* including emergency responses, only discussed theoretically and simulated in crew training on other submarine classes, were almost routine in 594 Tough World. A 594 Tough sailor had to be ready for absolutely anything at any moment." *(Related social media comment).*

"The phrase, "endured as frontline, first rate fast attack boats right up through their retirement" is what you've embodied in your book...," CDR Richard Severinghaus, USN (Ret), commissioning Commanding Officer, USS ANNAPOLIS (SSN 760), who served as a 594 Tough junior officer in USS GUARDFISH (SSN 612).

That all said, let's go then.

"Now Dive, Dive. Aooogah, Aooogah. Dive, Dive.

Diving Officer Make Your Depth
XXX feet. All Ahead Flank."

On with the story. . .

Prologue

We Go on Demand

Prologue

PCAN

*Saturday, August 24, 1985; Kennedy Space Center, Florida
at T-5 Minutes to launch, Space Shuttle Mission STS 51I*

"The damned countdown clock just stopped," exclaimed an exasperated GATO crew member.

"Well, I wonder what happened," replied another GATO crew member.

"This is Mission Control. The mission for today is scrubbed due to thunderstorms in the area. The mission clock will be reset, and we will launch tomorrow at the same time."

With that, about a dozen members of the crew of USS GATO (SSN 615) piled back into the Navy van and trekked back from the Kennedy Space Center, in the Merritt Island swamp, over to the ship, docked at Port Canaveral, out on the Atlantic side of the Intracoastal Waterway. Most of the intrepid

crew members who had ventured out in the pre-dawn hours to catch a glimpse – *from several miles away, in the swamp* – of the Space Shuttle Discovery's launch headed straight to the rack to get some sleep. You see, last night had been the first night in port after the stress of the annual weapons shoot and certification exam – and the crew had been out "steaming" in Port Canaveral. While they had had a brief swim call at sea after the weapons shoot and certification exam events had been completed, PCAN represented the first chance to really relax with the ship tied up to a pier.

For most of GATO's crew, the Friday night itinerary had included a stop to buy a T Shirt at the world-famous *Ron John* Surf Shop in Cocoa Beach, and then a *"well-lubricated"* dinner. Many, many beers were consumed; many sea stories were swapped. The stress associated with the annual weapons shoot and certification exam was "blown off" as the crew "steamed" the night away.

PCAN was a bit of a treat, you see, as Atlantic Fleet SSNs typically pulled in to PEV (Port Everglades, Fort Lauderdale) for the post-weapons shoot and certification exam liberty stop. Every Atlantic Fleet SSN sailor knows PEV like they know their homeport; PCAN was a bit of a *change of pace.* Usually only Boomers (strategic missile submarines, or SSBNs) pulled into PCAN. . .

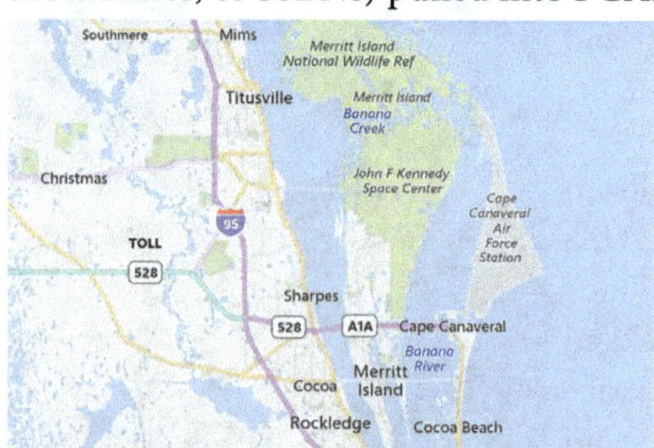

Despite not *"knowing"* PCAN, GATO's Officers quickly found *Captain Jack's* for dinner, right outside the gates of the Cape Canaveral Air Force Station, where the Navy PCAN pier is located. The enlisted crew on GATO also easily found *The Mouse Trap,* on Atlantic Avenue down in Cocoa Beach. Some say it is amazing that a submarine's crew can quickly find *"the right place"* to go, even in an "unfamiliar" port. Others would tell you that it is just another example of the natural, inherent tactical and strategic awareness that makes submariners, most particularly SSN sailors, so great at sea.

That night, Saturday night, the crew got another shot at PCAN's delights. Unusually, none of the Officers or crew had had any of their wives or girlfriends make the journey down to Florida for this trip. There were two key factors this time. First, this was late August – and GATO's homeport in Connecticut is generally much nicer in August than Florida is. The trip was much more popular in February, for sure. Not to mention all of the crew's kids getting ready to head back to school. Second, this was a relatively brief stop.

GATO had also spent a good bit of time in and around their homeport of New London in the months leading up to this trip. Over the last year the many years of GATO's *"hard running"* had *"caught up"* to the ship, and she had required some extended homeport maintenance work to keep her *ready* to *rock and roll.*

For instance, GATO had undergone an INSURV inspection about a year earlier. INSURV is a periodic evaluation of the ship's condition conducted by a centralized board of Navy experts. During the INSURV inspection the ship's rudder had jammed while the ship was at sea demonstrating hard turns. The failure had been caused by a pretty serious hydraulic system problem. To make matters worse, the rudder was turned hard over when it jammed – so GATO had had to limp home using the steerable Secondary Propulsion Motor to keep the ship going in kind of a straight line.

In another case, GATO had nearly sunk at the pier during waterborne maintenance on the ship's Main Ballast Tanks. So, with these and many other problems, the ship had had a great deal of maintenance completed in homeport to support the execution of a scheduled Fall, 1985 deployment. This was done despite the ship being scheduled to enter its second and final major shipyard overhaul the next Spring. Consequently, the ship had been "home" more than usual, as the GATO challenge had – *in real world terms* – become to simply *"get to overhaul"* in one piece.

In overhaul all known problems would be fixed and many equipment and system upgrades would be installed. At the end of the overhaul GATO would be in tip top condition, ready for another decade of *hard steaming* and highly effective service.

Now it was August, before a scheduled October deployment, and good 'ol GATO had actually run pretty damned well during the weapons shoot and certification trip. The backup air conditioners still leaked Freon, the 400 cycle motor generator sets were still finicky, and the ship's Head Valve was still cranky – and lots of other little things were annoying – but the ship had run pretty damned well. They had come a long, long way to get the ship into such (relatively) great condition, and these (relatively) minor remaining maintenance issues weren't going to get them down. But more about these *"little"* problems later, for now here they were at PCAN, with a highly successful weapons shoot and recertification exam behind them – and the crew was determined to get the most of it. After all, GATO was running well, and the crew had just done very well in the exam. Time to celebrate!

The next morning, Sunday, about a dozen intrepid GATO crew members – some of the same guys, some new ones – made the predawn trek back into the Space Center swamp to watch Discovery launch into orbit. By about 8:30 AM they were all back onboard GATO – one of the Space Shuttle's computers had failed late in the launch countdown. The shuttle would *finally* launch, but not until Tuesday morning. By then, GATO would nearly be back in New London, CT, starting its final maintenance upkeep period prior to deployment. GATO's plan, of course, was to fix those remaining "minor" nagging maintenance issues during the upkeep, and to have a great 72-Day Run to close out the year and to close out this operating cycle prior to overhaul.

In the ship's Wardroom, GATO's Officers were enjoying a late breakfast. Commander Rick Hanson, GATO's Captain, asked the ship's Executive Officer (XO) if the crew was all onboard yet. The XO went to check – *some of the crew had spent the night in town*

– but had all been supposed to be back by noon in advance of a scheduled 4 PM underway time.

The Captain then turned to the ship's Engineer Officer and said, "Eng, start the Reactor up now. I want to get underway as soon as possible. It's clear that we aren't going to see the damned Space Shuttle launch – *that guy isn't going anywhere soon* – so let's get the hell out of here now."

With that, the Captain then turned to the ship's Navigator and directed him to, "Call SUBLANT and get us cleared for an 11 AM or noon departure. Then call Port Operations and arrange tug support."

While he was the Captain, he could not get underway without clearance from the Duty Operations Officer at the Commander, Submarine Force, Atlantic Fleet (COMSUBLANT/SUBLANT) headquarters – who had "operational control" of GATO at the time. The Duty Operations Officer at the time happened to be an enlisted sailor, a Chief Quartermaster.

You see, SUBLANT keeps particular track of where each of the submarines under its operational control are at all times, and that responsibility fell to Duty Ops. So, Commander Hanson, in command of the mighty warship GATO, had to get the approval of a senior enlisted sailor to change his departure time. *Such is the world of nuclear submarining. . .* Positional authority can, and does, trump rank. Of course this was a mere formality designed to keep the ship safe, and approval would not be withheld unless approval would result in a submerged interference problem.

Each submarine's position and course are managed, you see, to minimize submerged collision risk. Also, *strictly for public relations purposes*, it also assists in locating a submerged submarine in distress to support "rescue" operations. *Ha, ha, good pabulum for the wives and mothers of the crew. . . Everyone who has ever worn dolphins knows that a SQUALUS-like rescue of a modern submarine in distress, while a nice fantasy, is extraordinarily improbable.* THRESHER. SCORPION. SAN FRANCISCO. CONNECTICUT. You stay safe by not letting yourself get into extremis, not by counting on some guy to come *"rescue"* you. Any *"rescue"* is going to start with yourself. You are a US Navy warship; stand tall, be safe and act like it.

While the SUBLANT clearance and tug support were being obtained, the crew was informally "mustered". That is, no formal muster or assembly was conducted – *several guys were still sleeping off the festivities from the night before, and their precious sleep was undisturbed until it was time to man the Maneuvering Watch to get underway.* Sleep is too precious on a submarine to waste on useless musters just to count heads. The whole crew was found onboard, and everybody was determined to be G2G (good to go).

Back aft, the Reactor was being started up and everything was going "by the book". Electrical Division Chief Andre Perot was the Engineering Watch Supervisor, and Mechanical Division Chief Ike Barnes was observing and "under instruction".

Barnes had only transferred onto GATO a couple of days prior to this trip and was not yet "qualified" to stand any watches. It had been almost 8 years since Barnes had been qualified on this type of Reactor Plant and Engineroom, and even that had been on a STURGEON (SSN 637) Class (newer model) submarine. Nonetheless, Barnes had been studying and reading and re-learning this type of plant in every spare moment. On submarines all crew members, even the most senior people (Officer and Enlisted) are re-quired, even if they had previously been qualified in a similar ship, to study hard and re-qualify on a new ship. In fact, as much as the Navy seeks commonality, even different ships in the same "Class" have small differences and quirks. Barnes, in accordance with Navy policy, would re-qualify on the trip back to New London.

As he walked around the propulsion plant spaces with Chief Perot, Chief Barnes gave his "instructor" a bit of grief for having gotten up early to head over the swamp to see the "launch".

"Andre, what in hell are you doing getting up at the crack of dawn to see that thing go – especially after it scrubbed 5 minutes before launch yesterday?"

"I don't know, it's just kind of cool."

"Well, think about this. We are on an OLD submarine, one that is more than READY for overhaul. Yet here we are. The Captain sez "let's go now" and we head back here, start her up and we are gonna go on demand. They might be going to outer space, but we are headed for inner space – and we are one fearsome warship. They get all of  the press; we are the Silent Service. Come on – latching and snatching the Control Rods and starting this Reactor up at will, and then heading out to the briny deep whenever we want to – GATO is much more impressive than that damned Space Shuttle. Not only that, we have, what, 90+ of these things in the Navy. . ."

"I still think that the Space Shuttle is kind of cool."

"Unlike the Space Shuttle, We Always Go on Demand,"

MMC(SS) Isaac "Ike" B. Barnes, VI
M-Division Chief
THE Mighty Mighty Warship USS GATO (SSN 615)
August 25, 1985

9

Preparation

The Greatest Danger to a Submarine is the Sea Itself

Chapter 1

POM Workup

Thursday, September 26, 1985;
Narragansett Bay Operating Areas.

"**E**merg," came the loud shriek from the ship's loudspeakers. At the same time the Emergency Blow Valve 6 inches above Chief Barnes' head opened and the rush of 4,500-pound air started screaming into the forward group Main Ballast Tanks. Upkeep had come and gone; GATO was underway for Pre-Overseas Movement (POM) workup, and the ship was *flooding?* WTF. Meanwhile, as the ship started to bang around like a child's toy – *it was now a mere 4,200 tons of men and steel being overwhelmed by the 130+ mph winds and up to 45-foot waves of a Category 4 hurricane* – the ship's Collision Alarm started sounding.

The Collision Alarm had obviously cut off the Chief of the Watch from his frantic announcement that he was initiating an Emergency Main Ballast Tank Blow. *No matter how many drills you do,* thought Barnes, *when the real thing happens, inevitably people get flustered by the real situation-related adrenalin, and things tend to happen a bit differently from the way that they are drilled.* The Chief of the Watch hadn't been supposed to announce, "Emergency Blow" – he had been supposed to *"just do it"* and to sound the Collision Alarm. They key thing is that he had actually executed the Emergency Blow and had rung the Collision Alarm.

This is not good, thought Barnes, as he jumped out of his bunk and into his pants and boots. *The ship is flooding, and we are right in the middle of the worst hurricane of the year.*

Moments later, as the ship banged around on to the surface in what was easily the worst part of the storm, he was out of the Chief Petty Officer's berthing area and in the GATO Bow Compartment. He noticed that the Bow Compartment to Operations Compartment watertight door was already closed and dogged shut. *So much for getting back to his Engineroom*, he thought. As he looked around, he also quickly noticed that he was the senior man in the Bow Compartment.

"This is Chief Barnes, and I am in charge in the Bow Compartment. Chief Perrot man the phones. Watson, get the compartment checklist and make sure that we are rigged for Flooding and General Emergency. Jones, make sure that everyone is out of the rack and let me know if there

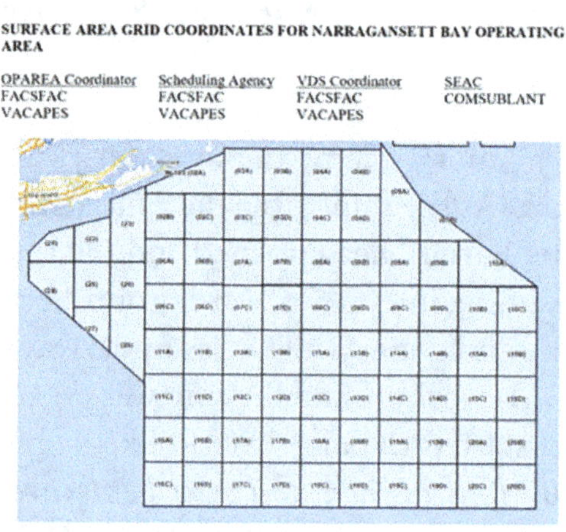

is any flooding down in the Diesel Compartment. And everybody, hold on, we are bobbing like a cork in this shit."

GATO was on POM workup in the Narragansett Bay Operating areas – a patch of the Atlantic south of Long Island that stretched almost to Delaware on the south side and out past Cape Cod on the east. She (GATO) was scheduled to depart on her 72-day WESTLANT deployment in a couple of weeks, and she was at sea this week with the Submarine Squadron 10 staff onboard to receive the Squadron's final approval for deployment. This meant that the ship was ready for war in all respects. In a week or so the Type Commander staff from COMSUBLANT would be on board for POM certification. For that trip not only would the ship Commanding Officer's reputation be on the line, but the Squadron Commodore's would be, as well.

Emergency Surfacing Test in Calm Seas
Now, Imagine doing this into the teeth of a Category 4 Hurricane. . .

During the POM Workup trip, originally scheduled for Monday through Friday, GATO and her crew once again did their thing with typical *Black Cat* style. In other words, going to sea on GATO was more like actually making sausage than watching a Hollywood movie about making sausage. Simply stated, it was sometimes messy and a bit ugly – but the results were always good. You see, as an *old boat* she had all of the *old boat blues. Yes, she ran pretty well, but the aches and pains of age are unavoidable.* The last ship of the 13 ship THRESHER Class to have been commissioned, GATO had also been *ridden hard and put up wet* more than a few times by her previous crews. She now needed lots of TLC on an everyday basis from an extremely sharp crew. Given the love, though, she was every bit the thoroughbred and would run with a bone in her teeth against any of them! GATO was, and always had been, a *HOT Boat.*

GATO had two main woes today. Neither one was enough to take her out of service, and each of these problems had already received a great deal of maintenance effort in unsuccessful attempts to correct the underlying issues. Unfortunately, like any two seemingly unrelated issues on a submarine, they could combine to create havoc. *In fact, they just had.* That, you see, is the fallacy of thinking that anything on a submarine is "unrelated." Nothing on a submarine is "unrelated" – everything *"matters"* to everything else. A more *"completely integrated and interdependent"* machine had never (before or since) been conceived.

The first *now-big* problem today was the Head Valve. Submarines can take in fresh air while submerged by sticking up a pipe above the surface of the ocean while they are at periscope depth. This pipe is called the Induction Mast. At the top of the Induction Mast sits the Head Valve. It has sensors that cause it to automatically shut if either a wave comes along and goes over the top of the Induction Mast or if the ship unintentionally goes any deeper. Occasionally GATO's Head Valve would stick open. All maintenance inspections and checks were absolutely good, though.

The other *now-big* problem today was the backup air conditioners. They leaked Freon when shutdown and were too noisy to routinely run at sea. Once again, extensive maintenance, and even a complete rebuild of the units during the just-completed upkeep, had failed to stem the leakage. Freon is bad stuff on its own, but when it is heated it can break down into really toxic gasses. This is not good in the completely enclosed environment of a submarine. *And don't go thinking that air conditioning is a luxury in a submarine, either.* You have a hot nuclear Reactor and lots of steam pipes running around the Engineroom. In addition, the Sonar Computers and other electronic equipment up forward had to be cooled, as well. All that heat is bad for every bit of the sensitive mission critical equipment onboard – *not to mention the crew.* Loss of air conditioning on a nuclear submarine is a genuine *big deal* problem. That is why there were backup units for the quieter steam-powered Main Air Conditioner.

As the Freon leaked out of the backup air conditioners the Freon concentration in the ship's atmosphere naturally went up.

Every few hours, or so, it would reach the limit on the Central Air Monitoring System and the ship would have to Ventilate. Basically, suck in fresh air through the Induction Mast and expel the bad air in the ship over the side using a blower. Annoying, and really not the way you want to deploy – *which is why a lot of effort had already gone into fixing this problem.*

On Wednesday of POM Workup week, the ship had gotten a message about Hurricane Gloria. It was the worst storm of the 1985 season in the Atlantic and was headed right for New London. All of the submarines in port in New London, and across the river in Groton, were being sent to sea in an emergency sortie to escape possible storm damage – a submarine deep below the surface is not as vulnerable to storm damage as she is when she is helplessly tied to a pier. As a result, GATO's operating area had been changed south so that the ships unexpectedly leaving port could submerge as soon as possible. The Navy was good about that – giving each submarine a safe haven where no other US or allied submarines are located. It helped reduce submerged collisions.

Now it was before dawn on Thursday, and the thick of the storm was approaching GATO. The Officer of the Deck (OOD) had gotten the Captain's permission to ventilate one last time before the storm got too bad so that the ship could ride out the whole storm down deep without having to worry about Freon levels in the atmosphere.

"This is the Captain. We have sustained flooding through the Induction Mast. Significant water has entered both the Torpedo Room from the Induction Sump drains overflowing into the Torpedo Room bilges and in the Control Room from the Induction Sump viewing window breaking under pressure. The flooding is stopped, and the ship's watertight integrity has been restored. During the flooding we Emergency Blew to the surface and used our air banks up and we would not normally submerge again until we had completed an air charge. We don't have time for that now, with the storm upon us, so I am submerging the ship to 400 feet.

We'll see how the ship rides there and get things cleaned up. Well done crew, you kept a bad situation from getting worse."

Moments later the voice of the Chief of the Watch came on the loudspeaker, "Now secure from Flooding and Secure from General Emergency. All stations report to Control. Now Dive, Dive!"

Note that, on an American nuclear-powered attack submarine in 1985, the OOD station when submerged is in the Control Room, and when surfaced in acceptable weather, on the Bridge (on top of the submarine's sail, which is the vertical protrusion from the top of the ship). Also note that on a submarine, during normal steaming underway (surfaced or submerged) there are only two Officers on watch. These are the OOD in Control or on the Bridge and the Engineering Officer of the Watch (EOOW), back in the Maneuvering Area (sometimes called "the box"). The other 3 senior watchstanders onboard are the Diving Officer (responsible for the ship's depth), the Chief of the Watch (who operates the Ballast Control Panel), and the Engineering Watch Supervisor, who is the senior enlisted nuclear trained (Nuke) operator back aft. While Officers all qualify on the Dive (Diving Officer), it is usually manned by the most senior Chief Petty Officers forward. The only exception is that the sole SSN "Pork Chop" (Supply Corps Officer) sometimes qualifies and stands watch on the Dive. The Chief of the Watch is manned by other forward Chief Petty Officers, and the Engineering Watch Supervisor is manned by the nuclear-trained Chief Petty Officers. Also, the very specialized position of Sonar Supervisor is manned by either the Sonar Division Chief Petty Officer or a senior Sonar Petty Officer. Note, as well, that there is no Junior Officer of the Deck (JOOD), and usually no separate Conning Officer. Finally, SSNs have no Tactical Action Officer (TAO), and no Combat Information Center Watch Officer (CICWO). SSNs don't even have a Combat Information Center! As such, during routine steaming hundreds of feet below the surface at night it is typical for the ship to be under the complete control of just two Officers, three Chiefs and the 20-odd men of the enlisted watch section – with everyone else asleep. Finally, including the Captain, XO, Hospital Corpsman, Yeoman, Supply Department cooks and Petty Officers and Ship's Engineering Laboratory Technician, there are only about a dozen people in the entire crew who are not on the 6 on, 12 off, 3 section watch rotation.

As soon as the loudspeaker went silent from that announcement it erupted again with the familiar sound of the ship's diving alarm, "AOOOGAH, AOOOGAH," followed by the Chief of the Watch announcing once again, "Dive, Dive!"

In the Bow Compartment Chief Barnes heard the expected sounds of the Main Ballast Tank Vent Valves opening up to expel the air from the Ballast Tanks so that the ship could submerge. After securing the compartment and making the report to Control he released the Bow Compartment emergency party. He and his buddy Chief Andre Perrot went back into the Chief's Berthing Area to finish getting dressed – neither man had put their shirts on when they had gotten out of the rack.

"Another GATO moment, for sure," quipped Perrot.

"I can feel the pressure on me now about those damned air conditioners going up by at least an order of magnitude. No way we deploy with this leakage," replied Barnes.

As the M Division Chief, and a Chief Machinist Mate, Barnes was responsible for all of the mechanical equipment in the Engineroom and Reactor Compartment. Perrot, also nuclear trained, was the E Division Chief, a Chief Electrician's Mate, and was responsible for all of the ship's electrical equipment. Between the two of them they caught the heat for about 85 percent of all of GATO's woes. Most of the other 15 percent went to the A Division Chief, a non-nuclear Chief Machinist Mate who was responsible for all of the ship's mechanical equipment (like the Head Valve) that didn't fall to Barnes. Both Barnes and Perrot had been on GATO for less than a year, and the upcoming 72-day run would be their first GATO deployment.

"I had better head aft and go ponder my *bad boys* down in Engineroom Lower Level," said Barnes.

"You'll Nuke it out, I am sure. I'll see you down there in a few minutes – I have to go check the brush rigging on my 400 cycle sets down there, too. Those damned 400 cycle sets are on their last legs. If we can get through this deployment, I'll be glad to see them go when we get to the shipyard for overhaul," said Perrot.

"You and me both. It will be great to make it to overhaul and see those antique 400 cycle sets, along with my ancient backup air conditioners, head off to the scrap pile where they both belong! See you down there," replied Barnes.

Twenty minutes later Barnes was standing in Engineroom Lower Level next to his recalcitrant backup air conditioners, pondering the equipment diagram that he could redraw in detail with his eyes blindfolded at this point. An idea was coming to him. It wasn't ideal, but, heh, this was GATO. His Engineroom Lower Level Watch, a kid named Martin from the world-famous Cleveland suburb of Parma, OH, approached him.

"Chief, I can't get the Evaporator to make water. Maneuvering is all over me because the coners let the Potable Water Tanks get real low up forward and Control is all over them to fill them, but the trip valve won't latch open. I tested the water that she's making, and it is good water, but the damned trip valve won't latch"

"How are your Reserve Tanks for the Engineroom looking," replied Barnes.

"Chief, I just finished filling them right before the flooding. We are good back here. I asked them then if they wanted Potable, but they said no. Now they are all over me to get the Evaporator re-started to make Potable, but the trip valve won't latch. I think there is something wrong with the solenoid," said Martin.

Just then Barnes spotted Chief Perrot climbing down the ladder into the Lower Level.

"Hey Andre, we have a problem with the trip valve solenoid on the Evaporator. Can you get one of your guys to take a look at it? Apparently the coners let the Potty Water tanks get low up forward and are all over us to make water," asked Barnes.

"How do our Reserve Tanks back here look?" replied Perrot. He might have been a Chief Electrician's Mate – *and on any non-nuclear ship the Chief Electrician's Mate wouldn't ever care about propulsion plant Reserve Tanks* – but Perrot was a good Nuke, and along with ship safety, always was concerned with anything that could have any implications on either Reactor safety or propulsion plant operations.

All Nukes are like that – while the enlisted Nukes are all specialists in one technical area, cross-rate knowledge is essential for everyone. For instance, despite not being qualified as Reactor Operators, both Chiefs had started up and shut down reactors during their training. Either one of them could start with $E=MC^2$ and calculate how many nuclear fissions were going on at any given time – or, in an emergency, safely operate any equipment or control panel in the propulsion plant.

"We are good. Martin just finished filling them before the flooding and asked them up forward if they wanted Potable, but they said no, and he shut the Evaporator down. Now they are crying for water."

"Typical. One of these days we ought to give them a lesson in what it takes to start up and shut down the Evaporator and maybe then they'll be a bit more considerate. I'll get my Auxiliary Electrician on it right away. For now, let's just keep it running dumping to the bilge until we find out how bad the problem is."

"I will tell Maneuvering. I have to go pump bilges overboard anyway, they are getting high as it is," said Martin.

With that Barnes folded up his air conditioner diagram and started to rehearse his pitch as he climbed the ladder to upper level. He knew that he should go to see LT Clark, his Division Officer, but fortunately Clark was in the box right now – on watch as EOOW – and unavailable for consultation.

The box was always restricted access, and the Nukes maintained a high degree of discipline about what went on in there – and limited it to strictly the business of operating the Reactor and the propulsion plant right now. Maintenance planning was done after watch, outside the box.

Now 99 percent of all submarine Officers are outstanding engineers, exemplary Officers, and great "operators" who are strong and effective leaders even under extraordinarily stressful circumstances. Clark represented the rest. A genuinely nice guy, very bright and a sharp engineer in his degree field, he had worked hard and made it through both Rickover's interview and a year of Nuclear Power School. His weakness, and it was obvious, was an inability to make a difficult, immediate, consequential life and death decision based upon imperfect and incomplete information – which is an essential skill, especially on an *old boat* like GATO. He also wasn't particularly strong in his ability to understand complex mechanical systems. It was clear to everyone that because of this LT Clark wasn't going to make it past his next major career event – the submarine nuclear Engineer Officer examination.

It seemed obvious, at least to Chief Barnes, that LT Clark should be a college professor, not a submarine Officer. This, not surprisingly, is what he ended up doing "after Navy." *Those that can, do; those that can't, teach,* thought Barnes.

In the meantime, he had been assigned to M Division and Chief Barnes. Not feeling like explaining his plan 6 times, Barnes had made the mental excuse that Clark was not available and that the backup air conditioner issue was urgent stuff. Barnes was headed to the Wardroom to find the ship's Engineer.

Called "Chief Engineer" or "CHENG" on other US Navy ships, on submarines the Department Head for the Engineering Department is known simply as the "Engineer" and is referred to as "Eng."

"Hey Eng, do you have a minute?" asked Barnes, as he spotted the Engineer.

"Sure, if you can tell me what is going on with the Evaporator. Control just called me and told me that we are going to have to secure Potable Water to the ship because the Evaporator is out of commission. How are the Reserve Tanks aft looking and what is wrong with that thing now?"

"Well, the Reserve Tanks aft are full. We just finished filling them right before the flooding and they called forward to see if they needed any Potable. They said no and we shut the Evaporator down. A little while ago they realized that they were almost out of Potable and ordered the Evaporator started. When we started her up the trip valve would not latch. Right now, we are making good water to the bilges and Chief Perrot has the Auxiliary Electrician looking into it. I don't expect this to be too serious of a problem. There is also no need to get crazy and to try to make good water with the backup unit – the capacity of that thing is way too low for our usage right now, and only a couple of my guys can even make that thing work. So, with that being a non-option, worst case is that we take the solenoid off of the backup unit and put it on the Evaporator – maybe an hour or so."

"OK. Get it fixed and keep me informed. Now about the Freon leaks. . ."

"That is why I am here. I have a plan, but it isn't completely by the book, and I am going to need help from the tender to get it fixed next week. I am pretty sure that we can isolate most of the Freon in the lower ends of the units, let whatever is in the upper ends leak out and then if we have to use them during the deployment, we'll be able to restore them in less than a half hour. To do it we have to replace these 8 valves because I know that the ones in the units won't hold. They are just worn out. So that is what I need. I need FULTON (the tender) to get us any kind of valves that fit – the right part number would be nice, but I don't care as long as they are refrigerant valves and will fit – and then recharge the units one last time. Then we can get through the deployment and get to the shipyard where the whole units can go to scrap."

"What is the alternative, Chief?" replied the Engineer.

"Well, we could go up to the Subbase or over to Electric Boat and drydock the ship. Then we could cut a hole in the side of the ship and remove these damned things and install something modern. Eng, I don't have a good alternative. We have done everything in the book, including a complete rebuild of the compressors, and there is no sealing these things up. It is like when I was on FULTON and the inspectors down at Gitmo wanted us to seal up the oil leaks in her ancient Diesel Engines. Not happening in this nuclear navy. We just have to deal with it, and we are down to our last draw of the deck. I can make this work, but I just need some support from the tender," Barnes said, making his ultimate plea/case.

"OK. That is the plan. What does LT Clark think of it?" came the Engineer's reply.

"He was in the box. I will tell him when he gets off watch."

"OK. I will brief the Captain and the Squadron. Now let's go get the Evaporator fixed while I deal with this Head Valve thing. It is starting to look ugly."

A short time later the Captain once again came on the ship's announcing system. Normally the Captain might make one announcement to the crew during a weekly operation like this. Lots of times, though, you don't hear the Captain on the ship's announcing system for months at a stretch. On deployment the ship's announcing system is not routinely used – the sound can actually be heard by a sensitive sonar system in close proximity. The fact that the Captain was making another announcement to the crew meant that this really was a GATO day.

"This is the Captain. We have recovered from the flooding and all damage was minor and is now repaired. About the biggest problem was the water that got into the ship's office and damaged some of our records. The Yeoman is working on that with the XO now. Unfortunately, we have some other problems.

"First, the Evaporator is out of commission, and we are out of Potable Water. The Reserve Tanks aft are fine, and the Engineer assures me that the Evaporator will be back in service soon. But until we get some Potable Water made the showers are secured and I have asked the cooks to minimize their use.

"The bigger problem is the Head Valve. As you know, we tried to ventilate again a short while ago when we were in the eye of the storm. Not only are our Freon levels getting too high, but our oxygen levels have gotten too low. We are safe, of course, because we have fully charged oxygen banks and a full load of oxygen candles onboard. I don't want to use either one, though, because I would like to save them for the deployment – particularly the oxygen banks. When we tried to ventilate again, though, we could not get the Head Valve to open. It was stuck open earlier, which caused the flooding. Now it won't open at all.

"It appears that even with the low pressure up above in the eye of the storm our ongoing air charge has sucked so much air out of the ship that the Head Valve can't overcome the differential pressure between the ship's atmospheric pressure and the outside atmosphere. The air banks are still too low for us to go deep, and the air charge is now secured, so I have restricted our depth to 400 feet. In the meantime, the Engineer and A Gang are working on a plan to break the vacuum in the Induction Mast between the Head Valve and the Hull Valve. If we can do that we can ventilate. This is going to take some time, though.

"So, while we are doing this and not wanting to have to start bleeding oxygen from the oxygen banks unless we are absolutely forced to, we have to minimize our oxygen consumption. To do this I want all Watchstanders to minimize your movement throughout your spaces. Do what you have to do to safely operate your equipment but no routine moving around – even for hourly log readings. Position yourselves where you have the best view of the majority of your equipment.

"Everyone else not on watch and not doing essential maintenance on the Evaporator or the Head Valve should go to your bunks and lie still. If we have to, I will bleed oxygen, but if we can successfully cut our oxygen usage rate, we can last an hour or so and hopefully get to a point on the trailing edge of the storm with the vacuum lock in the Induction Mast broken. That is all."

With that the crew did as the Captain had directed. For the first time in the careers of everyone onboard, including the embarked Squadron Chief of Staff (who himself had previously commanded an SSN), they employed a World War II submarine tactic to stretch the ship's oxygen supply. Kind of fitting for GATO, as the first USS GATO (SS 212) was the first ship of the 226 Fleet Submarines (GATO, BALAO & TENCH Classes) that took the war to the Japanese and won in the Pacific. Now the second GATO – the nuclear GATO – was using first GATO tactics to solve a problem not experienced by a US submarine in 40 years. Even more fitting as the current GATO was one of the very few nuclear-powered US submarines that was not equipped with an oxygen generator. These oxygen generators made oxygen from pure water and radically reduced the need to ventilate and conserve other oxygen supplies while submerged. GATO – *you had to love her and give her TLC and she would treat you fine.* GATO just wasn't an easy girl to love. Particularly today.

Two hours later, with the crew refreshed from an unexpected nap in the afternoon, the ship had ventilated, and the Potable Water Tanks were filling, and all was well with GATO. The Captain had requested the Engineer, LT Clark and Chief Barnes to join him and the Squadron Chief of Staff in the Wardroom. As Chief Barnes already knew, this was all show for the Squadron Chief of Staff. The Captain was onboard with the plan, and this was all for effect – to ensure that FULTON got on the job and got the refrigerant valves replaced, whatever it took.

Everybody knew that GATO's tender maintenance period (or upkeep) had ended over a week ago and that FULTON was now fully engaged in other work on other ships, including a big nuclear job on USS BILLFISH (SSN 676). Nobody wanted to make such a big deal out of the need for FULTON support of GATO that SUBLANT would find out and doubt GATO's ability to imminently deploy, but everybody knew that without FULTON's support GATO could not get the air conditioners fixed – and that deployment with the Freon leak would be bad judgment on everybody's part. *So, just a bit of liar's poker and a can-do attitude was all that was needed to responsibly get GATO out on deployment. . .*

Chief Barnes knew all of this all too well. His last duty station – just a couple of months ago – had been FULTON, in the Repair Department supporting GATO and the other ships in Submarine Squadron 10. GATO, by far, had been the hanger queen of the Squadron. One night when he had been the Repair Department Duty Officer on FULTON during one of GATO's upkeeps she had almost sunk at the pier due to a problem during Ballast Tank main-tenance. She took the most maintenance support and had the most challenging problems to deal with.

USS FULTON (AS-11) and her brood of
THRESHER Class Tended Units,
State Pier, New London, CT circa early 1970's

Of course, GATO was DUE for overhaul. Not the boneyard, just overhaul. As the last THRESHER Class ship to be commissioned, she was the last ship in the upgrade cycle. She was the ship with all of the oldest versions of all of the most troublesome equipment – most of which had already been scrapped or upgraded in the rest of the fleet. Squadron mate USS DACE (SSN 607) was older than GATO, and also a THRESHER Class ship – but she was more like a new LOS ANGELES Class (SSN 688) ship, in terms of her condition and equipment reliability, than like GATO. DACE had come out of overhaul a year earlier.

Barnes often thought that it was a cruel twist of fate that he had been assigned to GATO after FULTON. The only other alternative had been a new 688 in Pearl Harbor. He had commissioned a 688 class ship, USS LA JOLLA (SSN 701), prior to his duty on FULTON and loved the design and loved the ship. To Barnes 688's were ideal submarines. His wife did not want to move to Hawaii, though.

"So Chief, please explain your plan and tell us why you think it will solve our Freon problem," asked the Captain.

Barnes proceeded to explain the plan in detail and showed everyone on the equipment diagram why he thought that it would work. He was polite, respectful and not overly dramatic. Just the facts. He deferred to the Captain and Engineer, who asked questions and made points in favor of the plan while LT Clark sat quietly. Even the Squadron Chief of Staff played along with the charade that they were all having for themselves, asking the Chief a couple of questions. Everyone in the room, you see, knew each other quite well and all had a clear respect of each other's grasp of the technical details of nuclear submarining.

On the night that GATO had almost sunk at the pier last year it had been Chief Barnes, as FULTON's Repair Duty Officer, who had called the Squadron Chief of Staff at home to tell him about it and how they had solved the problem. LT Clark had been GATO's Duty Officer that night. Submarining is a family business and there are few secrets in the family – *especially about people and who you can trust with a plan.*

"Well Captain, it sounds like you have a good plan. I am going to send a personal message to the Repair Officer this afternoon and ask him to give this his full support even though we have to keep the BILLFISH job moving. As you know, Naval Reactors is on our tail watching that work very, very closely and neither the Commodore nor I want to have to call Admiral McKee (Admiral Rickover's replacement as the head of Naval Reactors since 1982) with any bad news on that job. Still, this is for the air conditioning shop to support, and it is a nuclear job on BILLFISH.

"Chief, this is a good plan. I am sure that you all will make it work out for GATO. This is a very important deployment for the ship and for the squadron.

"Captain, this has been one hell of a day!" finished the Chief of Staff.

With that the Wardroom conference broke up and Chief Barnes excused himself. A few minutes later he was in the Chief's Lounge, where the Chief of the Boat (COB) was putting an end to a silly discussion about returning to port.

"Now look, you guys, all of us would rather get home tomorrow like we were scheduled. But the Captain can't do anything about it. He did not order up the hurricane and sortie the fleet. All of the ships north of us are closer to port and will get first dibs on tug services for getting back into port. Unless one of you geniuses can pull a couple of available tugboats out of your butts for service on Friday, we will be home at 10 AM on Saturday morning and that is that," emphatically said the COB.

The next 24 hours passed calmly, routinely. It was almost as if the events of Thursday had never even happened. The ship even ventilated 3 times with no Head Valve problems. It was pure GATO.

Friday night the ship surfaced for Saturday's return to port and Chief Barnes made a visit to the bridge. Up on top of GATO's short sail the ocean was calm, and the air was crisp and clean. It was Fall, and Barnes never tired of his almost ritual bridge visits the night before returning to port. From above the ship, he looked back at the ship's wake and was simply amazed, for the gazillionth time, at what was going on below him. *A nuclear Reactor was smashing atoms and effortlessly making all of that wake.* The wow factor never escaped him. He could explain it all on a chalkboard for hours and hours, using diagrams and equations and waving his arms in energized, animated detailed explanation. He used to teach it at Nuclear Power School, after all. But up here, for a few quiet minutes, he got to be a kid filled with amazing wonderment once again. *WOW. God, I love this stuff*, he thought.

The Engineer was on watch as Officer of the Deck, up on the Bridge. They chatted casually for a couple of minutes about nothing in particular, watching the dolphins jump the ship's bow wake. *Yes, they really do that.*

Now if this had been an aircraft carrier you would have never found a Lieutenant Commander and a Chief Petty Officer shooting the bull. Particularly if the LCDR was on watch. But this was the submarine force, and more particularly, this was GATO. This was neither a lack of formality nor any sign of disrespect. On GATO everyone had this strange sense that their lives acutely depended upon the skill, knowledge, good sense, judgment and wisdom of everybody else onboard. It was a feeling that brought everyone close together in deep mutual respect. It was also a well-founded belief, because it was true. GATO was GATO, and she was a hard girl to love. She always, however, came through in a pinch. Always.

The crew was aware, of course, of the loss at sea of both USS THRESHER (SSN 593) and USS SCORPION (SSN 589). The loss of these two ships was a burden that every nuclear submariner carried very close. There was no aura of nuclear submarine invincibility. THRESHER shattered that myth, and her loss was pretty well understood – at least rationally. Emotions – something that hard-hearted submarine sailors rarely admitted to – were another matter. SCORPION was another matter entirely. There was the "official" story on SCORPION. But it was also widely known in the fleet that many on the crew considered SCORPION to have been a death trap due to deferred maintenance and the ship's generally shoddy condition.

Nobody felt that way about GATO. She was a true thoroughbred and ran hard and true. She just needed lots of love and TLC. So rather than being at all afraid of the ship, the crew looked forward to the upcoming 72-day run with great anticipation. There was a feeling that, given her chance, GATO would deliver and *kick ass* like a true champion. After all, this was the Cold War at its peak and submarines were the front line in America's fight. Let's get the FLOBs off the ship and let's get to it!

FLOBs, of course, are "free loading oxygen breathers" – non-productive submarine visitors who always want to catch a ride for a short trip near homeport. FLOBs are always first in the chow line, fill up the seats at the evening movie, take up a private bunk (making 3 guys share 2 racks, or "hot bunk"), eat your food, breathe your oxygen, drink your water, take Hollywood showers, and fill up your sanitary tank (i.e., "shit tank"). FLOBs are useless and not well regarded on the ship. Everyone works hard on an SSN; there is no tolerance for sloth or for FLOBs

Saturday morning Chief Barnes was back in the Engineroom on watch as the Engineering Watch Supervisor and tending to his Main Engines and other equipment. On a tour through Lower Level, he stopped to chat with Martin for a couple of minutes. He was a good kid. Only a few months out of Nuclear Power School, but the Chief was really impressed with his knowledge and work ethic. This was the kind of guy he loved to take under his wing and share some of his hard-earned wisdom with.

"You know Chief, I haven't been at sea very long, but I get the sense that Thursday was very unique," said Martin with some real insight.

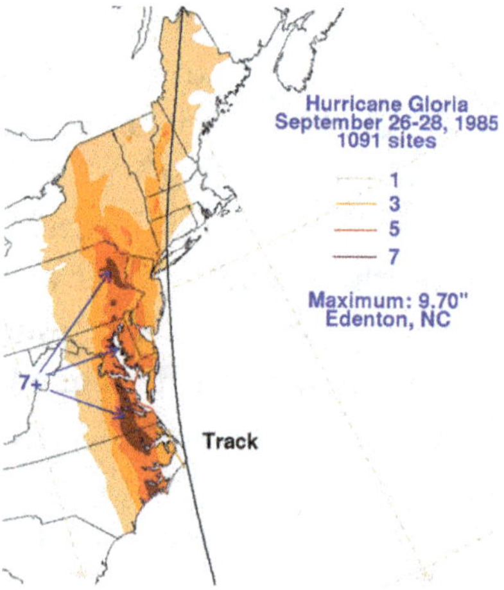

"You have got that one right, my friend. I have never seen anything like it myself. It just shows you that all the stuff they tell you in school about what a ship and crew together can do is really true," replied Barnes.

"Yeah, I get it. One minute we are flooding and emergency blowing into a hurricane. The next minute we are in the bunk because we don't have any oxygen left in the boat. An hour later we are certified by the Squadron as ready to deploy. Wow. Still, I think that someday somebody should write a book about Thursday. What a day!"

"Maybe so," replied Barnes, "maybe so."

Building a Nuclear Attack Submarine Force

Not as Easy as it Might Seem

Chapter 2

THRESHER, SCORPION & GATO

THRESHER
Wednesday, April 10, 1963, 220 miles east of Cape Cod

USS THRESHER (SSN 593) is conducting test depth certification operations following an overhaul at Portsmouth Naval Shipyard. THRESHER is the lead ship of a new class of nuclear-powered submarine and is the first second generation SSN designed for quiet operations. Following the heady, successful days of the 1950's with USS NAUTILUS (SSN 571) and her first-generation progeny, the Navy had moved quickly to the second generation designs. The USS SKIPJACK (SSN 585) and her 5 sister ships were the prototypes for the second generation – debuting both the single propeller, now classic, nuclear submarine teardrop hull shape and a new Reactor plant that would go on to be installed in a total of 98 submarines. But THRESHER was the real deal, with all the goodies, all the toys, all of the capability that the Cold War demanded.

Still less than two years old (she had been commissioned on August 3, 1961 and was only <u>615</u> days old at the time of her loss) THRESHER had a fast, furious and never-to-be-forgotten life. On that fateful Spring morning many lessons were learned, and nuclear submarining was changed forever as the Atlantic swallowed THRESHER and her 129 crew members. Of note, 17 of those on THRESHER that morning, and now forever, were shipyard workers or civilian contractors. Scheduled to have been in that contingent was Chief Ike Barnes' uncle Billy Barnes, who was a foreman at the shipyard. Submarines are a family business. He was an air conditioning expert and was to have observed operation of the ship's new steam powered air conditioning unit at sea – THRESHER had the first-ever steam-powered air conditioner on a submarine. The intermittent problems with the unit had been finally diagnosed pier side and were fixed before departure, though.

Reproduced below is an account of THRESHER's brief career and of her death from Wikipedia, the online encyclopedia.

Wikipedia is a crowd-sourced online Encyclopedia. The author neither validates nor provides comment on the accuracy of any of the material included in the Wikipedia articles copied in this book. The two Wikipedia articles are provided herein merely to provide context for readers who are not intimately familiar with American nuclear-powered submarine history. This is done in recognition that many such readers would consult this type of online article for additional context. Inclusion herein, then, is simply done as a time-saving service for the reader.

To Ensure Clarity for the reader, everything on the following pages is from Wikipedia. The end of the Wikipedia article will be designated with another comment. Source of following content: https://en.wikipedia.org/wiki/USS_Thresher_(SSN-593)

The second USS THRESHER (SSN-593) was the lead ship of its class of nuclear-powered attack submarines in the United States Navy. Her loss at sea during deep-diving tests in 1963 is often considered a watershed event in the implementation of the rigorous submarine safety program SUBSAFE.

She was named for a type of shark, which is harmless to man. It is easily recognizable because its tail is longer than the combined length of its body and head.

The contract to build the THRESHER was awarded to Portsmouth Naval Shipyard on 15 January 1954, and her keel was laid on 28 May 1954. She was launched on 9 July 1960, was sponsored by Mrs. Frederick Burdett Warder, and was commissioned on 3 August 1961, with Commander Dean L. Axene in command.

Photo # NH 97551   USS Thresher underway, April 1961

Early career

THRESHER conducted lengthy sea trials in the western Atlantic and Caribbean Sea areas in 1961 and 1962. These tests provided a thorough evaluation of her many new and complex technological features and weapons. Following these trials, she took part in Nuclear Submarine Exercise (NUSUBEX) 3-61 off the northeastern coast of the United States from September 18 to September 24, 1961.

On October 18 THRESHER headed south along the Atlantic Fleet. While in port at San Juan, Puerto Rico on 2 November 1961, her Reactor was shut down and the Diesel generator was used to carry the "hotel" electrical loads. Several hours later the generator broke down, and the electrical load was then carried by the battery. The generator could not be quickly repaired, so the Captain ordered the Reactor restarted. However, the battery charge was depleted before the Reactor reached criticality. With no electrical power for ventilation, temperatures in the machinery spaces reached 60 °C (140 °F), and the boat was partially evacuated. CAVALLA (SS-244) arrived the next morning and provided power from her Diesel Engines, enabling THRESHER to restart her Reactor.

THRESHER conducted further trials and fired test torpedoes before returning to Portsmouth on November 29. The boat remained in port through the end of the year, and spent the first two months of 1962 evaluating her sonar and Submarine Rocket (SUBROC) systems. In March, the submarine participated in NUSUBEX 2-62 (an exercise designed to improve the tactical capabilities of nuclear submarines) and in antisubmarine warfare training with Task Group ALPHA.

Off Charleston, SC, the THRESHER undertook operations observed by the Naval Antisubmarine Warfare Council before she returned briefly to New England waters, after which she proceeded to Florida for more SUBROC tests. However, while mooring at Port Canaveral, Florida, the submarine was accidentally struck by a tug which damaged one of her Ballast Tanks. After repairs at Groton, Connecticut, by the Electric Boat Company, the ship returned south for more tests and trials off Key West, Florida. THRESHER then returned northward and remained in dockyard for refurbishment through the early spring of 1963.

Loss

On April 9, 1963, after the completion of this work, THRESHER, now commanded by LCDR John Wesley Harvey, began post-overhaul trials. Accompanied by the submarine rescue ship USS SKYLARK (ASR-20), she sailed to an area some 350 km (220 miles) east of Cape Cod, Massachusetts, and on the morning of April 10 started deep-diving tests. As these proceeded, garbled communications were received over the underwater telephone by SKYLARK, indicating that after initial problems THRESHER had tilted and the crew were attempting to regain control. A few words were understandable, including the famous final phrase "... minor difficulties, have positive up-angle, attempting to blow." When the garbled communications --- which were followed by the ominous sound of pressurized air escaping --- eventually ceased, surface observers gradually realized that THRESHER had sunk. All 129 Officers, crewmen and military and civilian technicians aboard her were lost.

After an extensive underwater search using the bathyscaphe TRIESTE, oceanographic ship MIZAR and other ships, THRESHER's remains were located on the sea floor, some 8,400 feet (2560 m) below the surface, in six major sections. The majority of the debris is in an area of about 134,000 m² (160,000 yd²). The major sections are the sail (the raised tower atop a submarine's main deck), sonar dome, bow section, engineering spaces section, operations spaces section, and the tail section.

Deep sea photography, recovered artifacts, and an evaluation of her design and operational history permitted a Court of Inquiry to conclude that the THRESHER had probably sunk due to the failure of a weld in a salt water piping system, which relied heavily on silver brazing instead of welding; earlier tests using ultrasound equipment found potential problems with about 14% of the tested brazed joints, most of which were determined to not pose a risk significant enough to require a repair. High-pressure water spraying from a broken pipe joint apparently shorted out an electrical panel, which in turn caused a shutdown of the Reactor, causing a subsequent loss of propulsion. An inability to blow water from the Ballast Tanks was later attributed to excessive moisture in THRESHERs emergency high-pressure air flasks, which froze and plugged its own flow path while passing through the blow valves. This was later simulated in dock-side tests on the THRESHER's sister ship, TINOSA. During a test to simulate blowing ballast at or near test-depth, ice formed on strainers installed in valves; the flow of air lasted only a few seconds.

Unlike Diesel submarines, nuclear subs relied on speed, then deck angle (that is, driving the ship towards the surface), then deballasting to surface. Ballast tanks were almost never blown at depth; this could cause the ship to rocket to the surface out of control. Normal procedure was to drive the ship to periscope depth, raise the periscope and verify that the area was clear, then to blow the tanks and surface the ship.

At the time, Reactor-plant operating procedures precluded a fast Reactor restart, or even the ability to use steam remaining in the secondary system to "drive" the ship to the surface. Standard procedure following a Reactor "scram" (or sudden, abrupt shutdown) was to isolate the main steam system, cutting off the flow of steam to the propulsion and ship's service (electricity producing) turbines. This was done to prevent an over-rapid Reactor cooldown. THRESHER's Main Propulsion Assistant, Lt. Cdr. Raymond McCoole, was not at his station in the maneuvering room, or indeed on the ship, during the fatal dive. McCoole was at home caring for his wife who had been injured in a freak household accident -- he had been all but ordered ashore by a compassionate Commander Harvey. His replacement, Jim Henry, fresh from Nuclear Power School, probably gave the order to isolate the steam system after the scram (following standard procedures), even though THRESHER was at or slightly below her maximum depth and was taking on water. Once closed, the steam system isolation valves could not be reopened quickly. In later life, McCoole was sure that he would have delayed shutting the valves, thus allowing the ship to "answer bells" and drive herself to the surface, despite the flooding in the engineering spaces. Admiral Rickover later changed the procedures, allowing steam to be withdrawn from the secondary system in limited quantities for several minutes following a scram.

There was much (covert) criticism of Rickover's training after THRESHER went down, the argument being that his "Nukes" were so well conditioned to protect the nuclear plant that they would have shut the main steam stop valves -- depriving the ship of needed propulsion -- even at great depths with flooding in the engine room. Nothing enraged Rickover more than this argument. Common sense, he argued, would prove this to be untrue.

It's more likely that the engine room crew was overwhelmed by the flooding casualty, or simply took too long to contain it. In a dockside simulation of flooding in the engineroom, held before THRESHER sailed, it took the watch in charge 20 minutes to isolate a simulated leak in the auxiliary seawater system. At test depth, taking on water, and with the Reactor shut down, THRESHER would not have had anything like 20 minutes to recover.

THRESHER imploded (that is, one or more of her compartments collapsed inwards in a fraction of a second) at a depth somewhere between 1,300 feet and 2,000 feet. Those not injured by the flooding would have died in a split second.

Over the next several years, the Navy implemented the SUBSAFE program to correct design and construction problems on all submarines (nuclear and Diesel-electric) in service, under construction, and in planning. It was discovered during the formal inquiry that record-keeping at the Portsmouth Naval Shipyard was far from adequate. For example, no one could determine the whereabouts of hull weld X-rays made of THRESHER's sister ship TINOSA, nearing completion at Portsmouth, or, indeed, whether they had been made at all. It was also determined that THRESHER 's engine room layout was awkward, and, in fact dangerous, as there were no centrally-located isolation valves for the main and auxiliary seawater systems. All subs were subsequently equipped or retrofitted with so-called "chicken switches", which allowed the Engineer Officer of the Watch in the maneuvering room to remotely close isolation valves in the seawater systems from a central panel, a task that would have had to be performed manually on THRESHER. It's worth noting that such valves might not have been reachable during THRESHER's presumed flooding casualty: at such deep depths, the blast of water from even a small leak can dent metal cabinets, rip insulation from cables, and, in the case of a large break, split a man in half! (Water pressure at 1,000 feet is about 450 pounds to the square inch; imagine water shooting into a contained, confined area, packed with electrical panels, pumps, motors, and pipes at such high pressures, and you get a mind's-eye picture of what the crew was up against.)

Apart from SCORPION, the U.S. Navy has suffered no further losses of nuclear submarines.

The Navy has periodically monitored the environmental conditions of the site since the sinking and reported the results in an annual public report on environmental monitoring for U.S. Naval nuclear-powered ships. These reports provide specifics on the environmental sampling of sediment, water, and marine life which were taken to ascertain whether the submarine has had a significant effect on the deep ocean environment. The reports also explain the methodology for conducting deep sea monitoring from both surface vessels and submersibles. The monitoring data confirms that there has been no significant effect on the environment. Nuclear fuel in the submarine remains intact.

Details of the disaster

- 7:47 AM: THRESHER begins its descent to the test depth of 1300 feet.

- 7:52 AM: THRESHER levels off at 400 feet, contacts the surface, and the crew inspects the ship for leaks. None are found.

- 8:09 AM: Commander Harvey reports reaching half the test depth.

- 8:25 AM: THRESHER reaches 1000 feet depth.

- 9:02 AM: THRESHER is cruising at just a few knots (subs normally moved slowly and cautiously at great depths, lest a sudden jam of the diving planes send the ship below test depth in a matter of seconds.) Commander Harvey orders a course change: "Twenty degrees right rudder and five degrees down angle."

- 9:09 AM: It is believed that a brazed pipe-joint ruptures in the engine room. The crew attempts to stop the leak while the room is filled with a cloud of mist. Harvey orders full speed, upward tilt of 15 degrees, and emptying the Main Ballast Tank in order to surface. Due to Joule-Thomson effect, the pressurized air rapidly expanding in the pipes cools down, condensing moisture and depositing it on strainers installed in the system to protect the moving parts of the valves; in only a few seconds the moisture freezes, clogging the strainers and blocking the air flow, halting the effort to blow water out of the Ballast Tanks. The water leaking from the broken pipe most likely causes short circuits leading to an automatic shutdown the ship's Reactor. The vessel loses propulsion. Harvey orders propulsion shifted to a battery-powered backup system. Assuming that the flooding was contained quickly, the engine room crew begins to restart the Reactor, an operation that is expected to take at least 7 minutes.

- 9:13 AM: Harvey reports status via underwater telephone. The transmission is garbled, though some words are recognizable: "We are experiencing minor difficulties, have positive up-angle, and are attempting to blow." The submarine, growing heavier from water flooding the engine room, continues its descent. Another attempt to empty the Ballast Tanks is performed, again failing due to the formation of ice.

- 9:15 AM: SKYLARK attempts to contact THRESHER, gets no immediate answer.

- 9:16 AM: Garbled transmission received from THRESHER.

- 9:17 AM: A second transmission is received, with somewhat recognizable phrase "exceeding test depth ... nine hundred north". The leak from the broken pipe grows with increased pressure.

- 9:18 AM: SKYLARK detects a high-energy low-frequency noise with characteristics of an implosion.

On April 11, at a news conference at 10:30 AM, the Navy officially concluded the ship lost.

Officers and men lost with USS THRESHER (SSN-593)

The following crew members were lost with THRESHER (SSN-593). NOTE: the designator "(SS)" after an enlisted man's name and rate denotes "Qualified in Submarines", and entitles the man to wear the coveted silver dolphin insignia.

Officers
- Harvey, John W., LCDR, Commanding Officer
- Garner, Pat M., LCDR, Executive Officer
- Di Nola, Michael J., Lieutenant Commander
- Lyman, John S., Jr., Lieutenant Commander
- Collier, Merrill F., Lieutenant

- Smarz, John, Jr., Lieutenant
- Babcock, Ronald C., Lieutenant (Junior Grade)
- Grafton, John G., Lieutenant (Junior Grade)
- Henry, James J., Jr., Lieutenant (Junior Grade)
- Parsons, Guy C., Jr., Lieutenant (Junior Grade)
- Wiley, John J., Lieutenant (Junior Grade)

Enlisted Men

- Arenault, Tilmon J., ENCA(SS)
- Bain, Ronald E., EN2(SS)
- Bell, John E., MM1
- Bobbitt, Edgar S., EM2(SS)
- Boster, Gerald C., EM3(SS)
- Bracey, George, SD3(SS)
- Brann, Richard P., EN2(SS)
- Carkoski, Richard J., EN2(SS)
- Cayey, Steven G., TM2(SS)
- Christiansen, Edward, SN(SS)
- Claussen, Larry W., EM2(SS)
- Clements, Thomas E., ETR3(SS)
- Cummings, Francis M., SOS2(SS)
- Carmody, Patrick W., SK2
- Dabruzzi, Samuel J., ETN2(SS)
- Davison, Clyde E., III, ETR3
- Day, Donald C., EN3(SS)
- Denny, Roy O., Jr., EM1(SS)
- DiBella, Peter J., SN
- Dundas, Don R., ETN2(SS)
- Dyer, Troy E., ET1(SS)
- Forni, Ellwod H., SOCA(SS)
- Foti, Raymond P., ET1(SS)
- Freeman, Larry W., FTM2(SS)
- Fusco, Gregory J., EM2(SS)
- Gallant, Andrew J., Jr., HMC(SS)

- Garcia, Napoleon T., SD1(SS)
- Garner, John E., YNSN(SS)
- Gaynor, Robert W., EN2(SS)
- Gosnell, Robert H., SA(SS)
- Graham, William E., SOC(SS)
- Gunter, Aaron J., QM1(SS)
- Hall, Richard C., ETR2(SS)
- Hayes, Norman T., EM1
- Heiser, Laird G., MM1
- Helsius, Marvin T., MM2
- Hewitt, Leonard H., EMCA(SS)
- Hoague, Joseph H., TM2(SS)
- Hodge, James P., EM2
- Hudson, John F., EN2 (SS)
- Inglis, John F., FN
- Johnson, Brewner G., FTG1(SS)
- Johnson, Edward A., ENCA(SS)
- Johnson, Richard L., RMSA
- Johnson, Robert E., TMC(SS)
- Johnson, Thomas B., ET1(SS)
- Jones, Richard W., EM2(SS)
- Kaluza, Edmund J., Jr., SOS2(SS)
- Kantz, Thomas C., ETR2(SS)
- Kearney, Robert D., MM3
- Keiler, Ronald D., IC2(SS)
- Kiesecker, George J., MM2(SS)
- Klier, Billy M., EN1(SS)
- Kroner, George R., CS3
- Lanouette, Norman G., QM1(SS)
- Lavoie, Wayne W., YN1(SS)
- Mabry, Templeman N., Jr., EN2(SS)
- Mann, Richard H., Jr., IC2 (SS)
- Marullo, Julius F., Jr., QM1(SS)
- McClelland, Douglas R., EM2(SS)

- McCord, Donald J., MM1(SS)
- McDonough, Karl P., TM3(SS)
- Middleton, Sidney L., MM1(SS)
- Muise, Ronald A., CS2
- Musselwhite, James A., ETN2(SS)
- Nault, Donald E., CS1(SS)
- Noonis, Walter J., RMC(SS)
- Norris, John D., ET1(SS)
- Oetting, Chesley C., EM2
- Pennington, Roscoe C., EMCA(SS)
- Peters, James G., EMCS
- Phillippi, James F., SOS2(SS)
- Philput, Dan A., EN2(SS)
- Podwell, Richard, MM2
- Regan, John S., MM1(SS)
- Ritchie, James P., RM2
- Robison, Pervis, Jr., SN
- Rountree, Glenn A., QM2(SS)
- Rushetski, Anthony A., ETN2
- Schiewe, James M., EM1(SS)
- Shafer, Benjamin N., EMCM(SS)
- Shafer, John D., EMCS(SS)
- Shimko, Joseph T., MM1
- Shotwell, Burnett, M., ETRSN
- Sinnett, Alan D., FTG2(SS)
- Smith, William H., Jr., BT1
- Solomon, Ronald H., EM1
- Steinel, Robert E., SO1(SS)
- Snider, James L., MM1
- Van Pelt, Rodger E., IC1(SS)
- Wasel, David A., RMSN
- Walski, Joseph A., RM1(SS)
- Wiggins, Charles L., FTG1
- Wise, Donald E., MMCA(SS)

- Wolf, Ronald E., QMSN(SS)
- Zweifel, Jay H, EM2

Naval Observers

- Krag, Robert L., Lieutenant Commander, Staff, Deputy Commander, Submarine Force, Atlantic Fleet
- Allen, Phillip H., Lieutenant Commander, Portsmouth Naval Shipyard
- Billings, John H., Lieutenant Commander, Portsmouth Naval Shipyard Biederman, Robert D., Lieutenant, Portsmouth Naval Shipyard

Civilian Engineers and Technicians

- Keuster, Donald W., Naval Ordnance Laboratory
- Abrams, Fred P., Portsmouth Naval Shipyard
- Beal, Daniel W., Jr., Portsmouth Naval Shipyard
- Charron, Robert E., Portsmouth Naval Shipyard
- Critchley, Kenneth J., Portsmouth Naval Shipyard
- Currier, Paul C., Portsmouth Naval Shipyard
- DesJardins, Richard R., Portsmouth Naval Shipyard
- Dineen, George J., Portsmouth Naval Shipyard
- Fisher, Richard R., Portsmouth Naval Shipyard
- Guerette, Paul A., Portsmouth Naval Shipyard
- Moreau, Henry C., Portsmouth Naval Shipyard
- Palmer, Franklin J., Portsmouth Naval Shipyard
- Prescott, Robert D., Portsmouth Naval Shipyard
- Whitten, Laurence E., Portsmouth Naval Shipyard
- Jaquay, Maurice F., Raytheon Corporation
- Corcoran, Kenneth R., Sperry Corporation
- Stademuller, Donald T., Sperry Corporation

This is the end of the Wikipedia article on the USS THRESHER (SSN 593) loss. Source of the following content: https:// en.wikipedia.org/wiki/USS_Scorpion_(SSN-589)
*****

SCORPION
Wednesday, May 22, 1968, 400 miles southwest of the Azores Islands

USS SCORPION (SSN 589) is on its way home from a successful deployment to the Mediterranean Sea. In just a few days the crew and their families are to be reunited after a lengthy absence. While SCORPION was only just a tad shy of being 8 years old at the time of her loss on this fateful day, she was already an obsolete boat in a number of ways. To assess her relative "age" you must consider the following points:

At just under 8 years old, she had been in service for just 26 percent of the eventual 31-year life of the lead ship of her class, USS SKIPJACK (SSN 585). Calendar age isn't everything, though. Design age and relative degree of obsolescence is. The other 5 ships of the SKIPJACK Class, at this point, have been extensively updated and modernized – in particular, having received their SUBSAFE packages.

The entire 13 ship THRESHER Class, now all with SUBSAFE modifications, had been completed and commissioned. The last ship of the THRESHER Class to be commissioned, GATO, had been commissioned some 4 months earlier on January 25, 1968. *In fact, GATO's saddest mission in her first year of service was participating in the valiant, but hopeless, search for SCORPION in the area of her loss.*

Three ships of the STURGEON Class, the fully developed (and eventually 37-ship strong) second generation nuclear attack submarine class that incorporated all THRESHER lessons learned in its original design, were already commissioned and in service. These ships were USS STURGEON (SSN 637), USS PARGO (SSN 650) and USS QUEENFISH (SSN 651).

SCORPION was the only ship in the fleet to not have received the SUBSAFE modifications that were developed and mandated following the loss of THRESHER.

SCORPION was the very first submarine that had been used to prototype a reduced maintenance concept for attack submarines.

There were 3 concerns driving the development of the concept. First, as much as 40 percent of the available time for these early attack submarines was spent in the shipyard undergoing repairs, routine maintenance and modernizations/upgrades. The 60's were a chaotic time in nuclear submarine development, with thousands of lessons learned being developed and implemented in the midst of a frantic build program. One result, though, was too much time not on deployment. This was the Cold War, after all. Second, these maintenance periods were sucking up far too much of the Navy's Operations and Maintenance Budget line. Finally, there was the question of available shipyard capacity. Nobody wanted to either build more naval shipyards or qualify even more commercial yards for this difficult and technically complex work. What everybody in Washington really wanted for Christmas was to build new STURGEON Class submarines faster, as well as to keep building BENJAMIN FRANKLIN (SSBN 640) Class ballistic missile submarines even faster. In the submarine pecking-order the boomers (SSBN's) had always been top priority – with attack boats getting what was left. In 1967, as SCORPION entered Norfolk Naval Shipyard for what would be her final shipyard period, what was left for SCORPION wasn't much.

As SCORPION prepared for and conducted her Mediterranean deployment the crew made do with what had been provided to them. By all accounts they had a successful deployment and were going home on a relatively good note. That they didn't make it home is evidence of a tragedy whose real cause may never be known. Was it their own torpedo malfunction? Was it a problem with the ship's battery? Was it an aggressive act by a hostile ship? Or was it just plain bad luck with a ship that should have been better maintained and better equipped? What we'll always know, though, is that this business – submarining – is never to be taken lightly.

The following is an account of the SCORPION tragedy from Wikipedia, the online encyclopedia. Note: the same Wikipedia caution noted above also applies here.

To Ensure Clarity for the reader, everything on the following pages is from Wikipedia. The end of the Wikipedia article will be designated with another comment.

USS SCORPION (SSN-589) was the sixth ship of the United States Navy to be named for the SCORPION, (hence the Scorpius constellation on her insignia). She was a SKIPJACK-class nuclear submarine of the United States Navy. She was one of the few American submarines to be lost at sea while not at war and to date is one of only two nuclear subs the U.S. Navy has ever lost (both during peacetime). She was also the last nuclear sub lost by the Navy; the first was USS THRESHER (SSN-593), which sank in April 1963 off the coast of New England. SCORPION sank on May 22, 1968.

History of Service

Her keel was laid down on 20 August 1954 by the Electric Boat Division of the General Dynamics Corporation in Groton, Connecticut. She was launched on 19 December 1959 sponsored by Mrs. Elizabeth S. Morrison, and commissioned on 29 July 1960 with Commander Norman B. Bessac in command.

A new design

When new, the SKIPJACK class (of which SCORPION was a member) was the fastest, smallest, and most maneuverable of all U.S. nuclear submarines (at that time). Submerged, she could cruise at speeds of up to 30 knots — and probably faster. She was so fast that she could outrun most of the torpedoes that might ever be fired at her. She was so maneuverable and so fast that in Navy practice maneuvers, SCORPION could surface, attract the attention of surface warships, and then quickly disappear again and resurface miles away; when the surface ships participating in the maneuvers attempted to track her down, she moved into position for an easy kill.

The SKIPJACK-class subs were the first US submarines to blend a tear-drop shaped hull with nuclear propulsion. The Russians had streamlined their nuclear submarines at their first design. SKIPJACK subs such as SCORPION also featured retractable fittings on their hulls. All of the small projections typical of nuclear submarines could be retracted to reduce drag, reduce noise and to increase speed. SKIPJACK-class submarines were quite noisy however, and were probably readily tracked by their adversaries in Soviet nuclear subs.

1960 – 1967

Assigned to Submarine Squadron 6, Division 62, SCORPION departed New London, Connecticut, on 24 August for a two-month deployment in European waters. During that period, she participated in exercises with units of the Sixth Fleet and of other NATO navies. After returning to New England in late October, she trained along the eastern seaboard until May 1961, then crossed the Atlantic again for operations which took her into the summer. On 9 August 1961 she returned to New London, and, a month later, shifted to Norfolk, Virginia. In 1962, she earned the Navy Unit Commendation.

With Norfolk her home port for the remainder of her career, SCORPION specialized in the development of nuclear submarine warfare tactics. Varying her role from hunter to hunted, she participated in exercises which ranged along the Atlantic coast and in the Bermuda and Puerto Rico operating areas; then, from June 1963 to May 1964, she interrupted her operations for an overhaul at Charleston, South Carolina. Resuming duty off the eastern seaboard in late spring, she again interrupted that duty from 4 August to 8 October to make a transatlantic patrol. In the spring of 1965, she conducted a similar patrol in European waters.

During the late winter and early spring of 1966, and again in the autumn, she was deployed for special operations. Following the completion of those assignments, her commanding Officer received the Navy Commendation Medal for outstanding leadership, foresight, and professional skill. Other SCORPION Officers and crewmen were cited for meritorious achievement.

Overhaul

On 1 February 1967, SCORPION entered the Norfolk Naval Shipyard for another extended overhaul. However, instead of the much-needed complete overhaul, she got only emergency repairs to get her back on duty as soon as possible. The cost of that last overhaul was nearly one-seventh of those given other nuclear submarines at the same time. This was the result of concerns about the "high percentage of time offline" of nuclear attack submarines which was estimated to be at about 40% of total available duty time.

The reduced overhaul concept SCORPION went through had been approved by the Chief of Naval Operations on 17 June 1966. On 20 July, the CNO also allowed deferral of the SUBSAFE extensions, which had otherwise been deemed essential since 1963.

Loss of SCORPION

Disappearance

In late October 1967, SCORPION started refresher training and weapons system acceptance tests, and was given a new Commanding Officer, Francis Slattery. Following type training out of Norfolk, Virginia, she got underway on 15 February 1968 for a Mediterranean Sea deployment. She operated with the Sixth Fleet into May and then headed west for home. On 21 May, she indicated her position to be about 50 nautical miles (90 km) south of the Azores. Six days later, she was reported overdue at Norfolk.

The search

A search was initiated, but without immediate success. On 5 June, SCORPION and her crew were declared "presumed lost." Her name was struck from the Naval Vessel Register on 30 June.

The search continued, however. A team of mathematical consultants led by Dr. John Craven, the Chief Scientist of the U.S. Navy's Special Projects Division, employed the novel methods

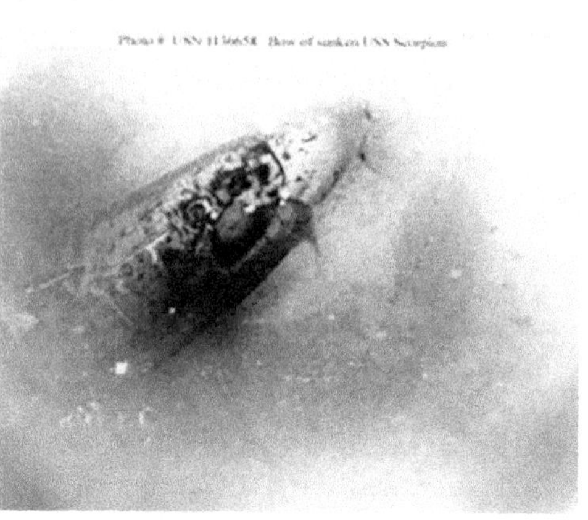

US Navy Photo 1958 of the bow section of SCORPION, by the crew of TRIESTE

of Bayesian search theory. These were developed two years earlier during the (successful) search for a hydrogen bomb lost at sea off the coast of Palomares, Spain, when a refueling Strategic Air Command B-52 collided with a KC-135 tanker and both crashed into the sea. At the end of October, the Navy's oceanographic research ship, USNS MIZAR (T-AGOR-11), located sections of the hull of SCORPION in more than 3000 meters (10,000 feet) of water about 740 kilometers (400 nautical miles) southwest of the Azores. Subsequently, the Court of Inquiry was reconvened, and other vessels, including the bathyscaphe TRIESTE, were dispatched to the scene and they collected a myriad of pictures and other data.

Cause of the loss

Although the cause of her loss cannot be determined with certainty, the explanation provided by the US Navy maintains that a battery of a Mark 37 torpedo was inadvertently activated during an inspection. The torpedo, in a fully-ready condition and without a propeller guard, began a live "hot run" within the tube. Released from the tube, the torpedo became fully-armed and successfully engaged its nearest target — SCORPION herself. Evidence for this includes the fact that the SOSUS network tracked the submarine moving back its original course, consistent with performing a 180-degree turn in an attempt to activate safety systems in the torpedo.

A theory later advanced is that a torpedo may have exploded in the tube owing to an uncontrollable fire in the torpedo room. The book ***Blind Man's Bluff*** documents the findings and investigation by Dr. John Craven, who had worked on the propulsion systems of the Mark 37. Craven discovered that a likely cause was overheating of a faulty battery. The silver-zinc battery used in the Mark 37 torpedo had a tendency to overheat, and in extreme cases, it would cause a fire that was strong enough to cause a low-order detonation of the warhead. Such a detonation may have occurred, opening the boat's large torpedo-loading hatch and causing SCORPION to flood and sink.

The explosion — later correlated with a very loud acoustic event recorded by SOSUS — apparently broke the boat into two major pieces, with the forward hull section, including the torpedo room and most of the operations compartment, creating one impact trench while the aft section, including the Reactor compartment and engine room, created a second impact trench. The aft section of the engine room is telescoped forward into the larger-diameter hull section. The sail is detached and lies nearby in a large debris field.

Environmental monitoring

The U.S. Navy has periodically monitored the environmental conditions of the site since the sinking and has reported the results in an annual public report on environmental monitoring for U.S. nuclear-powered ships and boats. The reports provide specifics on the environmental sampling of sediment, water, and marine life that is done to ascertain whether the submarine has significantly affected the deep-ocean environment. The reports also explain the methodology for conducting this deep sea monitoring from both surface vessels and submersibles. The monitoring data confirm that, by the standards of the U.S. Navy, there has been no significant effect on the environment. The nuclear fuel aboard the submarine remains intact and no uranium in excess of levels expected from the fallout from past atmospheric testing of nuclear weapons has been detected by the Navy's inspections. In addition, SCORPION carried two nuclear-tipped Mark 45 anti-submarine torpedoes (ASTOR) when she was lost. The warheads of these torpedoes are part of the environmental concern. The most likely scenario is that the plutonium and uranium cores of these weapons corroded to a heavy, insoluble material soon after the sinking, and they remain at or close to their original location inside the torpedo room of the boat. If the corroded materials were released outside the submarine, their large specific gravity and insolubility would cause them to settle down into the sediment.

`Secrecy`

The loss of SCORPION was a very traumatic event for the U.S. Navy and was one that has been successfully kept fairly quiet. Relatively little has been published about SCORPION, despite the loss of the 99 men who were aboard at the time of her sinking, and despite the fact that the boat contained a treasure-trove of highly sophisticated spy gear and spy manuals, two nuclear-tipped torpedoes, and her nuclear propulsion system. The best available evidence indicates that SCORPION sank in the Atlantic Ocean on May 22, 1968 after an explosion of some type, while in transit across the Atlantic Ocean from Gibraltar to her home port at Norfolk, Virginia.

Several hypotheses about the cause of the loss have been advanced; some debate whether an explosion ever actually occurred. Some have suggested that hostile action by a Soviet submarine caused SCORPION's loss; there was even speculation that the loss was somehow connected to the Bermuda Triangle. Shortly after her sinking, the Navy assembled a panel of submarine experts to investigate the incident and to publish a report about the likely causes for the sinking. The panel's conclusions, first printed in 1968, were largely classified. At the time, the Navy quoted frequently from a portion of the 1968 report that said no one is likely ever to "conclusively" determine the cause of the loss. The Clinton Administration declassified most of this report in 1993, and it was then that the public first learned that the panel believed that the most likely cause was a malfunction of one of SCORPION's own torpedoes. (The panel qualified its opinion saying the evidence it had available could not lead to a conclusive finding about the cause of her sinking.)

Blind Man's Bluff

In 1999, two New York Times reporters published ***Blind Man's Bluff***, a book providing a rare look into the world of nuclear submarines and espionage during the Cold War. One lengthy chapter deals extensively with SCORPION and her loss. The book reports that concerns about the Mk 37 conventional torpedo carried aboard SCORPION were raised in 1967 and 1968, before SCORPION left Norfolk for her last mission. The concerns focused on the battery that powered the torpedoes. The battery had a thin metal-foil barrier separating two types of volatile chemicals. When mixed slowly and in a controlled fashion, the chemicals generated heat and electricity, powering the motor that pushed the torpedo through the water. But vibrations normally experienced on a nuclear submarine were found to cause the thin foil barrier to break down, allowing the chemicals to interact intensely. This interaction generated excessive heat which, in tests, could readily have caused an inadvertent torpedo explosion. The authors of ***Blind Man's Bluff*** were careful to say they could not point to this as the cause of SCORPION's loss — only that it was a possible cause and that it was consistent with other data indicating an explosion preceded the sinking of SCORPION.

Red Star Rogue

In 2005, the book "**_Red Star Rogue_**: _The Untold Story of a Soviet Submarine's Nuclear Strike Attempt on the U.S._," by former American submariner Kenneth Sewell in collaboration with journalist Clint Richmond, claimed K-129 sank 300 miles northwest of Oahu on 7 March 1968 while launching her three ballistic missiles in a rogue attempt to destroy Pearl Harbor. The book is considered to be a circumstantial, sensational story.

Sewell claims that the sinking of SCORPION was caused by a retaliatory strike for the sinking of K-129, which they attributed to a collision with USS SWORDFISH (SSN-579).

In 1995, when Huchthausen began work on a book about the Soviet underwater fleet, he interviewed Admiral Victor Dygalo, who stated that the true history of K-129 has not been revealed because of the informal agreement between the two countries' senior naval commands. The purpose of that secrecy, he alleged, is to stop any further research into the losses of SCORPION and K-129. Huchthausen states that Dygalo told him to "overlook this matter, and hope that the time will come when the truth will be told to the families of the victims."

Present location

Today, the boat is reported to be resting on a sandy seabed at the bottom of the Atlantic Ocean in approximately 3000m of water. The site is reported to be approximately 400 miles southwest of the Azores Islands, on the eastern edge of the Sargasso Sea. The U.S. Navy has acknowledged that it periodically visits the site to conduct testing for

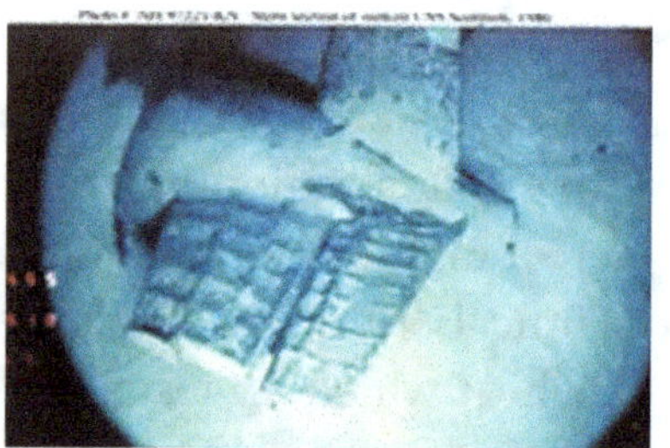

Stern section of SCORPION, seen in 1986 by Woods Hole personnel

the release of nuclear materials from the nuclear Reactor or the two nuclear weapons aboard her, and to determine whether the wreckage has been disturbed. The Navy has not released any information about the status of the wreckage, except for a few photographs taken of the wreckage in 1968, and again in 1985 by deep water submersibles.

The Navy has also released information about the nuclear testing performed in and around SCORPION site. The Navy reports no significant release of nuclear material from the boat. The 1985 photos were taken by a team of oceanographers working for the Woods Hole Oceanographic Institution in Woods Hole, Massachusetts. The circumstances of the Woods Hole mission show the high level of secrecy the Navy attaches to SCORPION; at the time the photographs were taken, the Navy and Woods Hole both maintained that the Woods Hole team was searching for the wreckage of the noted sunken ocean liner, RMS TITANIC. It was only after newspapers learned and reported that the Woods Hole team was also searching for SCORPION that the Navy admitted as much, and released some of the photographs taken during the expedition.

Officers and Men lost with USS SCORPION (SSN-589)

The following Officers and men were lost with SCORPION (SSN-589).

Officers
- Commander Francis Atwood Slattery, Commanding Officer
- Lieutenant Commander David B. Lloyd, Executive Officer
- Lieutenant Commander Daniel P. Stephens
- Lieutenant John Patrick Burke
- Lieutenant George Patrick Farrin,
- Lieutenant Robert Walter Flesch
- Lieutenant William Clarke Harwi

- Lieutenant Charles Lee Lamberth
- Lieutenant John C. Sweet
- Lieutenant (j.g.) James W. Forrester, Jr.
- Lieutenant (j.g.) Michael A. Odening
- Lieutenant (j.g.) Laughton D. Smith

Chief Petty Officers

- TMC Walter William Bishop,
  Chief of the Boat (COB)
- MMC(SS) Robert Eugene Bryan
- RMC(SS) Garlin Ray Denney
- RMCS(SS) Robert Johnson
- MMCS(SS) Richard Allen Kerntke
- QMCS(SS) Frank Patsy Mazzuchi
- EMC(SS) Daniel Christopher Peterson
- HMC(SS) Lynn Thompson Saville
- ETC(SS) George Elmer Smith, Jr.
- YNCS(SS) Leo William Weinbeck
- MMC(SS) James Mitchell Wells

Enlisted Men

- FTG3(SS) Keith Alexander M. Allen
- IC2 Thomas Edward Amtower
- MM2 George Gile Annable
- FN(SS) Joseph Anthony Barr, Jr.
- RM2(SS) Michael Jon Bailey
- IC3 Michael Reid Blake
- MM1(SS) Robert Harold Blocker
- MM2(SS) Kenneth Ray Brocker
- MM1(SS) James K. Brueggeman
- RMSN Daniel Paul Burns, Jr.
- IC2(SS) Ronald Lee Byers
- MM2(SS) Douglas Leroy Campbell
- MM3(SS) Samuel J. Cardullo

- MM2(SS) Francis King Carey
- SN Gary James Carpenter
- MM1(SS) Robert Lee Chandler
- MM1(SS) Mark Helton Christiansen
- SD1(SS) Romeo Constantino
- MM1(SS) Robert James Cowan
- SD1(SS) Joseph Cross
- FA Michael Edward Dunn
- ETR2 Richard Philip Engelhart
- FTGSN William Ralph Fennick
- IC3(SS) Vernon Mark Foli
- SN Ronald Anthony Frank
- CSSN(SS) Michael David Gibson
- IC2 Steven Dean Gleason
- STS2(SS) Michael Edward Henry
- SK1(SS) Larry Leroy Hess
- ETR1(SS) Richard Curtis Hogeland
- MM1(SS) John Richard Houge
- EM2 Ralph Robert Huber
- TM2(SS) Harry David Huckelberry
- EM3 John Frank Johnson
- IC3(SS) Steven Leroy Johnson
- QM2(SS) Julius Johnston, III
- FN Patrick Charles Kahanek
- TM2(SS) Donald Terry Karmasek
- ETR3(SS) Rodney Joseph Kipp
- MM3 Dennis Charles Knapp
- MM1(SS) Max Franklin Lanier
- ET1(SS) John Weichert Livingston
- ETN2 Kenneth Robert Martin
- ET1(SS) Michael Lee McGuire
- TMSN Steven Charles Miksad
- TMSN Joseph Francis Miller, Jr
- MM2(SS) Cecil Frederick Mobley

- QM1(SS) Raymond Dale Morrison
- QM3(SS) Dennis Paul Pferrer
- EM1(SS) Gerald Stanley Psopisil
- IC3 Donald Richard Powell
- MM2 Earl Lester Ray, Jr.
- CS1(SS) Jorge Luis Santana
- ETN2(SS) Richard George Schaffer
- SN William Newman Schoonover
- SN Phillip Allan Seifert
- MM2(SS) Robert Bernard Smith
- ST1(SS) Harold Robert Snapp, Jr.
- ETM2(SS) Joel Candler Stephens
- MM2(SS) David Burton Stone
- EM2 John Phillip Sturgill
- YN3 Richard Norman Summers
- TMSN John Driscoll Sweeney, Jr.
- ETM2(SS) James Frank Tindol, III
- CSSN Johnny Gerald Veerhusen
- TM3 Robert Paul Violeiti
- ST3 Ronald James Voss
- FTG1(SS) John Michael Wallace
- MM1(SS) Joel Kurt Watkins
- MMFN Robert Westley Watson
- TM2 James Edwin Webb
- SN Ronald Richard Williams
- MM3 Robert Alan Willis
- IC1(SS) Virgil Alexander Wright, III
- TM1(SS) Donald H. Yarsbrough
- ETR2(SS) Clarence Otto Young, Jr.

This is the end of the Wikipedia article about the loss of USS SCORPION (SSN 589).

*****

GATO
Thursday, January 25, 1968, General Dynamics
Electric Boat Division, Groton, CT

And then there were 13. On this beautiful, but bitterly cold January morning in the midst of the Cold War, USS GATO (SSN 615) *finally* entered the fleet under the command of CDR (later VADM) Albert Baciocco, Jr.

It had been an unusually long construction period that at times had seemed like it wasn't ever going to end. When THRESHER was lost on April 10, 1963, GATO was on the building ways. She was nearly ready for launch, but with the loss of THRESHER and the as-yet unknown lessons to be incorporated in her sister ships, all work was halted on GATO and her two sister ships then at Electric Boat – USS FLASHER (SSN 613) and USS GREENLING (SSN 614).

GENERAL DYNAMICS
Electric Boat Division
Eastern Point Road, Groton, Connecticut 06340 • 203 446-3129, 446-3514

NEW GOAL KEEPER - - - The nuclear attack submarine Gato, named for a World War II submarine that won fame as "The Goal Keeper" during operations in the Pacific, will be commissioned by the Navy Jan. 25 at the Electric Boat division of General Dynamics, Groton, Conn. Principal speaker at the commissioning ceremonies will be Rep. Craig Hosmer, of California, a member of the Joint Committee on Atomic Energy. Gato is the 29th General Dynamics-built nuclear submarine to be commissioned.

\# \# \#

1/23/68/6P/A-D-E

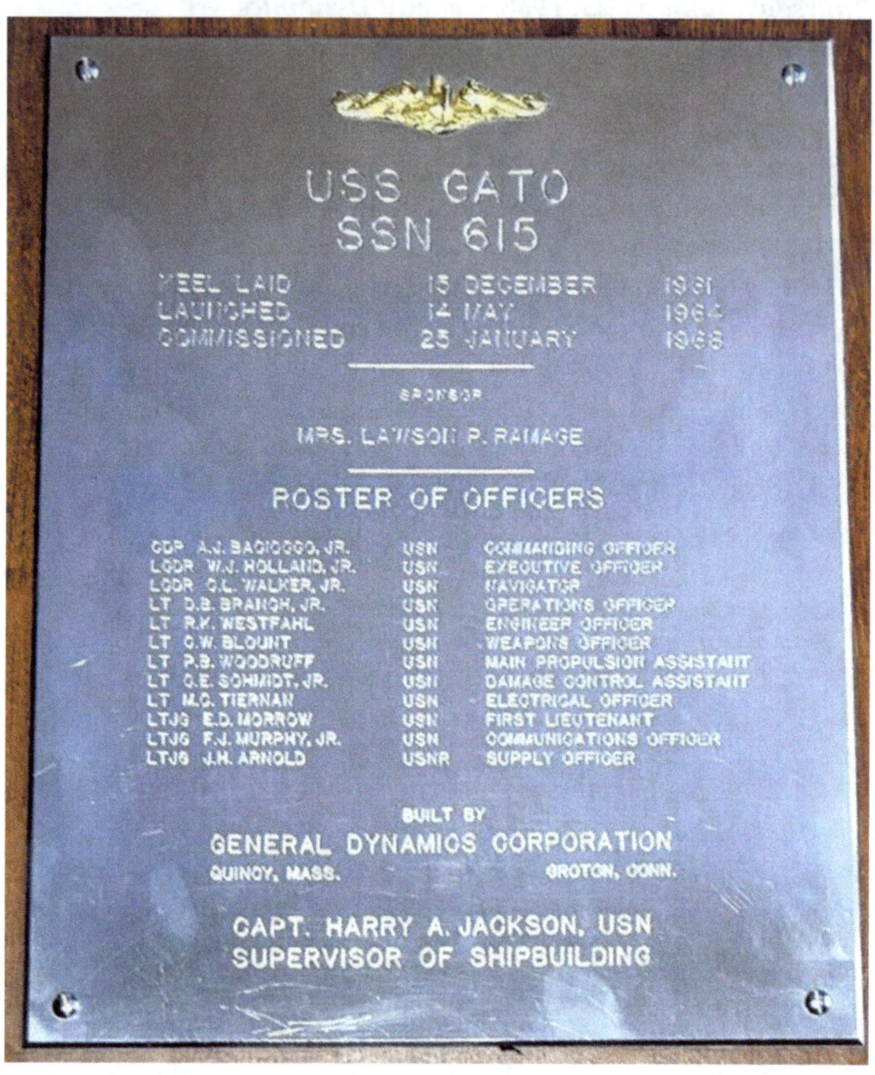
USS GATO
SSN 615

KEEL LAID   15 DECEMBER   1961
LAUNCHED   14 MAY   1964
COMMISSIONED   25 JANUARY   1968

SPONSOR

MRS. LAWSON P. RAMAGE

ROSTER OF OFFICERS

CDR A.J. BACIOCCO, JR.   USN   COMMANDING OFFICER
LCDR W.J. HOLLAND, JR.   USN   EXECUTIVE OFFICER
LCDR O.L. WALKER, JR.   USN   NAVIGATOR
LT D.B. BRANCH, JR.   USN   OPERATIONS OFFICER
LT R.K. WESTFAHL   USN   ENGINEER OFFICER
LT C.W. BLOUNT   USN   WEAPONS OFFICER
LT P.B. WOODRUFF   USN   MAIN PROPULSION ASSISTANT
LT C.E. SCHMIDT, JR.   USN   DAMAGE CONTROL ASSISTANT
LT M.C. TIERNAN   USN   ELECTRICAL OFFICER
LTJG E.D. MORROW   USN   FIRST LIEUTENANT
LTJG F.J. MURPHY, JR.   USN   COMMUNICATIONS OFFICER
LTJG J.H. ARNOLD   USNR   SUPPLY OFFICER

BUILT BY

GENERAL DYNAMICS CORPORATION
QUINCY, MASS.   GROTON, CONN.

CAPT. HARRY A. JACKSON, USN
SUPERVISOR OF SHIPBUILDING

.615
USS GATO
SSN 615
YELLOW
RED
YELLOW

USS GATO
SSN 615

Being the farthest along, though, work on FLASHER was restarted shortly thereafter and she was launched later that year. In the only simultaneous launch of two submarines from the same shipyard, FLASHER was launched on June 22, 1963, alongside USS TECUMSEH (SSBN 628).

(FLASHER is the ship on the left at the EB south yard ways in the photo below, as launch preparations are being made)

It was decided by the Navy that these three Electric Boat THRESHER Class ships would be highly modified with a "full" SUBSAFE package. The other ships in the THRESHER Class received lighter "modified" SUBSAFE packages. Since nothing on a submarine happens easily and since the extra weight of this "full" SUBSAFE package far exceeded the design margin for weight growth, this was a big problem. These three ships, unless something was done, would not float. You see, to achieve the exactly neutral buoyancy that a submarine needs to survive when submerged, it must weigh exactly the same amount as the volume of seawater that it displaces. Weight and balance are incredibly important in a submarine, which, in order to submerge, has far less "reserve buoyancy" than a surface ship. While extra lead is always added to a new design, so that it can be removed later in ship life as new, more capable, heavier equipment is added to the ship during modernization periods, the ships did not have that much margin in the original design.

The answer was to cut the ships in half after they were launched and to install a "plug" with the ship in drydock. It was an old procedure and had been most famously used when the original USS SCORPION hull was re-designated as USS GEORGE WASHINGTON (SSBN 598) while it was still on the building ways. The hull had been cut in half and the forward and aft sections had been separated so that the new missile compartment could be installed. As noted above – the boomers always had top priority.

In any event, FLASHER, GREENLING and GATO would get a 13-foot-long hull plug, installed just forward of the Reactor, and this would provide about 130 tons of additional displacement. This was more than enough to install the full SUBSAFE package and to have design margin at delivery for the eventual, inevitable ship modernizations over the ship's upcoming 30-year life.

The modifications to FLASHER were done at Electric Boat, and she was commissioned as the Navy's first SUBSAFE ship in a semi-reasonable period of time – on July 22, 1966. Meanwhile GREENLING and GATO sat, starting to rust into oblivion before they had even been completed! Because the building ways were needed for both STURGEON Class SSNs and for BENJAMIN FRANKLIN Class SSBNs, both GREENLING and GATO were launched in 1964 and were put alongside a pier at Electric Boat.

This was a crazy time for the Submarine Industrial Base as over an 8-year-long period during the 1960's the US Navy took delivery of a new submarine, on average, every 44 days. An incredible achievement, and a testament to America's then-industrial might – particularly as compared to the second decade of the 21st century when, despite everyone's best efforts, the Submarine Industrial Base was unable to ever deliver the desired 2 new submarines per year or to properly maintain the commissioned submarine fleet.

To put the 1960's submarine construction program all into perspective, consider these facts:

- While Electric Boat was building its three THRESHER Class submarines it also started, built and delivered twelve of its seventeen "41 for Freedom" SSBN ballistic missile submarines (shortest construction time at 580 days, or 1.59 years) and started, built and delivered two STURGEON Class SSN attack submarines.

- Quincy Shipbuilding had delivered its first submarine in 1908, and had built the world's first nuclear powered surface combatants, USS LONG BEACH (CGN 9) and USS BAINBRIDGE (DLGN/CGN 25). During the Electric Boat THRESHER Class construction program Quincy started and was building two STURGEON Class attack submarines. These ships, USS WHALE (SN 638) AND USS SUNFISH (SSN 649), were commissioned October 12, 1968 and March 15, 1969, respectively.

- The Electric Boat Thresher Class ships averaged 5.87 years in construction vs the Electric Boat "41 for Freedom" ships averaging 2.1 years in construction.

The table below, derived from official US Navy shipbuilding records, provides additional detail. *It is hard not to review this data and conclude that, from the jump, THRESHER Class ships were the so-called "red headed stepchildren" of the Submarine Force.* This, despite the fact that Thresher Class ships were more capable than either all preceding attack submarines <u>or</u> the succeeding STURGEON Class submarines. The price for this performance, of course, was the lack of much, if any, safety margin in the ship's design.

These *Apex Predators* lived at the very edge of the envelope. Mighty. mighty purebred *warships*, indeed.

THRESHER Class Commanding Officers knew how to get the most from these ships; this small 13 ship Class (with only 12 ships serving full ship lives) produced an inordinately large number of Flag Officers, from GATO's first Commanding Officer, Vice Admiral Albert Baciocco, Jr., USN(Ret) to USS DACE (SSN 607) Commanding Officer Admiral Kinnard McKee, USN(Ret), who relieved Admiral Rickover at Naval Reactors to the Navy's last active THRESHER Class veteran, Vice Admiral William Merz, USN(Ret), who retired from the Navy in late 2022, and many others. VADM Merz did not command a THRESHER Class ship but completed his first tour on USS HADDO (SSN 604) at the end of ship's life; he later commanded both research submarine NR-1 and LOS ANGELES Class attack submarine USS MEMPHIS (SSN 691). While under command of VADM Merz, MEMPHIS won the Battenburg cup as the best ship in the Atlantic Fleet. 594 Tough; *only the very best of the best sailed these demanding, high performance little ships.*

EB Sequence	"41 For Freedom" SSBN Names	SSBN	Builder	Keel Date	Date Launched	Date Commissioned	Launch to Commissuining Span (Days)	Construction Span (Days)	Construction Span (Years)
1	GEORGE WASHINGTON	598	EB	11/1/1957	6/9/1959	12/30/1959	204	789	2.16
2	PATRICK HENRY	599	EB	5/27/1958	9/22/1959	4/11/1960	202	685	1.88
3	ETHAN ALLEN	608	EB	9/14/1959	1/22/1960	8/8/1961	564	694	1.90
4	THOMAS A EDISON	610	EB	3/15/1960	6/15/1961	3/10/1962	268	725	1.99
5	LAFAYETTE	616	EB	1/17/1961	5/8/1962	4/23/1963	350	826	2.26
6	ALEXANDER HAMILTON	617	EB	6/26/1961	8/18/1962	6/27/1963	313	731	2.00
7	NATHAN HALE	623	EB	10/2/1961	1/12/1963	11/23/1963	315	782	2.14
8	DANIEL WEBSTER	626	EB	12/28/1961	4/27/1962	4/9/1964	713	833	2.28
9	TECUMSEH	628	EB	6/1/1962	6/22/1963	5/29/1964	342	728	1.99
10	ULYSSES S GRANT	631	EB	8/18/1962	11/2/1963	7/17/1964	258	699	1.92
11	CASIMIR PULASKI	633	EB	1/12/1963	2/1/1964	8/14/1964	195	580	1.59
12	BENJAMIN FRANKLIN	640	EB	5/25/1963	12/5/1964	10/22/1965	321	881	2.41
13	GEORGE BANCROFT	643	EB	8/24/1963	3/20/1965	1/22/1966	308	882	2.42
14	JAMES K POLK	645	EB	11/23/1963	5/22/1965	4/16/1966	329	875	2.40
15	HENRY L STIMSON	655	EB	4/4/1964	11/13/1965	8/20/1966	280	868	2.38
16	FRANCIS SCOTT KEY	657	EB	12/5/1964	4/23/1965	12/3/1966	589	728	1.99
17	WILL ROGERS	659	EB	3/20/1965	7/21/1966	4/1/1967	254	742	2.03
41.5% of the original "41 for Freedom" SSBNs, and all since, were built at Electric Boat - *12 were built start to finish during EB's THRESHER Class ship construction program*						Min	195	580	1.59
						Average	341	768	2.10
						Max	713	882	2.42

All Started after FLASHER and Delivered before GATO

EB Sequence	STURGEON Class SSNs Name	SSN	Builder	Keel Date	Date Launched	Date Commissioned	Launch to Commissuining Span (Days)	Construction Span (Days)	Construction Span (Years)
1	STURGEON	637	EB	8/10/1963	2/26/1966	3/3/1967	370	1,301	3.56
2	PARGO	650	EB	6/3/1964	9/17/1966	1/5/1968	475	1,311	3.59
3	BERGALL	667	EB	4/16/1966	2/17/1968	6/13/1969	482	1,154	3.16
STURGEON and PARGO were started after FLASHER and completed before GATO. BERGALL was 50% complete when GATO was commissioned						Min	370	1154	3.16
						Average	442	1255	3.44
						Max	482	1311	3.59

EB Sequence	THRESHER Class SSNs Name	SSN	Builder	Keel Date	Date Launched	Date Commissioned	Launch to Commissuining Span (Days)	Construction Span (Days)	Construction Span (Years)
1	FLASHER	613	EB	4/14/1961	6/22/1963	7/22/1966	1126	1,925	5.27
2	GREENLING	614	EB	8/15/1961	4/4/1964	11/3/1967	1308	2,271	6.22
3	GATO	615	EB	12/15/1961	5/14/1964	1/25/1968	1351	2,232	6.12
During Construction of these ships EB started & delivered (2) 637 Class SSNs During Construction of these ships Quincy started & built (2) 637 Class SSNs, these ships were delivered in 1968 & 1969						Min	1126	1925	5.27
						Average	1262	2143	5.87
						Max	1351	2271	6.22

So, as outlined above, GATO was a victim of this prioritization to take the easiest path to deliver the largest number of new submarines in the shortest possible time. Kind of sad, actually. GATO had had the wife of a World War II submarine hero – then retired Medal of Honor winner Vice Admiral Lawson P. "Red" Ramage – assigned as her ship sponsor. After the celebration and speeches about this and that on launch day, though, the pomp and ceremony was quickly forgotten as GREENLING and GATO became increasingly more incomplete, rusty spare parts bins for the active fleet.

Mrs. Lawson P. Ramage
Sponsor

USS GATO

The Gato, 21st nuclear submarine launched by Electric Boat in the past decade, is the third submarine to be launched here this year. An advanced design attack vessel, the Gato has specially designed anti-submarine warfare capabilities which will enable it to operate against submarines as well as surface ships.

When completed, the Gato will be 292 feet long and will displace 4,060 tons. She will operate at speeds in excess of 20 knots and will carry a crew of 10 officers and 100 men.

The Gato is one of 20 submarines of this type under construction or authorized.

The nuclear submarine Gato is named for a World War II submarine which was launched at Electric Boat in 1941. That Gato made 13 successful war patrols, sinking nine ships and winning the coveted Presidential Unit Citation and 13 battle stars.

Gato is a native Mexican name applied to a small species of shark found off the West Coast of Mexico and in the Gulf of California.

PROGRAM

National Anthem	United States Coast Guard Academy Band
Invocation	Capt. J. J. Tubbs (ChC) USN
Welcome and Introduction of Speaker	J. William Jones, Jr., President General Dynamics/Electric Boat
Address	Vice Admiral Harold T. Deutermann, USN Commander, Eastern Sea Frontier
Introduction of Sponsor	Mr. Jones
Christening	Mrs. Lawson P. Ramage

The Original USS GATO (SS 212)
During World War II

Soon it became intuitively obvious to even the most casual observer that these ships were not going to be completed at Electric Boat. *Not going to happen.* The Navy agreed with an Electric Boat proposal and the ships were moved to Quincy, MA where Electric Boat parent General Dynamics owned another shipyard. They were completed there. GREENLING was commissioned in November 1967 and GATO was commissioned two months later in January 1968. Meanwhile, USS HADDOCK (SSN 621) was finally completed *(longest construction period in the Class at 6.7 years)* at Ingalls Shipbuilding with the modified SUBSAFE package and was commissioned in December 1967 – making GATO the last THRESHER Class ship to enter service.

While they remained members of the THRESHER Class (at that point "officially" renamed the PERMIT Class for USS PERMIT (SSN 594), but always THRESHER Class to her sailors) the three Electric Boat ships ended up with a very distinctive profile. Because of the additional hull length and the way that it was integrated into the over-all ship design, the sail on FLASHER, GREENLING & GATO was obviously longer than on their sister ships. Among the cognoscente it was easy to identify these ships from just a quick glance in profile.

One notable event for GATO is the official ship picture taken during the ship's sea trials. Before GATO no US Navy submarine had been allowed to fly the stars and stripes when underway – only when in port. Someone finally realized, however, that nobody was kidding anybody about whose ships these were. GATO, therefore, was photographed at sea flying the US Flag from her sail.

GATO was put to work straight away. While many new ships spend significant time testing new gear and sometimes in develop-ing new tactics, etc. none of that was for GATO. She was almost a *blue-collar* SSN – straight to work. Do not pass go, do not collect $200. Go straight to work. *And work she did,* including participating in the search for SCORPION upon her loss.

Her early crews were highly competent and greatly skilled. GATO's commissioning Commanding Officer, CDR Albert J.

Baciocco, Jr., USN retired as a Vice Admiral; GATO's commissioning Executive Officer, LCDR W. J. Holland, Jr., later commissioning Commanding Officer of USS PINTADO (SSN 672), retired as a Rear Admiral. This, while notable, reflects the fact that by 1968 highly capable SSNs were less of a novelty and more of a front-line tool in the Cold War. Nobody ever forgot that we had an adversary, and that that adversary was pumping out new submarines at a horrific pace. Given all that happened in the geopolitical sphere in the early 60's, this was very serious business. By 1968, in fact, the rapid build program of that decade has established the SSN as a front-line player in the war. Nothing else was as effective in trailing the other guy's nuclear missile submarines. Nothing else could stop a nuclear ballistic missile attack by one of the other guy's submarines before it was ever launched. Between the time that he started making his preparations for missile launch and the launch of his first missile, one well-placed torpedo was all that it would take to save the world from nuclear Armageddon. It could most effectively be delivered by an SSN in-trail. So, trail they did.

Don't think for one single second that this was for the weak of heart. Unlike today, when absolutely everything feeds an insatiable 24-hour news cycle, there were more than a few times when Cold War SSNs returned home with tarps over their sails and/or dents in their hulls containing shards of titanium (a material not-then used in American submarines but used in certain other submarine fleets). No news here – *fix 'em up quick and get 'em back out on deployment or on Special Operations. There was a war going on. . .* If you don't KNOW that the Cold War was every single bit as tense and real as any war ever fought you simply were not there. <u>Thank a submarine veteran for giving you the opportunity to have been oblivious of this brutal reality</u>.

Speaking of reality, GATO was a true front-line player in this deadly game of cat and mouse from the moment that she first entered service. While on deployment "Up North" in the Barents Sea on November 15, 1969, less than two years after being commissioned, GATO collided (in one of the few publicly reported Cold War collisions) with the Soviet Submarine K-19 while in-trail and submerged at a depth of about 200 feet. K-19, the first-ever Soviet nuclear-powered submarine, was a Hotel Class ballistic missile submarine and had earlier had a serious, and deadly, Reactor accident at sea, south of Greenland, on July 4, 1961. This Soviet Reactor accident was later memorialized in the 2002 movie **_K-19, The Widowmaker_**, starring Harrison Ford and Liam Neeson.

Soviet Submarine K-19

In the collision K-19 had rammed GATO in the side at a relatively high speed. The entire bow of K-19 was destroyed, while GATO's damage was minimal. GATO continued her mission while K-19 was able to return to port on its own, was repaired and returned to service. And while this kind of collision did not occur on a daily basis, it also wasn't – as noted above – the only US/Soviet submarine collision during the Cold War. Not to mention the hundreds of cases of chicken – *exactly what you think is meant here* – where the ultimate collision was avoided by calmer heads on one side or the other overcoming the testosterone of the moment. Not surprisingly, Soviet missile submarine Captains did not like to be trailed. Just as clearly, American attack submarine Captains did not like to be detected by the Soviet missile submarine that they were trailing.

So it went for 17 years as GATO deployed, served on the front lines of the Cold War, and was truly *run hard*. During one notable operation, UNITAS '76, GATO became the first nuclear-powered submarine to circumnavigate South America, including a transit of the Panama Canal, on her way to overhaul.

The ship completed the first of two planned major overhauls in the ship's life, along with several more modest major maintenance periods during this time. Ever since SCORPION, the Navy had developed a much more effective maintenance and modernization program for the submarine force. This program actually achieved the balance that the SCORPION program had lacked.

This program was centered on how long the fuel was lasting in the ships – since refueling a submarine Reactor was major maintenance no matter how you sliced it. GATO had had a relatively new design Reactor core installed during her extended construction period. As a result, she only needed a single refueling during her life. This was conducted at Ingalls Shipbuilding in Pascagoula, MS.

As in all things GATO, she was notable here, of course, as well. Ingalls had built several nuclear-powered attack submarines and had also done major maintenance on SSNs. But with the rationalization of the submarine maintenance program and the slowing of the build rate as the fleet achieved critical mass, Ingalls was removed from the nuclear program. So the last THRESHER Class ship to be completed in her initial construction phase (causing obvious parts availability problems then) became the final nuclear-powered ship to be worked on in any capacity at Ingalls Shipyard. Go GATO!

This brings us to 1985. GATO is now a tired workhorse of the fleet.

Sometimes the hanger queen of Squadron 10.

Always exciting.

Ready for major overhaul number two – scheduled to start in the Spring of 1986 at Portsmouth Naval Shipyard.

All that stood between GATO and her badly needed overhaul was a little 72-day run.

GATO in Floating Drydock, Groton, CT

Finally, a brief note about scale. This book focuses on a single 69 day run – less than 0.7% of the eventually 28.3-year long service life of this single ship. These were, *as we'll explore in much more detail in the following chapters*, exceptionally consequential days in the life of this ship. Still, *make no mistake*, there were many, many other exceptionally consequential days in the service life of this single run-of-the-mill Cold War SSN. Just as there were many other ships doing the same, or similar, missions over many, many other exceptionally consequential days. The 13 ships in the THRESHER Class alone served for more than 318 ship-years of Class Service Life, as detailed below:

Commissioning Order	Decommissioning Order	Length of Service Order (Shortest to Longest)	Name	Hull Number - SSN	Shipbuilder	Commissioning Date	Decommissioning Date	Length of Service (Days)	Length of Service (Years)
1	1	1	THRESHER	593	PNS	8/3/1961	4/10/1963	615	1.7
2	6	13	PERMIT	594	MINS	5/29/1962	6/12/1991	10606	29.1
3	5	10	PLUNGER	595	MINS	11/21/1962	1/3/1990	9905	27.1
4	4	7	BARB	596	ING	8/24/1963	12/20/1989	9615	26.3
5	2	2	DACE	607	ING	4/4/1964	12/2/1988	9008	24.7
6	3	3	POLLACK	603	NYSB	5/26/1964	3/1/1989	9045	24.8
7	8	11	TINOSA	606	PNS	10/17/1964	1/15/1992	9951	27.3
8	7	9	HADDO	604	NYSB	12/16/1964	6/12/1991	9674	26.5
9	10	6	FLASHER	613	EB	7/22/1966	5/26/1992	9440	25.9
10	9	4	GUARDFISH	612	NYSB	12/20/1966	2/2/1992	9175	25.1
11	12	8	GREENLING	614	EB	11/3/1967	4/18/1994	9663	26.5
12	11	5	HADDOCK	621	ING	12/22/1967	4/7/1993	9238	25.3
13	13	12	GATO	615	EB	1/25/1968	4/25/1996	10318	28.3

# Built	Shipbuilders		Length of Service (not including THRESHER)		
2	PNS	Portsmouth Naval Shipyard (ME)	Average	9636.5	
2	MINS	Mare Island Naval Shipyard (CA)	Shortest	DACE - 9008	24.7 Years
3	ING	Ingalls Shipbuilding (MS)	Longest	PERMIT - 10606	29 Years
3	NYSB	New York Shipbuilding (NJ)	Difference	1598	4.4 Years
3	EB	Electric Boat (CT) (Long Hull Version)			

Note: Technically, USS JACK (SSN 605) is listed as a member of this Class, but this ship had an unusual one-of-a-kind test Engineroom/Propulsion Equipment Design and was, as a result, 20 feet longer than a standard THRESHER Class ship. Because it was a prototype ship it is not included here.

Recall that in late 1985 there were 99 SSNs in the active US Navy fleet. In short, then, **<u>it took many, many exceptionally consequential days at sea to win the Cold War</u>**.

Certification for War

Ready to Protect the Nation

Chapter 3

POM Certification

Thursday, October 10, 1985, Narragansett Bay Operating Areas

There are three attack submarine squadrons homeported in New London in 1985. Submarine Squadron Two is the workhorse attack submarine squadron assigned to the submarine base. Of course, the Submarine Base New London is actually (and always has been) located on the east side of the Thames River in the town of Groton, CT. The other Subbase squadron is Submarine Development Squadron Twelve. DEVRON 12 got the newest submarines, and while they did occasionally humble themselves enough to do "routine" submarine deployments they also specialized in developing new attack submarine weapons employment and general operating tactics. As a result, they thought of themselves as being something quite special. And then there was Submarine Squadron 10, located at State Pier on the West side of the Thames River and actually in the City of New London.

While the other guys had the Submarine Base and all of its facilities for support, Squadron 10 had the USS FULTON (AS 11) for its support. FULTON was an ancient submarine tender. To put it in perspective, when the Japanese had struck at Pearl Harbor in 1941 FULTON had been at sea in the Pacific. FULTON participated in combat during the Battle of Midway, rescuing nearly 2,000 survivors from USS YORKTOWN (CV 5) while under fire during the battle. She supported the original USS GATO (SS 212) during that war. Now 46 years old, FULTON is still soldiering on.

Thames River, looking North at the Bridges, Viewed from State Pier, New London, CT

FULTON and her Squadron 10 brood of submarines had been located in New London, away from the Subbase, for a logical reason. There is a major railroad and Interstate highway bridge over the Thames River just north of State Pier. Any problem with either bridge (and the rail bridge has to be opened for submarines to pass) would strand everything at the Subbase, which was a couple of miles farther north on the river. There was no other way out.

So, with shore facilities that consisted basically of a parking lot at the head of the pier, with the smallest and oldest submarine tender around, and with their physical separation of a couple of miles and the width of the river from the center of the submarine universe, Submarine Squadron 10 thought of itself as being just a bit independent of the politics and whatever. Not outcasts. Not cowboys. Just a bit independent. You could detect an attitude, if you looked for a moment. . .

This afternoon found three SSNs in the same Narragansett Bay Operating Area (NBOA) section for the POM Certifications of both GATO and USS AUGUSTA (SSN 710), with USS SKIPJACK (SSN 585) also participating.

Today's exercise was far bigger than simply certifying two SSNs for deployment. Onboard GATO was the Commodore of Squadron 10 and the SUBLANT Chief of Staff. Onboard USS SKIPJACK (SSN 585) was the Commodore of Squadron 2. Onboard AUGUSTA was the Commodore of DEVRON 12, and another senior Officer from SUBLANT. Yes, this was more, much more, than simply certifying GATO and AUGUSTA for deployment. This was for all the stakes in the unofficial but extremely important squadron reputation wars. Today we were playing for all of the marbles. High stakes – careers depended on the outcome of today. Everybody knew it, too.

Normally you would not find three submarines assigned the same NBOA safe haven. As part of its submerged interference and routing rules, the Navy wisely provides separation whenever possible. It makes a lot of sense, as these ships do not have windshields. You are flying blind, sometimes at very high speeds, underwater. Today, for this anti-submarine warfare training exercise, however, separation is only provided vertically. It is an accepted risk of live training.

GATO actually has the deepest test depth rating of the three submarines, so she is assigned to depth zone deep. What it means is that GATO can go anywhere in that NBOA horizontally, but unless there is an emergency, she has to stay down close to her test depth. SKIPJACK, being oldest and having the shallowest test depth rating, gets depth zone shallow. SKIPJACK can go from the surface down to a specified relatively shallow depth. That leaves AUGUSTA for depth zone middle. For fairness, the 3 depth zones are the same vertical size.

AUGUSTA is a brand-new LOS ANGELES (SSN 688) class ship getting ready for her first deployment. She is a *hot rod* and can outrun everyone else in the exercise. While AUGUSTA is fast, in terms of top speed, she was yet to earn a reputation as a *Hot Boat*. To earn that moniker, of course, AUGUSTA had to actually deploy and *do* something notable. This would be a relatively good deployment for AUGUSTA; it would not be until her next deployment that AUGUSTA would become *notorious. . .*

Of the three ships participating today GATO is actually the slowest in terms of top speed. Until LOS ANGELES came along in 1976, SKIPJACK held the American submarine speed record – but no more. To get that speed, the 688's have more powerful engines and a slightly thinner hull than their THRESHER & STURGEON class predecessors – giving them slightly less depth capability. 688's also have the best sonar, the best electronics and are quieter than all prior ships. By all rights, this should be a cake walk for AUGUSTA today.

SKIPJACK is old in years but has been updated and modernized. Some things are hard to modernize, though. She has very little quieting in her design and because of the basic architecture of her hull and sonar sensor placement she is limited in her passive sonar capability. Not arcane or archaic and still both capable and lethal, but the advance odds are still that SKIPJACK will not last very long in today's contest.

GATO, of course, is the wild card today. Last weekend the Commodores of Squadron 10 and DEVRON 12 had seen each other at the Officer's Club up at the Subbase. Of course there are few secrets in the family and everybody *KNEW* about GATO's little adventure during POM workup a couple of weeks ago. It was already a *great* sea story. It hadn't been so great to *live*, but *in the telling* it had quickly become a legendary sea story. Is there any wonder that the two Commodores found themselves wagering a bottle of fine alcohol and some equally fine cigars on the outcome of the POM Cert exercises? Especially since DEVRON 12 was sending their newest boat, which everyone *knew* was aching to build a great reputation, up against GATO?

The setup was simple. It was a classic game, and everyone already knew the rules. Intel from other assets has reported multiple enemy submarines in a certain area and your job is to clear that area. Pretty simple. Stay in your depth zone. Detect the enemy submarine and then start trailing him. Do target motion analysis so that you can plot a firing solution for your torpedoes. Don't get detected yourself. Use all of your own cunning, skill and anything else available (like potentially available ocean thermal layers) to hide with pride while you simultaneously attack with panache. A wonderful game. As soon as you lock a legitimate firing solution in your Fire Control

Computer that target is simulated gone. First guy to get them both wins. Remembering that the other two guys are trying to do the same thing at the same time as you. Drama.

At this point, as the exercise begins, the tension in the ships is palpable. Submarine warfare is individual combat. The hundred-odd guys on each submarine act as a highly lethal, but single, unit. You don't have a wingman to cover your six. You are standing naked on the stage in Times Square on New Year's Eve and hoping that nobody notices you – there is no place to hide. *This is it, baby, and you are on your own. Have you got it to go?* Entire careers come down to moments like this. Let the adrenalin flow!

On GATO, as on the other two ships, the Captain has a bit of a swagger as the exercise begins. These guys are at the top of their games – the pinnacles of their professional lives. When the command assignments came down, they were not relegated to the back-bench command of a ballistic missile submarine. No, they got SSNs. The home of *real* submariners. **S**aturdays, **S**undays and **N**ights – on an SSN it doesn't matter when. *We've got you covered, baby. You are ours for the taking!*

As the exercise proceeds GATO maneuvers around, on the prowl for a juicy target. The whole tracking party is focused on the Captain and on the Sonar Room. The Captain has the Conn – is actually driving the ship. Outside of the Control Room and Sonar Room, everyone else on the ship is as quiet as a mouse in church. In this world, dropping the seat on a toilet can mean detection – *and death.*

Back in the Engineroom Chief Barnes is in Upper Level, quietly talking to Martin. While Martin stands his watches in Lower Level, and will for the whole 72-day run, he is working on his qualifications to stand watch in Upper Level – which is a generally preferable place to be.

They are discussing the procedure to start up and warm up a steam turbine engine. If not done correctly, you can destroy the turbine. As a result, it is not a trivial training point. And more than just knowing the procedure, Barnes is explaining the details of "why" it has to be that way and "what" exactly happens (from a physics point of view) if you do it wrong. In nuclear power plant operations, knowing the "why" is just as important as knowing the "what." That is because someday there may come a time when something happens that isn't covered in the operating manuals. If you know the "whys" you can hopefully quickly figure out the necessary "what" well enough to stem whatever problem, you are having. It might even save the ship one day.

In the box, or Maneuvering Area, the four watchstanders are crowded into their stations. One man is at the throttles for the Main Engines. Between him and the two guys up in Control who are operating the rudder and the planes, they are directly controlling the ship's motion. Interestingly, and following long established submarine tradition, the Throttleman is an Electrician's Mate – not a Machinist Mate (as on skimmers (surface ships)).

Another man is at the Reactor Control Panel. Operating the Nuclear Reactor is actually a lot easier than it might seem at first blush. These Reactors are well designed and actually kind of user-friendly. But, of course, this is a very senior watchstation and the Reactor Operator has years of learning many, many "whats" and "whys" under his belt before he takes a seat at this control panel.

The Electrical Operator runs GATO Power & Light – he has pretty much ultimate control over everything on the ship except for the few air powered items and the battery powered flashlights. The Electrical Operator needs to be sharp and on his toes at all times.

These three guys are all enlisted sailors. Their immediate boss on watch is the EOOW – one of the two watchstations on the ship normally manned by Officers.

This afternoon LT Clark is the EOOW. While he would never have been assigned as EOOW during the annual Reactor Safeguards Examination, he is the obvious choice today. But he really would have rather been up in Control. As such, this afternoon he is just a bit miffed at having been stuck back in the box by the XO. As a result, he has the Electrical Operator manning the phones and listening in on the tactical communications circuit. This is giving everyone an update of the action as it unfolds.

It has already been over an hour without a sniff of anything. The predictions of SKIPJACK falling early were wrong. Her crafty Captain has obviously somehow turned SKIPJACK's natural liabilities into some kind of effective tactical advantage. On the other hand, there is no sign that GATO has been detected by the other guys either.

As GATO comes out of a turn the communications circuit erupts with a report, "Conn, Sonar, new submerged contact designate Sierra 1 bearing 323 relative. Working classification, but it sounds like an American SKIPJACK Class submarine"

The Captain immediately replies, "Sonar, Conn, Aye. Chief, let's get a bearing rate on this guy."

And so, the hunt begins. Over the next 40 minutes GATO does target motion analysis – a technique used to apply three-dimensional geometry to solve the problem of transforming a relative bearing to a defined moving point in space. At the end of the process SKIPJACK is logged as a kill.

"Jock is one hell of a crafty skipper. I knew he was the right guy to put in SKIPJACK," commented the SUBLANT Chief of Staff to the Squadron 10 Commodore.

"Yes, I knew him when he was Engineer on PARGO. Jock is a good man," replied the Commodore.

SKIPJACK's Captain's career took a boost today. While his ship was beaten, he beat long odds and lasted a lot longer in the fight than he was expected to. Against less capable and noisier adversaries he could easily have won. His career did continue well. He later got command of a TRIDENT missile submarine, back in the days when this assignment was a real career boost, and eventually got the job as SUBLANT Chief of Staff himself before he retired.

GATO had passed her first test and had done so without being detected by AUGUSTA. *But where the hell were they?* Was this thing going to end in a draw?

Onboard AUGUSTA they had also "bagged" SKIPJACK at about the same time, and they were similarly searching for GATO.

Back on GATO, the report went in, "Conn, Sonar, transient noise in the water. Sounds like someone slammed a shitter door. I am trying to pick this guy out of the clutter. . ."

With that, some careless sailor had slammed the door in the bathroom stall and AUGUSTA was detected. Everything matters on a submarine. 45 minutes later it was over. GATO had won it all.

The three Commodores exchanged pleasantries and congratulations for GATO on the underwater telephone and the exercise was over. Soon GATO was on the surface and headed back toward New London.

As they cruised along toward Long Island Sound, the ship's announcing system erupted, "GATO, this is the SUBLANT Chief of Staff. I want to congratulate each and every one of you, along with your Captain, on a fine exercise. You have demonstrated, without doubt, in true *Black Cat* style, that you are fully ready for your deployment next week. I wish you good hunting and Godspeed as you head out to WESTLANT, and I know that you are going to do us proud!"

As GATO pulled in to port the next morning the whole crew had the swagger thing going. Hot stuff coming through. 688 slayers arriving! It was, for a moment anyway, the Hollywood script – and GATO was the star of the show.

Meanwhile, onboard AUGUSTA, nobody was at all happy about GATO having gotten them in the exercise. This was serious business for everyone in the crew, not just for the Captain. The careless sailor who had revealed their position was identified by the Chiefs; he had only been onboard for a few months and was not yet fully qualified in submarines. So, as AUGUSTA headed up to the Submarine Base on their return trip from POM Cert a certain young non-qual was re-educated through some well-earned *dungaree justice* in the meaning of *"personal patrol quiet"*. It was effective training, as the young man never slammed a shitter door onboard ever again – even tied up to the pier.

GATO and AUGUSTA were both ready for their deployments and were now certified for War.

USS AUGUSTA SSN 710

72 Day Run

Gentlemen, these will be the Greatest Days of our Lives

Chapter 4

Underway

Monday, October 14, 1985, Day 1, State Pier, New London, CT

There are a number of other submarines going to sea from the New London area today – Mondays were always busy – and in order to give the ships only going out for few days more time to do their exercises and tests GATO was assigned a 3 PM underway time. The tugboats drove the underway and return schedules in New London. As a result, the routine was a bit leisurely this Monday morning.

Normally the Reactor is started up during the night so that by the time the crew arrives at 6 AM the ship is on its own electrical power and connected to the pier only by the 4 mooring lines, the single shore telephone line and the boarding brow (so that people can come onboard and leave the ship). Today, however, the Reactor is still shutdown overnight and the Duty Section – the crew that was onboard overnight (about one third of the crew – enough to get underway in an emergency, and enough to handle any situation import – is always onboard an SSN) actually got some sleep.

By mid-morning the word was announced over the ship's announcing system, "The Reactor is Critical."

The first time that some people hear that term they freak out a bit. Who in hell wants to be anywhere close to a *"Critical"* Nuclear Reactor, anyway? But it is actually a physics-based term, and it technically means that self-sustaining steady state nuclear fission is underway in a controlled fashion in the Reactor. In other words, the Reactor needs to be Critical in order to release the energy that you need to power the ship's electrical and propulsion engine demands. Critical is a good thing – a very good thing. Today's Criticality is intended to be continuously maintained for the next 72 days. Not a problem – it could be maintained a lot longer than that, if desired. But, of course, in true GATO style, the Reactor will be shut down a couple of times well before the scheduled end of the 72-day run. *But more about all of that later...*

Chief Barnes is up on the pier with his family. His four kids range in age from almost 5 to 8 years old and this is his second major deployment this year. He had deployed to Italy with FULTON for 6 months starting January 2. Yes, even a ship as old as FULTON deployed during the Cold War. His twins turn 5 in a couple of weeks, so they had had their 5th birthday party over the weekend. Barnes had found over the years that saying goodbye for a deployment was something best done the night before at home, but the late in the day underway time had complicated matters today and his oldest son had wanted to see the ship actually sail away.

This was the case with many of the crew's family. While it was only 72 days to WESTLANT and not 6 months to the Mediterranean Sea, it was still a very big deal. Especially since Day 72 was Christmas Eve. And this time there were no stops scheduled, either. None of the crew's wives and girlfriends would be flying anywhere to meet the ship. None of that this trip. While GATO may get a stop in somewhere sometime, none was scheduled.

Chief Andre Perrot was also up on the pier with his latest girlfriend. He had only known her for a month or so, but he had known "of her" for some time. Andre, you see, had a second and a third life outside of the Navy. A slight man, very French in his features, with a sexy mustache, Andre moonlighted as a Disc Jockey for private parties. Andre DJ. He also, on occasion, made a few bucks as a male dancer. That had all started when Andre had been on the crew of special research submarine NR-1.

In any event, he had met this girlfriend at a wedding that he had done about a month ago and they had hit it off hot and heavy. He also had just bought a new car and had decided to give it to this girlfriend "for safe keeping" during the deployment. It was a decision not made lightly, and he would second guess himself every single day that GATO was deployed, but he had committed.

Down below, the ship was a hubbub of last minute activity. Once the brow was lifted off, they would be on their own. Everybody onboard was thinking of what they might have left behind that they would need that they might be able to get in the last few moments alongside the pier. But the ship was ready.

GATO had a full load out of weapons with live warheads – war-shots – *no exercise shots on this trip*. She also had stores for 90 days. While the food would not be from a gourmet palate on the last few days (maybe even just peanut butter crackers) the cooks were committed that they could feed the crew for 90 days without restocking. As a result, every passageway forward of the Reactor Compartment had food stored in the aisles. There were two layers of cartons, each with 4 large cans of something, everywhere. The freezer was packed in the order in which the frozen food would be eaten – there was no walking into it, at least yet. And the normally open passageway where the ship's torpedoes had been loaded through and into the torpedo room from the Weapons Shipping Hatch above was closed off with web netting and filled to the overhead with food. Finally, because it was fall and they were going into WESTLANT and not down to the warm Caribbean, the Forward Escape Trunk, up in the Bow Compartment, had a full load of eggs. It was the auxiliary chill box, unless the ship was going to warm waters.

Deployments are also times of change in a ship. A number of crew members were scheduled to get out of the Navy or transfer off the ship during the deployment period, so they would not be going along on the run. Keeping with longstanding tradition these guys had all had "the duty" the night before – had been part of the one third of the crew onboard overnight – and the Nukes among them had been part of the crew that had started up the Reactor that morning. One of them was a young sailor named Anderson.

He was a First Class Machinist Mate and had been on GATO since he had left Nuclear Power School over 4 years ago. Anderson's big claim to fame, at least over a beer in a dive bar in some exotic liberty port, was that he had gone to High School in Ossining NY with Martha Quinn and had briefly dated her. Martha Quinn was, of course, one of the original six Video Jockeys (VJs) on MTV. Guys of a certain age, particularly in that dive bar setting, generally considered Martha Quinn to be *HOT*. So, as a result of actually *(no shit)* having briefly dated her, part of her celebrity had rubbed off on Anderson.

Anderson was also one of the "old men" on the ship, as the crew usually served approximately 3-year long stints on any given ship. Since he had decided not to reenlist, signaling that he would be leaving the Navy when his six-year obligation was up, he was left assigned to GATO until the end of his enlistment. That was the deal – go to Nuclear Power School and get a great education but agree to a six-year minimum enlistment in exchange. Many guys, like Chief Barnes and Chief Perrot, had committed to stay in well before their first enlistments were up and as a result, had completed shorter tours on their first ships. Anderson was getting out, but he loved GATO and the crew. It was a misty-eyed morning for him – *a big part of his life was coming to an end today.* Men and their ships…

He approached Chief Barnes, who was with his family on the pier, "Hey Chief, we have got a couple of problems down below. What is the tender doing up in the sail?"

"Anderson, you kill me. Are you sure that you don't want to reenlist and come with us? You are done, but *you* won't be *done* until we back out without you. Are you sure that you don't want to come with us? It is not too late – the XO is right over there. . . The sail, well, the damned Head Valve failed its pre-underway checks last night. Stuck open, do you believe that? The tender is checking it out again, because now it works just fine," replied Barnes.

"Chief, you almost have me, but you know that I head back to finish college, starting in January, I need to get home and established. Maybe I'll be back as an O Ganger (Officer), who knows. But for now, I am off and back to college. Anyway, we have two problems down below that you should go check out. First, there is a very small steam leak on the inspection cover of XXX steam valve. You might make it through the run without having to fix it, but I doubt it. That valve has been a problem before, but it has been a while since the last time it caused trouble for us. The other problem is the Main Air Conditioner. I think that you have an air leak in the mechanical seals on one of your pumps. She is making some cold water now, but she's just not right," reported Anderson.

"Thanks. There is nothing that we can do about the steam leak if we want to get underway today. I guess that we'll just have to watch it and decide as we go. If we get a liberty port maybe, I'll fix it then. The air conditioner is a bigger problem – I had better go check it out. Thanks, once again. And don't be a stranger. You have been a great asset to this ship and both GATO and the Navy will miss you."

With that they said their final goodbyes and Anderson stepped away to watch HIS SHIP back out and head down the river without him. Barnes said his final goodbyes to his family, with hugs and kisses all around and promises of seeing them at Christmas, and he headed down below.

Arriving in Engineroom Lower Level, Chief Barnes spotted Martin. They discussed the air conditioner problem. Barnes started studying the diagram, but he already knew what it all meant. He had been the top student several years ago at the week-long specialist school for this equipment. Of course the GATO version, with the old Auxiliary Sealing System, had only been a footnote in the course. Even then, 8 years ago, there were only a few of that version left in the fleet. Today GATO had the only one – *the very last one*. There was a good reason why the sealing system had been updated – and this was it. GATO, of course, would get the upgrade in overhaul next year. Not a help today, or for the next 72 days. *What to do?*

As Chief Barnes pondered his options, the Engineer came down the ladder.

"They told me that you were down here, Chief. All I want to know is whether we can go or not?" asked the Engineer.

It was 2:30 PM and the tugs were arriving. It was decision time.

"I assume that you know about the steam leak, too," replied the Chief.

"Yes, and I also know about the Head Valve and Chief Perrot's problem with #2 400 cycle set," was the reply.

"OK. I will figure this thing out, and we'll deal with the steam leak later if it gets too bad. We can go," was Chief Barnes' assessment.

With that the Engineer nodded and turned to head up the ladder. He had to go talk to the Captain. He shook his head in resignation. He had actually left the Navy after his first tour only to have decided that life after Navy wasn't nearly as much fun. His return to the Navy assignment had been GATO. All the fun he could ever ask for, and a bit more.

The Captain was steely on the outside and a jumble of emotion inside. This run would make or break his career and largely determine if he was selected for promotion to Captain or not. You see, his naval rank was Commander. As Commanding Officer of the ship his title was Captain, but he only had 3 gold rings on the sleeve of his dress blues. Like all Commanders, he wanted to get the 4th gold ring and be a Captain. And this trip was *it* for him. The POM Cert had been a good start, but failing to back out and head down the river on-time would negate all of that, and more. The lasting impression that all Commanding Officers want to leave as they head out for deployment is one of crisp confidence and complete readiness. Not possible if you left late.

"Well, Commodore, we are ready to go," he reported to the Commodore, his boss, on the pier.

The Captain was the only member of the deploying crew who was not already at their Maneuvering Watch watchstations. The tugs were tied up and the Harbor Pilot was climbing up to the bridge. The ship's Yeoman had sent off his final crew list and other departure dispatches. The Main Engines were warmed up. You could, in fact, see the gentle swishing of water around the stern of the ship as the engines were gently rocked forward and aft to keep them ready. The crane was connected to the brow. All that was left was for the Commodore to make his final comments to the Captain and for the Captain to climb up to the bridge.

"Have a great run, Rick. I will be watching your progress and am sure that you'll deliver great results for the Squadron. See you at Christmas," was the Commodore's final admonition to the Captain.

Both the Captain and the Commodore realized that the Commodore's chances for making Admiral would be affected by GATO's results. Commodores are judged on the performance of the ships in their squadron, so while not quite as directly an impact as on the Captain's own promotion potential, it did matter. The Commodore had 6 other submarines and a tender under his command, which also impacted his performance rating. Still, this was an important deployment for both GATO and for him.

"Thank you, sir, see you at Christmas."

Five minutes later, at exactly 3 PM, the last line was taken in and the Main Engines were ordered to Back 1/3 speed. GATO was underway.

In the Crew's Mess – *as was GATO tradition* – the then-already-classic Willie Nelson song *On the Road Again* was playing on the Crew's Entertainment System. Some guys sang along with Willie as the ship made the turn and headed down the river and out to sea.

Fifteen minutes later the ship had passed Electric Boat, the shipyard where it had been built so many years ago and where it had had some maintenance done on the Main Engines last year. Electric Boat was on the Groton side of the river. The line handlers had stowed everything topside and had come below. The Weapons

Shipping Hatch, the ship's main hatch for personnel access, was now closed. 110 eager men, with the exception of the Officer of the Deck and the two lookouts up on the bridge, were all now inside the ship.

The ship quickly fell into an underway routine. This is to say that about one third of the crew was on watch, operating the ship, one third of the crew was preparing to go on watch in a couple of hours, and one third of the crew was hitting the bunks. While it was only mid-afternoon, the people who were hitting the bunk now would be on watch tonight from 1:30 AM to 7:30 AM. If they didn't get some sleep now, they would be sleep deprived for days. Sleep is one of the most precious commodities on an SSN at sea, and crew members of all ranks learned this very early on their first ships. Once the Weapons Shipping Hatch indicates shut on the Ship Control Panel any good submariner is ready for the bunk, if available.

And so it went, with watches changing every 6 hours. Six on and 12 off, the body quickly adjusted to an 18-hour quasi-circadian cycle. Before and after each watch change there was a meal – four times a day. It was one of the two ways that you could tell what time of day it was. Breakfast food, lunch food, dinner food and mid-rations (soup and sandwiches, crackers, etc.) differentiated the time of day. The other way to tell was to go up into Control. If the Control Room was rigged for red, with all red lights and no white lights on – or if the Officer of the Deck was wearing red wrap around goggles, then it was dark in the outside world on the surface. The adaptation of the OOD's eyes to red light was a significant help in giving him immediate night vision in the periscope, if needed.

On deployment the ship typically shifted to Greenwich Mean Time (GMT) as soon as it deployed. Each of the 24 time zones in the world is universally represented by an alphabetic letter, and GMT is Z, or Zulu, time. It is the time zone reference used by deployed ships in their reports and in orders that they receive, so shifting to Zulu time made life a bit easier.

As each watch ended, starting the first night after the evening meal, the XO met with the off going watchsection in the crew's mess and gave the same briefing.

"Well, we are finally on deployment. Thanks for all of the hard work on everyone's part in getting the ship ready. I want you all to know that the next 72 days will be the greatest days of our lives.

"As soon as we get submerged and clear the NBOAs we will be on station – and on patrol. As you know, quiet is king. There will be no drills or training events on patrol, and everyone needs to practice personal patrol quiet at all times. You all saw what the actions of one errant sailor cost the AUGUSTA in our POM Cert exercise. Don't you be the one who blows it for all of us – especially since this is no exercise.

"Now, as to what we'll be doing and what you can say about it when we get home. . . We are deploying to the Western Atlantic Region in order to evaluate the capability of a nuclear-powered attack submarine to conduct extended independent submerged operations in the open ocean. That's it. I know that it is the same "cover story" that we always use, but that is it. If there are no questions, I need everyone to sign your personal briefing statement and turn them in to me now."

And that was it. It was all to be a big secret. And interestingly enough, on this patrol GATO would conduct an extremely important surveillance and gather key intelligence that was vital to the National Interest while trailing something new – and do it over a several week period – and about 80 percent of the crew would be totally oblivious to what was going on when they did. *But nobody knew that now, and there will be much more about that later. . .*

Back in the Engineroom Lower Level Chief Barnes and a couple of his senior men were coming to a conclusion on the Main Air Conditioner. The alternatives were a bit ugly, but there was an elegantly simple patch job that they could do that could maybe hold them even for the whole run. The by-the-book repair was to replace the mechanical seals in several auxiliary pumps – there was no way to know which guy was leaking. They had the parts onboard, but the problem was access. These little pumps were buried way out by the hull, under lots of piping.

Normally it would be a week-long job with tender support to remove all of this piping interference in order to gain access to the pumps. Plus, with all this piping removed the ship's engines and electrical generators would have to be shut down and the ship would have to be on the surface. Not happening. The other bad alternative was to send the smallest guy in the ship crawling out there to the pumps. Not good, either, on two counts. First, the only guy who could possibly fit out there without interference removal was one of Chief Perrot's Electrician's Mates. The guy was fresh out of Nuclear Power School and barely knew where his bunk was – much less how to change a delicate mechanical seal.

So, it came down to option three – the patch job. Not in any book, and only 95 percent likely to work, it could be done in a half hour – then they would know. Better yet, they could do the patch job with the unit still limping along in operation. One thing was for certain, though, they were not going to do this deployment running those leaky, noisy backup units. GATO's success on this deployment absolutely depended upon keeping the Main Air Conditioner up and running – and running well.

Chief Barnes set out for the Wardroom to brief LT Clark and the Engineer. This was a complicated plan to explain, despite its simplicity of implementation. He thought to himself that, generally speaking, despite the elegance of the system, any problem with a machine that uses steam to make cold water tends to be complicated to explain to anyone who is not intimately familiar with how it works. Further, to his knowledge nobody had ever tried such a fix before. He was sure, though, that if it did not work, they wouldn't further degrade the machine more than it was already degraded; in other words, the machine wouldn't run any worse. In that regard it was a low risk plan. Still, they hadn't even gotten past Race Rock in Long Island Sound yet – a key waypoint on the way out. It was early in the run to be doing this kind of repair. As a result, it ultimately took longer to sell the plan than it took to implement it. But it was still Day 1, and they deserved some good fortune. The plan worked as advertised.

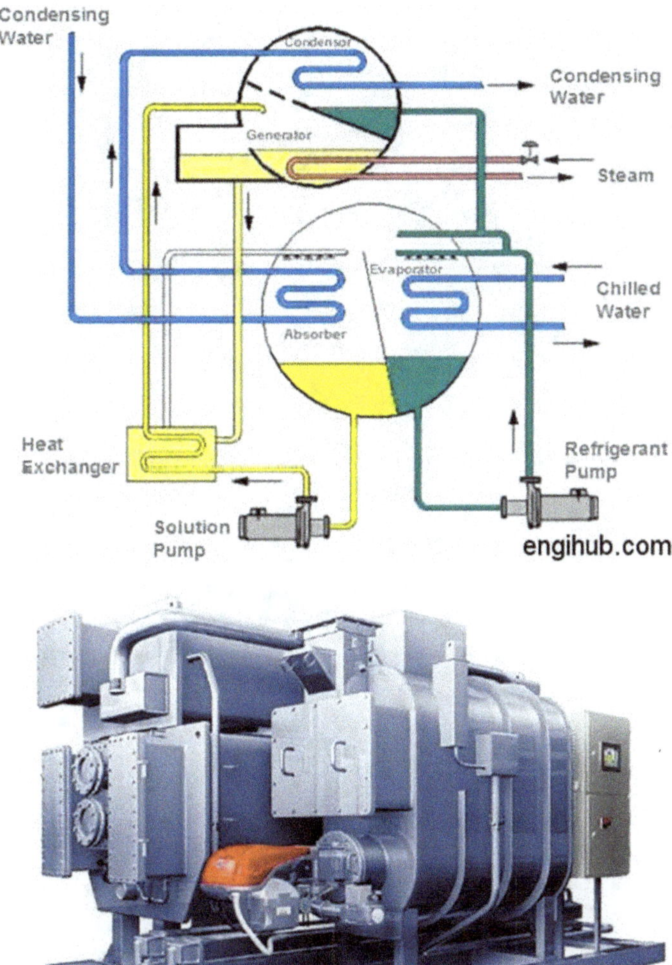

Steam Powered Air Conditioning System Complexity, as Seen in a Typical Commercial Unit
(NOT GATO's System, but the same laws of physics & chemistry still apply)

Chapter 5

Halloween

Thursday, October 31, 1985, Day 18, On Station, WESTLANT

More than two weeks out of port, GATO had fully slipped into the routine of deployment. She had put some miles behind her, and about once per watch she was coming to periscope depth to talk to the satellite. Position reports were sent, and intel was exchanged, along with a routine housekeeping traffic exchange.

The ship had moved *Up North*, along the GIUK gap – the Greenland, Iceland, United Kingdom gap. If some guy was coming down from the North, he had to pass through the GIUK gap, and GATO was in position to pick him up.

As part of the underway routine GATO had ventilated to get fresh air while transiting North, even though they were already "on station." Now, though, they were bleeding oxygen from the oxygen banks. The Freon leak had subsided as expected. Because of this they could now go an extended period on the same internal atmosphere using only the ship's Atmosphere Control Equipment. Ventilating was a noisy event – not to be done up here except as absolutely necessary. Chalk up one major success for GATO's crew, confirming that the "last draw of the deck" had worked as planned and solved the Freon leak problem.

Of course, on the other hand, the damned Head Valve was acting up once again. While no Captain likes to have to report this kind of issue to his operational commander, this one had to be reported

– and was. Still, not a "return to port" problem. Just an emergent issue that required attention if attention was available. Some people were surprised by the attitude, but there were lots of maintenance issues on a submarine that would keep you from getting underway, but which would not result in you returning to port if they developed while you were already underway.

Today is Halloween, and the crew is feeling mischievous after a couple of weeks at sea. As a result, the routine was changed tonight. Normally after the evening meal and after the Crew's Mess is cleaned up a movie is shown in the Crew's Mess area. The crew eats, trains and relaxes in this area, which is also used for staging damage control efforts, when required. Similarly, the Wardroom served as the ship's operating room for use by the sole Hospital Corpsman onboard in an emergency. Every place/thing on a submarine does "double duty" if possible.

Today, in 1985, we have just entered the age of video – the Beta vs. VHS wars are booming. The ship's movie stock, therefore, is still big bulky film reels and used the old, noisy Bell & Howell projector. Curses to anyone who broke a projection bulb, too! Not tonight, though.

Tonight, we have costumes and *trick or treat*. Everyone not on watch either put on the costume that they had brought or improvised with whatever was onboard (mops made fine wigs…) and got into costume. Everyone then went around, trick or treating in the Wardroom, the Chief's Quarters, in Sonar, Radio, and the Torpedo Room. Candy for the kids, all around. Remembering that the average age onboard was 21, and that the Captain was only in his mid-thirties, it went over well. Fun was had by all. It was a great break in the routine of the patrol.

Chief Barnes and Sonar Chief Barry Joseph manned the Chief's Quarters, handing out the candy and other goodies. They had a Betamax player in there, and they had two whole movies onboard. One was a cheese making tutorial, extolling the virtues of European cheeses and explaining how they got the holes in Swiss Cheese (natural gas bubbles, of course). The other one was a hilarious comedy starring Dan Akroyd. ***Doctor Detroit*** quickly became a cult favorite in the Chief's Quarters on GATO.

Ike and Barry played ***Doctor Detroit*** tonight, handed out candy and shot the bull. While Barnes was closest to his nuclear compatriot Chief Andre Perrot, he liked Joseph. Good guy, for a coner. Coners, of course, are those sailors who worked up in the nose cone of the ship. Joseph was a great Sonarman, too. He had been the one who had caught the transient noise on AUGUSTA. Ike trusted Barry's technical wisdom in the same way that he trusted his own wisdom about everything related to the propulsion plant.

At the same time, Barry thought that the Nukes were often just a bit too full of themselves with their self-defined aura of importance. He also thought that some of them tended to whine too much about how hard they worked. After all, they always got the maximum reenlistment bonuses. . . Nonetheless, Barry liked Ike – a pretty regular guy, for a Nuke. After all, Ike seemed to really know his stuff back aft and actually paid attention to what was going on in the rest of the ship – where all of the *real* mission-critical work is done.

In other words, Ike and Barry respected each other's capability, experience and wisdom. They enjoyed each other's company, despite their very different jobs. They both realized that a truly great crew requires experience, wisdom and overall excellence in every area from the messcooks to the Captain. They both also knew that this was the best, most capable crew that either one had ever been part of. No pretentions, and not "perfect" – just the excellence that only can be achieved through consistent dedication and very hard work.

"So, Barry, what do you think we'll be doing, because we haven't done much more than smash some uranium atoms so far on this trip," asked Barnes.

"Well, Ike, things are quiet. Intel has no hits for us. It is a big dark quiet ocean. It is not our fault, and the Captain still feels good. We have not had to pull in anywhere and a lack of targets isn't his fault. Something is going to come up pretty soon," replied Joseph.

"I hope so. We both know that this run is it for the Captain. After this he takes GATO to overhaul and then halfway through overhaul, he gets relieved. As we both know, Captains can only earn negative points if something goes bad in overhaul. For him to earn the positive points that he needs to make Captain he needs to bag something good on this trip," said Barnes.

"Roger that. But I am not worried," replied Joseph.

Unknown to the Chiefs, the ship had just received new orders. It seemed that the wife of one of the forward Electronics Technicians was having serious problems with her pregnancy back in New London. Because GATO was not engaged with a contact, because the Head Valve was acting up once again, and because Petty Officer Winston's wife was having the pregnancy problems the ship's operational commander had just directed GATO to head to Holy Loch, Scotland.

Known as Site One in the Submarine Ballistic Missile community, there was a submarine tender in Holy Loch. While SSNs rarely stopped there, it wasn't unheard of. The plan was for GATO to pull in one afternoon, let Winston leave to fly home, have the tender look at the Head Valve that evening and then to get underway again early the next morning. The Reactor would not be shut down, and none of the crew would leave the ship. Just a drive-by.

Chapter 6

Holy Loch

Sunday, November 3, 1985, Day 21, Holy Loch, Scotland

In the submarine world, even the SSN part of the submarine world, Holy Loch is a special place. Many SSN sailors have had the misfortune of having been assigned to an SSBN (missile submarine) and others have stopped at Holy Loch on similar drive-byes. It was well known as a beautiful place, with very friendly people. More than a few SSBN sailors have returned from a posting to Holy Loch with a gorgeous Scottish wife. Beyond the special bond between the United States and the United Kingdom, Holy Loch was a special place for submariners.

Photo # NH 69856   USS Hunley at Holy Loch, April 1966

GATO pulled alongside USS HUNLEY (AS 31), the tender currently assigned to Site One (as Holy Loch was known in the strategic missile world) and berthed outboard of an SSBN in the midst of refit. Everything is "special" to the boomers, so an *upkeep* to anybody else is a *refit* to a boomer. HUNLEY had boomers on both sides of her – she was fully engaged in her support mission.

As soon as they were tied up the Squadron 14 people on HUNLEY provided the details of Winston's trip home, and he got to call his wife and tell her that he was coming home. It was sad for him on two counts. First, he would lose that baby. Second, he had really looked forward to the run – and nothing much exciting had happened yet.

At the same time the tender's experts were immediately up in the sail, inspecting the Head Valve. It was probably the most inspected valve in the US Navy by this point. Next year in overhaul, as a result of all of this trouble, the ship would get an entirely new Induction Mast and Head Valve assembly. But that, like everything else on the overhaul work list, didn't do much good for GATO today.

Back in the Engineroom both Chief Barnes and Chief Perrot had their guys working. The Reactor was still up and running, and the ship was still making its own electricity, but she was tied to the tender and there were no sea motions. The Shaft was also not turning.

"The Shaft" is a definitive term on a submarine. There were literally hundreds of machines on GATO that had shafts in them from small to big. But when somebody on a submarine spoke of *the Shaft*, it only meant one thing: the propeller shaft. It is a hollow steel shaft, a couple of feet in diameter, filled with hard packed sand. It runs from the back end of the Main Engines all the way out to the ship's propeller. There was a lot of equipment in the ship whose ultimate purpose was to simply turn that Shaft.

It was also one of the largest penetrations in the submarine's hull. You are a few hundred feet, or more, from the surface and you have a two-foot hole in your ship? Yep. So, sealing the hole, with the shaft being able to turn freely and quietly, was no small task. Which brings us to the other infrequently talked about reality of submarines: they leak.

The fact of the matter is that water is always leaking into a submarine at sea. The only real questions are how much and where. The objective is to have it be very little leakage and only from those places where the leakage is designed in. Like the seals on any seawater pump shaft and on the propulsion shaft.

At her age and in her condition (DUE for overhaul) GATO leaked a lot more seawater in than the average ship. It created two problems. First, all leakage into the ship has to be pumped back out. That pump, the Drain Pump, is a noise generating piece of equipment. On station you wanted to run it as little as possible.

The second problem was that the ship's Diving Officer of the Watch spent all of his time trying to maintain the ship at around neutral buoyancy when submerged – at least close enough that the Trim Pump could catch up to it when you slowed down for evolutions like a trip to periscope depth. You see, submarines are a bit like an airplane when they are moving through the water. The hull creates lift when the ship has any appreciable speed on, and this can mask the fact that you are seriously negatively buoyant (which can easily be caused by too much water in the bilges).

If you have to slow down quickly or come to periscope depth in an emergency, you might be so heavy overall that the fairwater and stern planes cannot create enough lift to keep you at your desired depth at slow speed. In other words, unless you take the drastic step of blowing ballast (something you only want to do if you are surfacing) you could sink if you lost propulsion and were too heavy overall – and even more particularly if you were heavy aft (making the stern hang low).

All of this was well known to qualified submariners and it led Chief Barnes to tell everyone that his Main Engines were the most potent depth control device on the ship. It also led him to be fanatical about keeping the bilges as dry as possible. And that meant being fanatical about fixing seawater leaks. Nothing good ever came from a seawater leak, was the way that he put it to his men.

Today, they were working on the shaft seal. It was something that could not easily be done at sea, so he was taking advantage of being in Holy Loch to do the work.

Chief Perrot had his guys working on #2 400 cycle set. The ship had two of these machines and needed one on service at all times. This provided the electrical power to the Combat Control Systems up forward, and the whole ship was pretty useless on patrol without those computers. They had been running #1 since they had left New London, but she was getting noisy in one of her bearings. Some seawater had been spilled on the bearing and as Chief Barnes always said, nothing good ever came from that. Still, #1 was OK for now. But would she last the whole trip? Chief Perrot was having his doubts.

That had them working on #2, which was operable, but which had problems with its brush rigging. Something called the "neutral plane" had shifted and unless they found the new null point the brushes would spark when the machine ran. Like seawater leaks, sparking brushes never led to anything good. Of course both units would be scrapped next year in overhaul and GATO would get the new, smaller, lighter and much more reliable units that had made their fleet debut about ten years ago. Once again, GATO had the only old design units left in the entire fleet.

So, it went. Since the crew was not allowed to go topside while inport, to many of them the Holy Loch stop was like still being underway – except with the Weapons Shipping Hatch open. 18 hours after her arrival GATO silently slipped back out to sea. The tender had blessed the Head Valve after finding nothing wrong with it. The cooks had gotten some fresh veggies and milk. The Nukes had fixed the Shaft Seal leak and had made some progress on #2 400 cycle set (good thing, as it would be needed later) and GATO was back on station. The Captain and the whole crew felt great, having successfully escaped the siren song of maintenance availability. You see, GATO loved her maintenance – and they had convinced her not to demand any big maintenance during the brief stop. Any significant maintenance in Holy Loch would have killed the whole trip. But instead, GATO had figuratively sailed between Scylla and Charybdis, and was back on station.

Chapter 7

Clunk

Wednesday, November 6, 1985, Day 24, On Patrol, WESTLANT

GATO was on its way to a new hunting area, and there was intel that some guy would be coming down in a few days. While nothing was around them now, and while they were doing nothing but a transit, there was a palpable air of expectation throughout the ship. They had been preparing for the "Big Mission" for seemingly an eternity, and now it was almost upon them.

LT Clark had convinced the Captain to let him stand Officer of the Deck, at least while they weren't engaged with anybody. As a result, the usual OOD for that watchsection, the Weapons Officer, LT Wallace, was back aft standing EOOW. Each Officer had to stand at least two EOOW watches per month to stay "proficient" and thus qualified, so it was convenient for all concerned.

It was the midwatch, from 1:30 to 7:30 AM – the middle of the night. GATO was scheduled for a routine trip to periscope depth to talk to the satellite. No big deal. No ventilation, nothing exotic. Slow down, come up, clear baffles, put up the periscope and SATCOM antenna and a few minutes later head back deep to resume transit course and speed. With no contacts anywhere and with deep water in every direction nothing could have been more routine, *or so everyone thought . . .*

LT Clark had decided, on his own initiative, that since nothing was going on they could afford to get in a little watchsection training during this evolution. He thought that he would impress the Captain by showing a little initiative. . . But it seems that he had forgotten about being on station on patrol, and not in a training regime. . . So, he decided to shift off the Main Engines and to do the satellite check-in evolution on the Emergency Propulsion Motor. The EPM was designed for just this kind of situation. If the Main Engines failed for any reason, the EPM was the ready backup.

So, he ordered the shift in propulsion. He *should have waited* until the Diving Officer of the Watch had checked the ship's trim at slow speed, but LT Clark had a satellite schedule to catch and would miss his window if he did not hustle. It, of course, ended up as a perfect example of that old saw about *prior planning preventing piss poor performance* – and LT Clark had not done his 6P planning very well tonight. . .

Back aft, Chief Barnes was on watch, and he got his two involved watchstanders to do their thing. Under his breath he muttered to himself "I hope Clark knows what the Hell he is doing."

The EPM came online just fine, and they started answering engine orders on this unit. Everyone noticed, however, that the stern was starting to hang very, very low. The ship was developing an increasing up angle, as the EPM was ordered to full power ahead. The bilges were dry, but the Reserve Tanks were full . . .

Well, the EPM is no Main Engine – to put it simply. Up forward, instead of being near periscope depth the Diving Officer of the Watch was pumping overboard with the Trim Pump at full speed and he was *losing the battle* as the ship slid backwards *deeper* and *deeper* and *deeper* in depth. He had obviously been very heavy – *tens of thousands of pounds* – heavy overall (negatively buoyant) before slowing down and it had been masked by the ship's transit speed. He was in no condition to be attempting a trip to periscope depth on the EPM, and he needed some speed to regain depth control while he pumped the Trim Tanks (in particular, from the After

Trim Tank) overboard to achieve the neutral buoyancy required for slow speed periscope depth operations.

LT Clark silently watched the whole mess unfold.

"Officer of the Deck, I can't hold depth with the EPM, I need the Main Engines. Passing 500 feet and going deeper," reported the Diving Officer of the Watch.

"Maneuvering, Control, shift propulsion to the Main Engines," ordered LT Clark.

Meanwhile, back in the Engineroom, Chief Barnes had realized that something was wrong – something was very badly wrong. He had sent one of his guys over by the Shaft Seals to read a seawater pressure gage to see how deep they were.

"Chief, we are 600 feet and going deeper fast," came the report.

At the same moment, over the announcing system in the Engineroom came the order, "Shift Propulsion to the Main Engines NOW." Not only was it literally screamed into the propulsion plant announcing system, the simple use of any loudspeaker system on patrol emphasized "EMERGENCY."

As the seconds ticked off the Engineroom crew flew through the steps. *Of course, what little good the EPM was doing was lost as it had to be shut off as step one.*

Then, when they hit the Clutch to reengage the Main Engines it rejected. Things had just gotten worse. Much, much worse. The Clutch DID NOT ENGAGE. But even worse yet, the *Anti-Recycle Light* came on – demanding a three-minute Clutch cooldown period before another engagement attempt could be made. "Goddamned accumulator leak," swore Barnes. "*This thing is gonna be OVER in three minutes,*" he thought.

At the rate they were getting deeper, they could all easily be dead in three minutes, and Barnes knew it. No time for consultations or considerations or getting permission. Everything had gone to Hell in a handbasket; GATO was in the midst of an uncontrolled depth excursion (a polite way to say that they were quickly sinking) and the only option right now was ACTION.

Inventing an emergency procedure on-the-fly, he directed one guy to hit the override on the Clutch Hydraulic Pump and another guy to manually position the solenoid valve.

"Alright. One, two, three: GO," as he coordinated the manual override of all interlocks and safeties.

It was time to *go for the gusto*, and he was pulling out all of the stops . . . hoping that she'd engage . . .

Up forward, both realization and panic were setting in there, as well. LT Walsh, the ship's Damage Control Assistant, had just entered the Control Room and immediately understood the situation. He was about to order an Emergency Blow . . .

LT Clark, the OOD, was like a deer in the headlights – frozen and unable to speak.

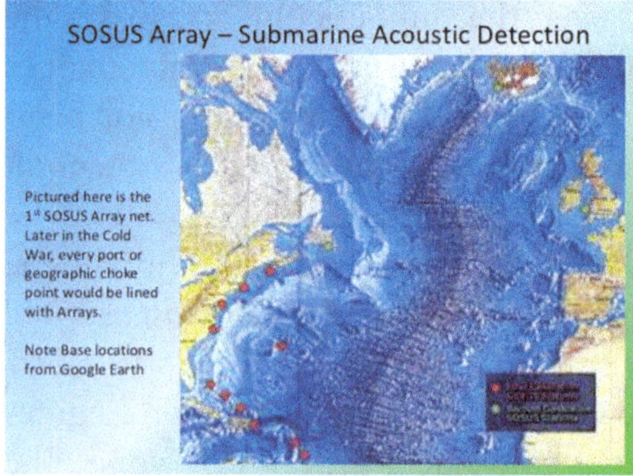

Back aft there was a loud crash and a bang, and the Main Engines jumped on their foundation. The Clutch hadn't synchronized very well... but it *was* engaged. The engagement was abruptly felt throughout the ship – and heard for hundreds of miles beyond the ship.

"Tell them they have Main Engines," yelled Barnes to the guy on the phones.

As the report went in, steam poured into the Main Engines – the throttles had been immediately whipped wide open once the "Clutch Engaged" light came on. Everything worked exactly as designed. The screw bit hard and the ship shot forward, back up from near test depth. GATO's propulsion plant, as always, did its thing. The Shaft accelerated quickly.

As the ship regained depth control, everyone who had known what was going on was trying to overcome their personal adrenalin overdoses. Chests were beating wildly, and people were *beyond* themselves – reliving their very recent *near-death* experience. This was far worse than the flooding during Hurricane Gloria, and everyone knew it. *Holy Shit Batman, we are lucky to be alive.*

In the moments following the event, for some strange reason, Barnes thought to himself that while a completely different cause and corrective action set had been involved, the only thing on film that came *even close* to representing what they had just been through is the flooding scene in the 1968 movie **Ice Station Zebra**.

Meanwhile, in Norfolk, Virginia there was an immediate recognition of something wrong in the Atlantic... *But, more about that later.*

When they got off watch that morning the Captain convened two critiques after breakfast. Every time that something goes wrong during the operation of the ship there is a critique to determine exactly what happened when, why and what was going to be done so that that never happened again.

At the "public" critique the scenario was played out. It was clearly obvious that everything had cascaded badly when the attempt was made to go to periscope depth on the EPM without first getting the ship properly trimmed.

Chief Barnes was then questioned about why the Clutch had not engaged the first time that it had been cycled to restore the Main Engines. He explained that there was a nitrogen accumulator on the Clutch Hydraulic System, and it had a slow internal leak. There was no easy way to tell how much nitrogen had leaked out, so they were recharging it weekly to be sure it would properly operate when needed. It was due to have been recharged on the day watch today. And, yes, the accumulator was on the overhaul work list.

There was some grimacing about the Clutch and some discussion about the emergency engagement procedure that they had created on the spot and its impact on the Clutch, but the Captain and Engineer decided to accept Chief Barnes' recommendation that they recharge the Clutch Accumulator daily instead of weekly for the rest of the trip and to hold training for the other watchsections on how to do an emergency Clutch engagement. With that the Nukes were off the hook.

The Captain also held a private critique with LT Clark in the Captain's Stateroom – the only really private place on the ship. Nobody knows what was said, but the whole crew noticed that LT Clark never stood another OOD watch again, surfaced or submerged, unless the Captain was awake and in the Control Room with him.

That day he had forever become Clunk.

Chapter 8

SUB-MISS

Wednesday, November 6, 1985, Day 24 Routine Mid-Watch, Keflavik, Iceland & Norfolk, Virginia

GATO's little near-death adventure had not gone unnoticed. In addition to almost sinking, GATO had also missed her scheduled satellite check-in. These things happened sometimes, particularly when engaged with a contact – but GATO was in transit. . . The fleet command in Norfolk was concerned but would wait until GATO missed the next orbit of the satellite before raising any alarm bells.

At the same time as the scheduled satellite check-in Chief Barnes and the Engineroom crew had smashed the Clutch back into engagement – *with a massive bang, and almost ripping the engines off of their flexible foundation.* In sonar terminology, this created a "hot noise" all over the North Atlantic. A hot noise like this – with that kind of frequency, amplitude and duration – did not occur in nature. It was a man-made noise, and the SOSUS alarm bells started ringing. . .

SOSUS, the Navy's Cold War Sound Surveillance System, was deployed around the oceans to assist in tracking Soviet missile submarines. There were shore monitoring stations around the rim of both the Atlantic and the Pacific, and the one in Keflavik, Iceland had just gone nuts.

This was communicated to fleet command in Norfolk and some quick analysis was done. GATO had missed her scheduled satellite check-in, and the noise was in the general vicinity of her transit course. . . Was this a "SUB-MISS"? Did we have another SSN missing in the Atlantic??? The Fleet Duty Officer, a young LT who had just completed his first tour of duty on a ballistic missile submarine, wondered if he should call the Admiral and send out a "Navy Blue" (Emergency) message to the Pentagon and the whole fleet???

Of course, the Fleet Duty Officer thought, there was virtually nothing that could be done if, indeed, GATO had gone missing. The ship was in deep water, thousands of feet deep, and if GATO had gone down, she had imploded long ago.

The Submarine Rescue Unit in San Diego made nice press and made Congressmen and mothers *feel* better. That, he thought, was *something* for all of the money they spent on it. What else could anyone do in a case like this?

So, thought the Fleet Duty Officer, it *is* getting toward morning. If I don't hear from GATO on the next satellite pass, I will call the Admiral. . .

Of course, on GATO the Captain understood the urgency of doing a "routine" satellite check-in call on the very next satellite pass. . . The very last thing that he wanted was for anyone outside of the ship to think that there was anything unusual going on. . . He wasn't going to "hide" anything, but he wasn't going to advertise this little adventure, either.

That was why GATO's Executive Officer had personally supervised LT Clark's transit up to periscope depth and the "routine" check-in with the satellite on the very next pass. No fooling around with the EPM this time. Strictly professional and by-the-book.

In Norfolk the Fleet Duty Officer finally relaxed when he got word that GATO had done a "routine" check-in with the satellite. Better, still, GATO hadn't mentioned anything about any problems onboard. Maybe the hot noise was something created by the *other guy*. Who knows? It didn't correlate with anything, but stuff sometimes didn't make sense, right?

He was relieved of watch in the morning and headed off home to get some sleep. He had nothing of significance for either his relief (the next Fleet Duty Officer on watch) or for the Admiral.

Just another routine night in the North Atlantic during the Cold War...

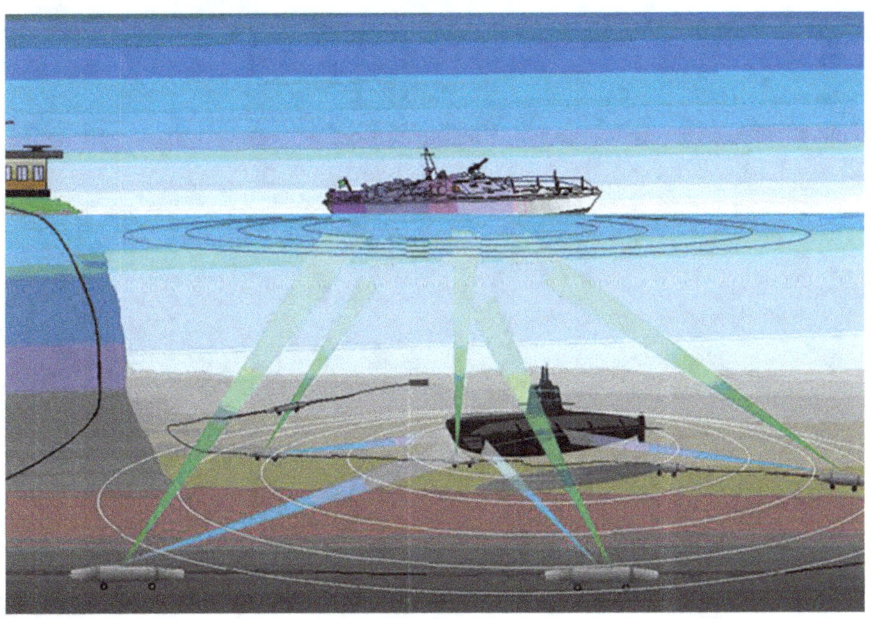

Chapter 9

M Division Night

Saturday, November 9, 1985, Day 27, On Patrol, WESTLANT

Outside of the submarine the crew is the crew, and they are all GATO. Within the ship there were healthy rivalries between the various segments of the crew. Each Division had its own specialized training and each job had unique demands. One way, of course, of settling the age-old question of who is the better sailor is to put the different groups on a level playing field and have them do the same thing. Softball games at the ship's summer picnic – things like that.

Chief Barnes knew of another way to pump up the *esprit de corps* of his guys. You see, he and Chief Joseph (Sonar) had the largest crews onboard the ship. M Division had to operate and do all of the maintenance on the engines and other mechanical equipment, as well as each man having to personally maintain a razor sharp nuclear knowledge. And they had to do it in the hottest, dirtiest area of the ship. Barry Joseph's guys, on the other hand, really didn't have a big workload in port and at sea worked in a cool, quiet space looking at computer screens all watch. Coolness provided, of course, by the M Division air conditioners.

At sea when not on patrol the Nukes were constantly doing training drills of what to do if this or that happened. For instance, they practiced what to do if the Reactor had an emergency shutdown at sea (called a SCRAM) all the time – though that nearly never happened. Most of the crew had never been at sea for a real (non-drill) SCRAM. Lots of work, no sleep. And when not doing drills, there were the nearly endless off-watch refresher training lectures on everything imaginable. They could all calculate from memory, for instance, what would happen to all of the various systems onboard if you simply moved the Control Rods in the Reactor a tenth of an inch in either direction.

On patrol, it was another story. The Nukes were expected to turn the Shaft, keep the lights on, send Potable Water forward on demand, keep the ship cool and to be quiet doing all of this and to be otherwise generally unobtrusive. Don't let anything break. So, on one hand it led to a bit of relaxation. The heat was off. The glory hounds up forward were getting all the attention. But like kids in a big family, they wanted some recognition that – *hey* – we are still here, too.

The answer was M Division Night in the crew's mess. Chief Barnes cut a deal with both the Chief of the Boat and with the Chief Cook, Chief Walter Williams, to have his guys cook and clean for the evening meal on Saturday night. It would be a feast like none other. Kind of cool, too, because it was Chief Barnes' 13th anniversary in the Navy – though he kept that detail to himself.

During the week Barnes and Williams had planned the menu. It would be chicken cordon bleu, with all of the fixings. Cake for dessert. *Let them eat cake*, had been Ike Barnes' half-serious thought. Willie had gotten his menu approved by the Supply Officer and the XO and it was official.

The next step, of course, was advertising. The posters went up. While this had been done on other ships, GATO hadn't done this in many years. It worked, too. All week the boys from M Division got that swagger thing going. They all knew that next week this guy would be coming down and the glory hounds up forward would be in heaven as they picked up the contact and went into trail. This week, though, was M Division night in the Crew's Mess.

During the week the anticipation built steadily. In the end it was almost more about the fanfare and anticipation than it was about the meal. But it was a wonderful meal. Chief Barnes and Chief Williams started cooking as soon as the Galley was cleaned up following the noon meal. Martin and a couple of other guys from M Division joined in as soon as they had gotten cleaned up following the morning watch. Chief Perrot and Chief Nelson, the nuclear Electronics Technician chief, graciously agreed to split Chief Barnes' afternoon watch – with Chief Perrot staying on an extra 3 hours after a break to eat lunch and with Chief Nelson coming on 3 hours early for the evening watch (with a break for THE MEAL). The Nukes hung together, and Barnes really appreciated the support.

The cooks on a submarine have a tough, frequently unappreciated job. Four meals a day, making the stores load last an entire run, and doing it in a Galley the size of a broom closet. They really appreciated the evening off and did not at all mind being "shown up" with a gourmet submarine meal cooked by the Nukes.

The other most unappreciated people on the ship are the messcooks. This is, simply, a *nasty* job. The messcooks prepare the mess area for the meal, served the meals family style, and do all the cleanup, including dishes and washing the floors on their hands and knees after each meal. Unlike cruise ships, which occasionally succumb to outbreaks of food-borne illnesses among their passengers, Navy cooks deservedly take great pride in keeping their crews both well fed and healthy.

Virtually all the enlisted people on the ship got a "chance" to messcook. The only ones who avoided it were the Nukes who had stayed at Nuclear Power School to be instructors after their graduation. These guys typically arrived at their first ship as First Class Petty Officers and were thus immune. Everyone else got it, though. Third and Second Class Petty Officers who arrived at the ship having never been to sea usually got a 30 to 45 day stint in the Galley, depending on the available messcook backlog. Non-Petty Officers, the lowest three enlisted paygrades, typically got to enjoy a 90 day stint.

Sometimes it got almost comical. A couple of months ago Chief Barnes had had to pull one of his guys, Bob Mazzucchi, off of messcooking during a meal to head back aft. Mazzucchi was the only nuclear trained welder onboard and he had been needed to go back and fix a pinhole leak in a steam drain line on one of the steam turbines. Mazzucchi laughed about it – two and a half years of intense training (he had gone to Nuclear Welding School after Nuclear Power School), and he had to finish the dishes before he could go do an emergency weld repair at sea! But that was part of the unique joy of the crew – 90 percent of them had some kind of advanced skills training, yet the dishes still had to get done.

As the afternoon wore on the anticipation grew. Barnes had set expectations very high for his guys, but he knew that they would measure up. Besides, what other Division had the chutzpah to put it all out there and cook for the crew? How could this go badly? Chief Williams was a jewel and made sure that it all came together. He appreciated the respect that Barnes was showing his cooks by even doing this and he was committed to making it a success. Maybe he could get the rest of the old goats in the Goat Locker (Chief's Quarters) to make this an every Saturday night event. *That would be sweet.*

As the Messenger of the Watch went around later that afternoon to wake up the oncoming watch section, he had a special message for those he was waking up. M Division was cooking dinner, and nobody wanted to miss that meal... Most of the people up forward, the coners, were counting on a bust. It would give them reason to harass the Nukes for the rest of the trip, and long beyond. Friendly jeers and sneers could be heard in the chow line just before the Mess Decks were opened for the meal.

In the Wardroom the Officers ate the same meal as the crew. The ship only had one little Galley and the Mess Decks for the crew were on one side, while the Wardroom was on the other side of the

Galley. As the Captain sat down – *nobody sits in the Wardroom until the Captain is seated* – Chief Barnes entered from the Galley/Pantry area to serve the meal. It was received to high acclaim. A few weeks later, in fact, the XO led the ship's Officers in doing the same thing for the crew – having an Officer's night of cooking for the crew. That night, however, they also auctioned off the seats in the Wardroom for dinner to the highest bidder, with the proceeds going to the ship's recreation fund. Mutual respect among all aboard. Camaraderie. *Submarine Style.*

Out in the Crew's Mess the jeers and sneers were quickly replaced with grudging compliments. This was a really good meal. The cake was an unexpected bonus, too.

Chief Williams and his cooks were beaming from ear to ear as the M Division crew laid it on thick about how difficult it had been, but how satisfying it was, to have put out a "good meal."

Ike Barnes knew he had a hit on his hands. This is what submarining was all about. This was his third SSN tour of duty. He had been here less than a year, but this was the most fun and the tightest, closest crew he had served with. His first crew had been fairly typical for a relatively new 637/STURGEON Class ship – competent and professional, but not as "tight" as a crew can only get by executing multiple deployments together. That ship had been in DEVRON 12 and was more than 12 years old before it went on its first real deployment.

His second ship had been a new construction ship, USS LA JOLLA (SSN 701). He had been on LA JOLLA for more than 5 years, and when he left there had been only one other crew member still onboard who had been there with him on day one of the crew's existence. LA JOLLA was a great ship, but with all of the crap associated with construction, commissioning, homeport change from New London (where she had been built) to San Diego, and everything else, the crew had never deployed and had never coalesced. *Still, Barnes absolutely loved that 688 Reactor and propulsion plant design...*

Easily 80 percent of his frustrations with GATO could never exist on a 688 because of the radical design improvements. It was dramatically different. But there was truly something about "old boat" sailors, *particularly old "594 Tough" boat sailors.* They were *closer* to their ships; they were better in a pinch. They had to be – *they got more practice at being in a pinch...*

So, almost halfway into the trip M Division night was a huge success. High fives all around. It was as if the ship was finally ready for the next phase of the adventure.

Chapter 10

Big Contact

Sunday, November 10, 1985, Day 28, On Patrol, WESTLANT

"Conn, Sonar, I have a new contact bearing 064, designate Sierra 1, possible submerged Soviet submarine," was Chief Barry Joseph's report.

"Sonar, Conn, designate this contact as Master 1, this is our guy coming right down from where we expected him to be," replied the Captain.

The foreplay was over. If ever there had been a lot of foreplay, this was the time. All the crap associated with getting ready for the run . . . almost a month underway . . . an unscheduled drive-by at Holy Loch – all of that was over. They were in the game now! This is what they had trained for and worked for and searched the ocean for a month for. *This was the main event.*

The Captain maneuvered GATO deftly to get a solution on this guy and then to take up trail in his baffles. Once GATO was in his baffles, pretty much directly behind him, it would be very, very hard for this guy to detect GATO. The game was to hang close, listen, watch, wait, record it all – and not to become an entry in this guy's Master Contact Log. And, of course, if he gave any indication of making preparations for a hostile missile launch . . .

GATO's Captain smiled from ear to ear. His ship was doing it. As the hours passed, everyone fell into the routine of trail and

GATO did not let him down – either the ship or the crew. For him, this moment had started almost 20 years earlier, when he had reported for plebe summer at the Naval Academy in Annapolis, MD. He had been in high school at the time of the Cuban missile crisis, and he knew that he had wanted to go to sea. It was the Navy, after all, that had put up the blockade that had ended the crisis. He had a love of math and science, and the idea of nuclear-powered submarines was very attractive to him. He majored in nuclear engineering at Annapolis. He initially was concerned – *and a bit self-conscious* – about the fact that he had an immune system disorder – *alopecia universalis* – and thought that his complete lack of body hair could keep him from entering the Submarine Force.

When the time came for his class to indicate their preferences for duty, Rick Hanson had no doubts in indicating submarines. All of the various warfare communities recruited hard at Annapolis. But he had done one of his summers on an SSN and that was all the confirmation that he had needed. He listened politely to the aviators – who would have gladly taken him even with his nuclear engineering degree. He skipped the Marines. He respected them but had no interest in that service branch for himself. He wanted to be a submariner. His alopecia turned out to not be a problem, but there still was a hurdle: Rickover.

So, it was with a bit of trepidation that Midshipman Hanson and his fellow potential Nukes got on the bus for the short ride down to Arlington, VA and to the headquarters of Naval Reactors. It was an event in the career of every submarine Officer that was never forgotten.

Naval Reactors (NR) is the organization responsible for nuclear propulsion within the Navy. The head of NR in the 21st century is a full Admiral, usually one of the top 4 or 5 Admirals in the Navy in terms of seniority. Back when Midshipman Hanson made his initial visit it was then-Rear Admiral Rickover. Uniquely he held the designation as Deputy Commander of the Bureau of Ships for Nuclear Power and as a Deputy Director in the Atomic Energy

Commission. In the 21st century the organizations have changed names, but the dual hated position still has leverage both within the Defense Department and the Energy Department.

Rickover held final say over all Officers assigned to his program. To get to that decision point a candidate first had to have exceptional credentials and college grades. Rickover shrewdly knew that the ultimate success of his whole life's work would be determined by the quality of the men that he allowed to command nuclear-powered ships. He wanted only the best.

The process on interview day involved very senior executives from the NR staff interviewing each candidate on a wide range of subjects. Anything was open game, including philosophy. After several of these one-on-one interviews the candidates were put in a windowless room and were told to be quiet. The interviewers would caucus and some of the candidates were asked, one by one, to leave the room with a staffer. Unbeknownst to the candidates still in the room, these early departures were the ones who had not *made the cut* to see the Admiral. They were thanked for their time and interest in nuclear power and asked to wait on the bus for their buddies who would be seeing the Admiral.

Rickover interviews are famous. They could be lengthy and grueling, and Rickover could demand promises and follow-up and all sorts of things. Hanson's interview was less dramatic. He had great grades and class standing at Annapolis, had done well in the first-round interviews, and was exactly the kind of guy that Rickover cherished for his program. It only lasted 5 minutes, involved a couple of questions, and included only two scowls from the old man. *Hanson was in.*

Following graduation from Annapolis and a brief vacation to get married to his high school sweetheart, Hanson had reported to Nuclear Power School at Bainbridge, MD. Years earlier, during WWII and Korea, it had been the Recruit Training Center for enlisted women entering the Navy. Now, Nuke school was the big action on the Base. Located at very top of the Chesapeake Bay, it was a gorgeous location in a rural setting. Not many distractions from the very intense graduate-level studies. After 6 months of 12-hour school days in Bainbridge, he had then gone off to Windsor, CT to the prototype of the USS TULLIBEE (SSN 597) for the second phase of Nuclear Power School.

TULLIBEE was a one-of-a-kind electric drive submarine whose Reactor had been designed by Combustion Engineering Corporation near Hartford, CT. As was the practice in the early days of the program, a full scale working submarine prototype with Reactor, engines and everything else was built to test the design before the ship was built. Other prototype sites were in West Milton, NY, where the General Electric designs were tested, and Idaho Falls, ID, where the Westinghouse designs were tested.

At the end of his second very intense 6 months of training at Windsor then-Ensign Hanson stood for his qualification board orals. He had already completed and passed an 8-hour-long closed-book written final exam, and now he was taking his 4 hour-long orals. During the orals anything – *going back to the first day at Bainbridge* – was fair game. Sitting in judgment at the orals was the Commanding Officer of the Training Unit, a civilian engineer from Combustion Engineering, a personal representative of Admiral Rickover and a Lieutenant who was an instructor at this phase of training. Any member of the orals Board could, individually, end the candidates' Nuclear Power Program career by failing them on just one of the exam sections. There were exam sections on each element of the propulsion plant.

Ensign Hanson did very well on his Oral Board and was congratulated by the Commanding Officer. A couple of weeks later he got a personal note from Admiral Rickover, also congratulating him on his excellent performance. These were all great signs – Rickover congratulatory notes were rare.

His new wife and he packed up for the 50 mile move down to New London with a light heart and with great hope for the future. He was off to Submarine School, and he was a *hot runner*. The six months of submarine school were almost a vacation compared to the intensity of a year of Nuclear Power School. He learned all of the basics of how the ship worked and practiced damage control in the wet trainer. Here real flooding is simulated, and the trainees get really wet doing emergency repairs. He went through the escape trainer, doing a free ascent to the surface in the famous escape tank. He also learned the basics of target motion analysis and weapons control in the attack simulator. While he lived and breathed nuclear power, Hanson knew that the attack simulator was where the rubber met the road. Do well and impress the instructors there and, along with his good nuclear performance, he would be sure to be on the "A" track.

"A" track Officers had a career path that generally started on an SSN, included a cross-over tour as Engineer Officer on an SSBN, and then an Executive Officer (XO) tour and command on an SSN. "B" track Officers generally got the opposite. While it was not cast in stone, it was hard to overcome your initial slotting. If you wanted command of an SSN, you really wanted your first tour to be on one. Hanson got USS BERGALL, (SSN 667) and was jumping with joy. He wanted to stay in New London and BERGALL was a New London boat – and it was brand spanking new STURGEON Class ship. It still had the new boat smell . . . Awesome.

Over the three years on BERGALL Ensign Hanson progressed to Lieutenant (Junior Grade) and then to Lieutenant. He quickly mastered the art of submarining and earned respect from both his peers and from the enlisted men onboard. He earned his dolphins, having passed his final oral examination with the Squadron Commodore early, and set to work on his Engineer Officer qualifications.

With the help and support of his Commanding Officer, the Squadron Engineer and the refresher course at Sub School, LT Hanson worked hard to master the intricacies of the submarine Engineer Officer courses. It was, effectively, a compressed post-graduate level version of Nuclear Power School. The coursework here, of course, did include lots of equations and diagrams and procedures. But it was a lot more than that – and this "more" frequently proved to be the hardest part for young Officers to "get."

The *more* was the demonstration of appropriate engineering judgment and/or wisdom. What to do when the books run out of advice and the ship is far from port. Now, it was not that the books were short of guidance and direction. If you took all of the technical and operating manuals used for GATO's Reactor and propulsion plants, it would fill a couple of shelves about 15 feet long each. Page after page after page of details, procedures and drawings. But the day could come when the crew of a ship had to decide what to do for an eventuality that had never been foreseen. That is when the judgment thing was so important.

The Engineer Officer Exam was a two-day affair at NR Headquarters. It involved written as well as oral examinations but did not include visiting with the Admiral. You only saw Rickover for your initial screening to enter the program and during your pre-command training period. Hanson did fine and was sent back to BERGALL as a fully qualified LT, ready for his next assignment.

He got a *hot runner* assignment and went back to Nuclear Power School, this time at West Milton, NY. It was a good couple of years and included the joyous birth of his first child. Soon they were on their way back to New London. This time he bought a nice house in the town of Gales Ferry, just north of the submarine base, and reported to USS LAFAYETTE (SSBN 616) as the Blue Crew Engineer Officer.

With his assignment to an Engineer Officer job, he got a "spot promotion" to Lieutenant Commander. The trips to Holy Loch and the Strategic Deterrent Patrols went by like a blur. The boomers were well maintained, and LAFAYETTE had all of the most recent modernizations done in her last, and recent, overhaul. Nothing too out of the ordinary. While on LAFAYETTE Hanson noted three personal milestones. First, his second child was born. Unfortunately he was at sea for the blessed event – you could not get your wife pregnant and then be there for the delivery if you were on a standard

SSBN patrol cycle. But that was part of the price that the submarine force paid for Freedom in the Cold War. Second, he did get early selection to Lieutenant Commander – so his rank was no longer "positional" based upon his job. Finally, he qualified to command submarines. All in all, a very good tour.

Reflecting his very high nuclear community standing, he was asked to be a junior member of the Nuclear Propulsion Examining Board (NPEB) for the Atlantic Fleet for his next job. It meant a move to Norfolk and frequent trips to sea, but it was a real plum assignment. The Hansons rented their house in Gales Ferry to some junior Officers and headed to Virginia.

The NPEB is the group that goes around to each nuclear-powered ship (and to each boomer crew) once per year to administer the annual Reactor Safeguards Exam. It is the capstone of about 3 months of intense preparation on the part of a crew and can determine the career paths for the ship's three senior Officers (Captain, XO, Engineer). Blow a Reactor Safeguards Exam and you have blown your career. *No deposit, no return.* Only the best nuclear Officers in the fleet were selected to do these intense three-day exams on each ship, and Hanson had made the grade. He was on a phenomenal career arc.

Following this highly successful tour, Hanson was assigned as Executive Officer on USS ARCHERFISH (SSN 678). ARCHERFISH was a *hot* New London boat, and this was a great assignment. They did a couple of great special operations (60 to 90-day deployments without port calls, with focused objectives) and made a real name for themselves in the community. XO is normally a miserable assignment for an Officer – it is not only tough to be second in command, the XO also has to deal with all sorts of administrative challenges and issues. Officers generally felt that the best day of their XO tours was the last one. Not only because it was over, of course, but because it meant that they were headed to command. Lots of work to build a Commanding Officer. Finally getting there was so sweet.

With his promotion to full Commander and selection for command of GATO, Hanson headed off to the Prospective Commanding Officer pipeline. It involved courses at the Sub School and a stint back at Naval Reactors. It also involved courtesy calls down in Norfolk at the headquarters of the Atlantic Submarine Force. One thing that the Commander of the Atlantic Submarine Force, the senior operational submariner in the Navy and a Vice Admiral, told him always stuck with him.

COMSUBLANT told the young Prospective Commanding Officer that he needed to be acutely aware that when he was in command the entire crew would be watching absolutely everything that he did and said. Every facial gesture and grunt would be analyzed in an attempt to gain insight into the Captain's state of mind and thoughts. COMSUBLANT told Hanson, as he told all new Commanding Officers, to be careful what messages he sent to his crew and to learn how to carefully script and broadcast the exact messages that he intended. In closing the Admiral told him that for some new COs this was the hardest lesson to learn and that failure to learn it and master the art of effective "command communications" and "command presence" had ruined more than a few once-promising careers.

With all of that done, and with his family moved back into their house in Gales Ferry, Hanson reported to the Commodore of Squadron Ten in New London. After a couple of days, including introductions to the squadron staff, he was on the pier to watch his ship return from sea. It had been out on a short operation providing support to the P3 Antisubmarine Warfare planes out of Brunswick, ME. GATO had been the rabbit and the planes had tried to find and chase her.

Commander Hanson had some time in port to meet with the departing Commanding Officer and both the Wardroom and the Crew. He got "turnover" information from the departing skipper and advice on all manner of things. This was followed by a week at sea for routine training, where Hanson got a chance to observe the ship in action at sea. On this trip he was 100 percent observer – not yet in command. But everyone had played to him anyway. Like a great future Captain, he didn't say much or do anything to undercut the departing CO. He heeded COMSUBLANT's advice on command communications and kept it all very close to his chest.

The big day came, and it was a beautiful day. His parents, and his wife's parents, had flown in from Wisconsin for the ceremony. The crew mustered topside in their dress uniforms and the Commodore presided. First, the departing CO was praised for his achievements in command. Today was a swansong for him, even though he had lots of career left, leaving your first command is a day that will live with you forever. He had done well and was awarded with a commendation and Legion of Merit medal. With that award presented, the departing CO got his chance to make his departing remarks and to provide his closing admonitions to the crew and to his successor. Finally, he read his orders.

Once that was done, Commander Hanson stepped to the microphone and read his orders and turned to the departing CO, saluted him and said, "I relieve you, sir"

The departing CO returned the salute and replied, in time honored fashion, "I stand relieved."

With that the complete mantle of command had shifted from one man to another. GATO had a new CO.

It didn't really hit Hanson until later that night, after the party at the Officer's Club had ended and after he had seen off his visiting family members. He was in bed with his wife at home up in Gales Ferry when it hit him. WOW. Like many before him, and many to come after him, he suddenly felt the awesome weight of his responsibility. He had been training and working so hard since he had left high school for this very day. His wife, wise to the ways of the Navy, understood when he told her that he needed to go out for a drive.

He knew that the last thing in the world that he should do right then, the most damaging to his career, would be to actually go visit his ship. He was the Captain, but if he showed up now, at 10 PM on his first day in command, it would reveal a break in his command presence. Captains just didn't show up unannounced on their ships at 10 PM. So, instead he drove down the Groton side of the river, near the WWII Submarine Memorial, and looked over across the river to State Pier. There she was, and everything was fine. GATO, his ship, was fine.

He went home to Gales Ferry and he and his wife conceived their third child that night. What a day.

That all happened 18 short months ago. God, how a command tour flew by! And through the luck of the scheduling gods, here he was on his first major deployment in command.

This guy was his, and he was on top of the world.

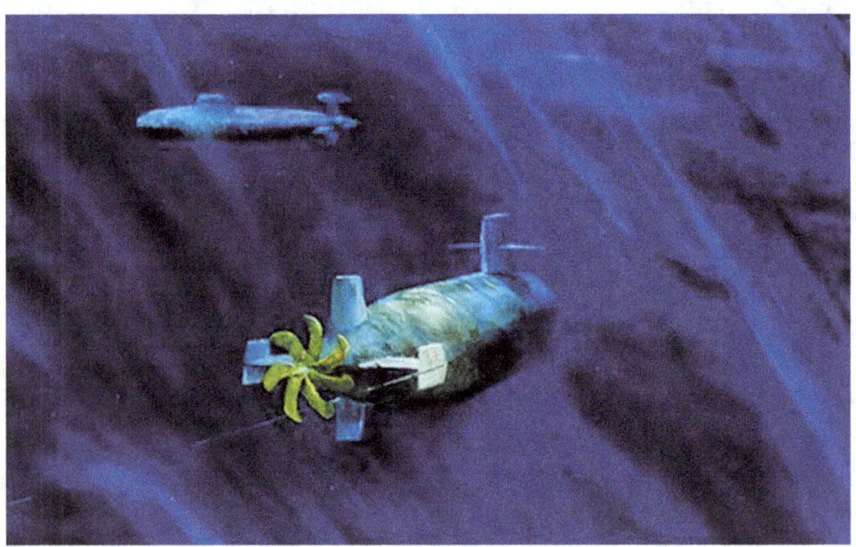

Chapter 11

In Trail

Thursday, November 14, 1985, Day 32, On Patrol, WESTLANT

GATO had rapidly fallen into the "routine" of trailing a Soviet missile boat. It almost felt like "finally" – but it surely also felt "great."

It had taken an almost herculean effort over the last year to get the ship ready for this trip, and the first 4 weeks of the trip had been unfulfilling – and more frustrating with each passing day. Their persistence had been rewarded, however, when they took this guy in trail on Day 28.

Now it was Day 32, the 5th day in trail, and it had become "routine" once again. GATO, you see, was no rookie at this. The ship was now well into its second decade of trailing these guys. In fact, as discussed earlier, less than two years after GATO's commissioning she was busy trailing the Soviet ballistic missile submarine K-19, when it had actually rammed GATO.

In the ship's Control Room, there was a real buzz and a focused intensity. The ship's Weapons Control System was manned and fully operational – along with the Torpedo Room crew, GATO was ready at any moment to fire a "snapshot," warshot in the event that this guy started making preparations to launch one of his nuclear tipped ballistic missiles. There was no more serious mission in defense of

America, and everyone on GATO knew it, felt it, and was proud to be "up to the task."

Back aft, in the propulsion plant, everything was quiet – both literally and figuratively. Everything was working well and nothing too unusual was going on.

- The Main Air Conditioner continued to make cold water – crazy patch job, and all.

- #1 400 cycle set continued to make power for the Combat Control Systems, despite the steadily degrading bearing.

- No new seawater leaks had started, and the existing seawater leakage was reasonable, controlled and not getting any worse.

- The small steam leak that had been identified when the Plant was being started up was not nearly as small now – *steam leaks always grow over time* – but it was still not a safety or equipment hazard and they still planned to fix it should they get a port visit. Maybe – *but maybe not* – they'd get through the whole run without having to fix it while deployed (either in port or at sea). Either way, not an immediate issue.

Being good Nukes, the Nuke Chiefs – Chief Barnes, Chief Perot and Chief Nelson – were taking advantage of the "quiet" steady-state trouble-free operations to work with their watchsections to advance their training objectives.

Since it takes a new crew member more than a year to become fully qualified on all assigned watchstations and on the ship overall (i.e., become "Qualified in Submarines" and be allowed to wear the coveted dolphin insignia on their uniforms), there was always train-ing to do. As the senior enlisted Nukes, getting their people fully qualified was one of the Chiefs' missions.

The Nuclear Power Program provides great training materials, including a variety of "T Manuals." These T Manuals are basically graduate level theory and practical design manuals.

Chief Barnes was talking to a couple of his watchstanders, in between their rounds to monitor their equipment, about advanced theory. One of the things he was discussing was the benefits of listening closely to each piece of equipment operating under various conditions and watching the trends/correlations in the various operating parameters of each unit/system. His point was that once you "know" your systems and equipment you can spot a problem in a unit 20 feet away simply by hearing/feeling the difference in how it is operating, or with a quick look at the various operating parameters. Finally, he also pointed out how the values of operating parameters for one system can tell you what is going on in another system in another part of the propulsion plant.

Still, it was actually a pretty "boring" time around the propulsion plant. With everything operating pretty much as designed, and with a steady power level trailing this guy, there wasn't much to do except to monitor conditions and to do the routine daily operating maintenance on everything, like shifting and cleaning oil strainers.

During times like these, when everything got especially boring, Chief Barnes always tried to both *spice it up* and to remind his watch team of what they were really doing each time before they took the Watch. When his watch team finished each meal before starting their Watch period, the Chief would say something like, "it's time to head aft guys, and to exercise the distinct privilege of operating a submerged nuclear propulsion plant."

They'd all smile and give him crap, but he also knew that it served as a simple reminder that they were both distinctly privileged to be standing these watches on this mighty warship, and that their shipmates and, indeed, the entire Nation, had placed great trust in their skill, dedication and attention to detail in the operation of the plant.

One of Chief Perot's points to his guys, in his own effort to combat the issue of boredom, was how the operation of a nuclear propulsion plant can sometimes be characterized as seemingly end-less hours of complete boredom – *punctuated by moments of extreme excitement.* His point was that "boring is good" – but we can't let it lull us into complacency. We must be ever vigilant so that if something unusual happens we will be mentally alert, sharp and at the "top of our games" to prevent an undesirable outcome.

> *The reality of Chief Perot's "seemingly endless hours of boredom – punctuated by moments of extreme excitement" sentiment – is, in fact, expressed in this book in the fact that there are gaps in this sea story narrative of more than two weeks without comment. Routine operation of the ship is just that, routine. Like any great story, we don't focus on the routine, but on the unusual action and events which best tell the intended big story.*

The same "boring is good" truth had overcome the crew up forward, as well. Truth be told, the absolutely most boring mission on earth is to operate a nuclear ballistic missile submarine on Strategic Deterrent Patrol. Since November 1960, when USS GEORGE WASHINGTON (SSBN 598) started the world's first nuclear ballistic missile submarine Strategic Deterrent Patrol, thousands of nuclear ballistic missile submarine patrols have been completed by several Navies without a single nuclear ballistic missile being launched in anger. The US Navy, only one of the navies which conduct these patrols, celebrated its 4,000[th] successful Strategic Deterrent Patrol in September 2014. A US Navy poster celebrating this milestone is provided, for reference, on page 144.

"Hiding with pride" – as the Boomer sailors call it – is excruciatingly boring. GATO's current reality is that keeping one of these guys in trail is only a little bit less boring. The trail guy (GATO, in this case) has to be sharp to detect turns – but even that becomes boring. These nuclear ballistic missile submarines tend to patrol in a designated "box" in the ocean, so even their turns become a bit predictable.

It is into this routine that GATO has fallen. Everyone was "sharp" – but after 6 days in trail, this guy was predictable and not very exciting. Then again, they all realized that *this is the mission.* They had trained for it; they were up to it, and they were doing it.

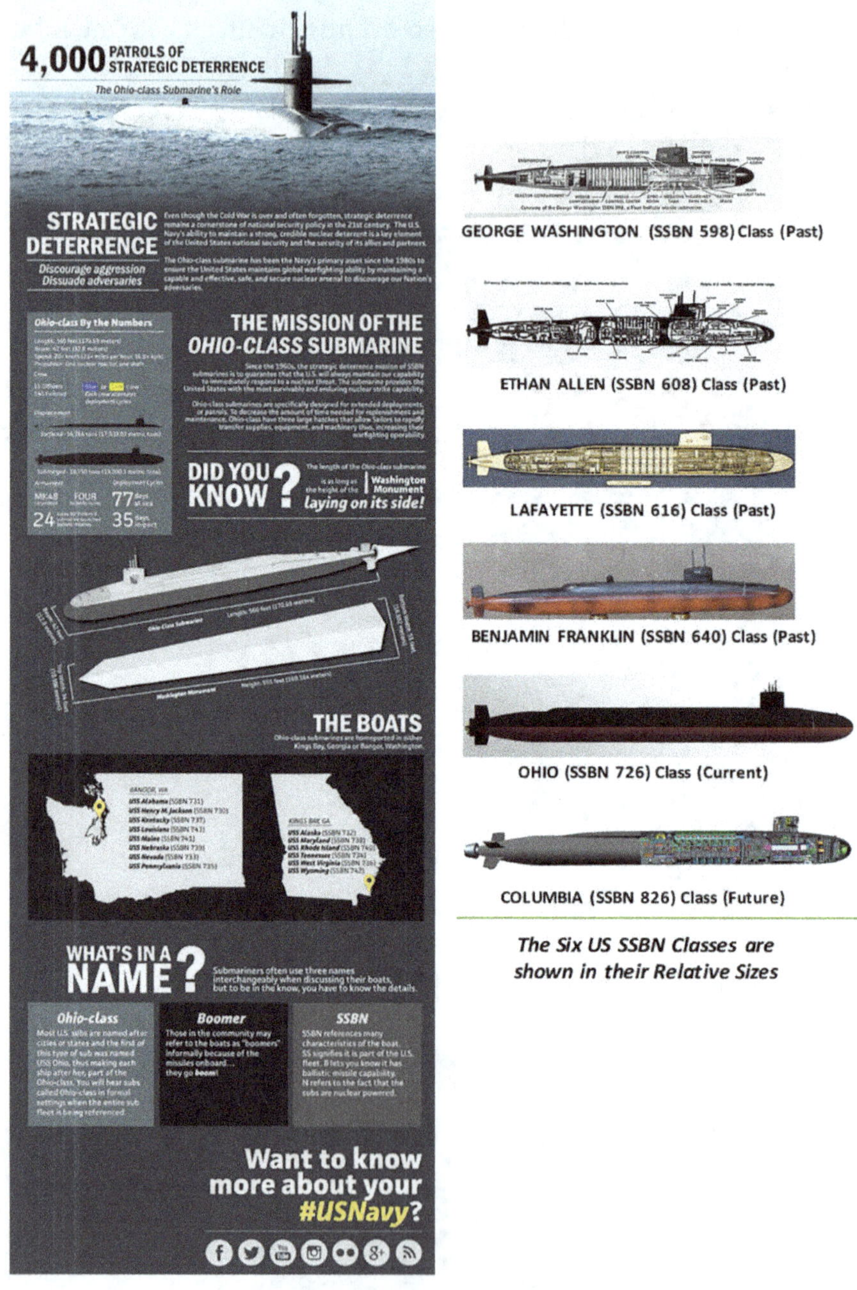

The Navy chart to the left can be accessed online at:
http://navylive.dodlive.mil/2014/09/19/4000-
patrols-of-strategic-deterrence

Chapter 12

Grape. . . Or Orange?

Friday, November 15, 1985, Day 33, On Patrol, WESTLANT

It was the midwatch – the most routine of the routine times during the mission. LT Clark was back in the box standing EOOW and Chief Barnes was the Engineering Watch Supervisor. As Barnes toured Engineroom Lower Level he stopped to chat with his guy Simpson. Simpson had been out of Nuclear Power School a bit longer than Martin – he had been in the class ahead of him – but was also a young guy "learning the ropes" on how to operate the plant and the ship.

"Chief, I kind of get what you have been saying about knowing your equipment. I have noticed that the Evaporator is using more steam and producing less fresh water. I wonder what is going on???"

With that the two of them took a detailed look at the operating logs to review the various parameters. They confirmed, as Simpson had "felt," that, despite all operating parameters being "in spec," the Evaporator wasn't tip-top. Barnes knew, from experience, what was going on – but he helped Simpson to "figure it out" for himself with a series of helpful questions and hypotheses. It turned out that the heat transfer surfaces inside the machine were getting scaled up.

There was a Navy-specified treatment chemical that they added to the feedwater to keep the machine from scaling-up – and Simpson verified that they were religiously treating the machine. As they then discussed, the "right" solution was to shut the machine down, partially disassemble it and then clean the internal heat transfer surfaces. Of course, this wasn't going to happen on station. So, what to do?

Barnes knew of a potential "interim" solution – but had never had to try it himself. It was an old fleet legend among submarine nuclear Machinist Mates. But both of the other two ships that he had previously served on had had much newer equipment and were not susceptible to this age-related issue. He told Simpson about it and said that he would get permission to try an experiment and that Simpson would be put in charge of the experiment, once he got it approved.

When he got to the upper level Engineroom, Barnes went into the box to relieve the EOOW, so that he could make a tour of the propulsion plant. As they "turned over" Barnes explained to LT Clark that the Evaporator was showing some signs of poor performance – nothing of immediate concern – but that he wanted to discuss an experiment to remedy the problem after they got off watch and had had breakfast.

When they got together after watch Barnes brought Simpson with him to meet with LT Clark and the Engineer, who had coincidentally been in the Wardroom. Barnes had Simpson explain how he had identified the performance degradation in the Evaporator and then Barnes talked about his conceptual experiment. Basically, he explained that he'd heard of using Bug Juice Mix to treat the Evaporator instead of the Navy-approved treatment chemical. He wanted to try it for a couple of days, and he made the sale.

Bug Juice Mix, of course, is the mix that the cooks used to make the non-carbonated drinks in the coolers in the Crew's Mess. Granulated flavored and sweetened crystals. The big question, of course, was Grape or Orange? They would try each flavor for 2 days and see. The chemistry, interestingly, is that Bug Juice has a slightly acidic pH – and was expected to dissolve/knock some of the scale free – where it would be washed overboard with the brine wastewater in the normal course of operations. This, conveniently, was the opposite of the unit's feedwater – straight from seawater – and its slightly alkaline pH. Just a mild chemical shock to restore normal operations.

With the Engineer's approval Barnes and Simpson then visited with Chief Williams, the head cook. Of course, at this point Willie would gladly do *anything* for Ike. He agreed and told them that he had much more Grape on hand than Orange. For some reason, GATO's crew seemed to love Orange Bug Juice.

Simpson set up the experiment, starting with Grape. After just one day the Evaporator was running so much better that they never tried the Orange – and were able to reduce the Grape treatment level below what they initially tried. Another GATO success. Of course, another major worklist item for when they got back to port (cleaning the machine out internally).

**Commercial Surface Ship Evaporator
(Not GATO's Equipment)**
*(notice how "out in the open" this equipment is when
installed – not so in a submarine, where layer upon
layer of piping, wiring and equipment is installed all
around every piece of equipment in the ship)*

Chapter 13

Lost Contact

Saturday, November 16, 1985, Day 34, On Patrol, WESTLANT

GATO had been running hard for the last 34 days and the Reactor Controls Equipment was due for a little planned maintenance. It was one of those things like an oil change – you could put it off, but you eventually had to do it. It only took 30 minutes to do, but the catch was that you had to shut the Reactor down to do it. And, yes, of course, the need for this particular periodic maintenance did not exist on the new 688's. *But let's not forget, this stuff had been designed in 1954. . .*

Saturday morning, the sixth day in-trail, GATO got a message from their operational commander telling them that they should expect to remain in-trail on this guy for the foreseeable future. Armed with that knowledge, the Captain called the Engineer into his Stateroom.

"Eng, I want to do the Reactor Controls maintenance this afternoon. While we could do it on the Battery, I don't want to take any chances, so I want to do it with the Diesel Engine running to provide electrical power. We'll get directly behind him and back way off, so he won't detect us. I'd like you to brief your people and be ready to go at 3 PM."

"OK, Sir, but you know we could let this maintenance go and do it when we are no longer on this guy. The worst case is that we have to write NR a letter about it when we get home, but it is clearly within your discretion to do that."

"I have considered that, but I don't want to be writing letters to NR about this maintenance. This guy has no idea that we have him, and he has been very predictable. I am convinced that we can get this done and maintain trail."

"Yes, sir. We will be ready to go by 3 PM."

At 2:45 everybody had been pre-briefed. The maintenance team was on station and all necessary watchstanders were in place. Essentially the entire nuclear crew was back aft either standing by to do the maintenance or acting as assistants to the guys actually on watch.

The ship came to periscope depth and prepared to snorkel. The Head Valve, which had to let in the air for the Diesel Engine, did not act up and passed its pre-snorkel test. Everything was looking good.

Now GATO had a unique Diesel. All of the noise cuts taken from outside the ship indicated that something was seriously wrong with it – like maybe a warped engine block. Rumors were that a few years ago someone had improperly snorkeled and had flooded the engine with seawater – which can easily warp things. Seawater doesn't compress very well . . . but the engine had been torn down and inspected by the Fleet Diesel Inspector and it met all physical specifications. It also always started and ran well under load. Just a bit noisy. Nonetheless, when GATO went into overhaul next year the Diesel was already slated to be replaced, lock stock and barrel, with the spare engine owned by the Navy. The Navy usually bought one spare of something major like this for each ship class and kept it for the life of the class. Since GATO was the "newest" THRESHER Class ship and would be the last one to go through major overhaul, upon the Fleet Diesel Inspector's recommendation the spare engine was slated to go into GATO at overhaul.

Who knows what it was today. Was it the unique noise of the Diesel? Was it just fate? Whatever it was, this guy detected GATO about 3 minutes after the Reactor was shut down. He boogied on out of there and GATO, with a shutdown Reactor, could not follow. You can't go very fast on the Diesel.

Thirty minutes later the maintenance had been successfully completed and GATO's Reactor was Critical once again. With the Main Engines back online GATO took off in the last known direction looking for her lost contact. For about 30 minutes GATO burned up the sea zooming this way and that in a hopeless search for the now alerted target.

On the plus side, the Clutch had worked fine when shifting to/from the EPM for the evolution.

At the one-hour point after the contact was lost the Captain called in to the operational commander and reported the bad news. No other assets had the guy. This was B–A–D.

For the rest of the day GATO conducted a search along what they thought was a good search pattern. No joy.

By midnight it was obvious – *that guy was long gone.*

The Captain, human as he was, had just seen 20 years of his life go down the tubes. His career was toast. *What the hell had gotten into his mind?* Run the Diesel – was he *frigging nuts,* or *what?*

Pity the poor Officers of the Deck. In time honored tradition they had to report their relief to the Captain at the end of each watch period. He had retreated to his stateroom and was in a foul mood. He basically bit the head off each of the OODs as they dared enter his lair to report their reliefs. The whole ship went into a blue/black funk. *The general attitude was something along the lines of how nobody would be surprised if they called them home early after this boneheaded play.*

Requiem for a Submarine Captain

Chapter 14

The Other Guy Gets a Vote, Too

Sunday, November 17, 1985, Day 35, On Patrol, WESTLANT

GATO's Captain spent a great deal of time thinking about how he had let that guy "slip away". His entire focus, and appropriately so, was on his own – and his ship's – performance. After all, he couldn't do anything about any of the other guy's actions, so he could only control what was going on onboard his own ship. In the end he concluded that while doing the Reactor Controls maintenance was appropriate, he shouldn't have run the Diesel. The Main Storage Battery had plenty of capacity to support the maintenance, and he had been *too conservative* in his planning. He'd never *do that* again...

Nonetheless, these guys don't come along every day, and he was now gone. Trailing these guys is, after all, *the mission*. It is why they were there, to begin with, and now he was gone. Any way you sliced this mess up, it was UGLY.

What the Captain didn't really consider at that moment is that the "other guy" gets a vote, too. Further, despite the then-current caricatures in popular culture, Soviet nuclear ballistic missile submarine Captains were every bit as professional, committed, dedicated and focused as were American submarine Captains. They wanted to win, too.

Further, despite all of the crew's ruminations about the "boring routine" of trail, the fact of the matter is that trailing a Soviet nuclear ballistic missile submarine during the Cold War was a nerve-wrack-ing form of Battle, just like the Cold War itself was an endurance test that required nerves of steel and an enduring commitment. This form of Battle was like dancing on the edge of a razor sharp knife and doing it for weeks at a time – uninterrupted. Consider:

1. Having 100+ guys live together inside a steel tank hundreds of feet below the surface of the ocean, with many tons of pressure on the outside of the tank surface, in and of itself, is an incredible technical and logistical challenge.

2. Having that steel tank (the hull is affectionately known as the *"people tank"* in submarine lingo) enjoy independent freedom of movement in three axes – and at incredible speeds – with no outside view or support is an even greater technical challenge, requiring an exceptionally complex machine.

    Let's face facts, folks. There are no navigation references underwater, and there is no way to "see" where you are going. Still, you have the confidence to "let her rip" and to travel at very high speeds. Yes. Yes, indeed.

3. Recognizing that even momentary lapses in the execution of the technical and logistical challenges outlined in #1 and #2 above have already been so significant as to have – *on their own* – claimed the lives of many fine people doing exactly what you are doing, sometimes in exactly the same design unit as you are in – *ignoring the additional pressures that accrue from any third party actors like Soviet submarines with nuclear ballistic missiles that can "light the fuse" on the end of the world* – and then completely isolating these 100+ guys for months at a time, from the world at-large creates an

abnormally intense psychological stress level on everyone involved.

4. Add to the mix of technological, logistical and psychological challenges involved in simply being on patrol, that adversarial Soviet submarine with nuclear ballistic missiles that can "light the fuse" on the end of the world – and then add the requirement to "stay close" but without being detected and to "be ever-ready" to fire a "snapshot" warshot upon his preparation to launch his missiles – and to have that snapshot warshot be released in time to prevent that missile launch from occurring, and you have anything but a routine, boring job. *You have a crew dancing on a razor-sharp knife edge, uninterrupted, for an extended period of time.* <u>*To do this it takes audacity, commitment, faith in your ship, faith in your training and skill, and an enduring faith in your shipmates.*</u>

Since psychologists seem to be fixated on "coping mechanisms" for high stress situations, we offer the Cold War SSN sailor, convincing himself – because "all of it" is too great "to process" – that it is a manageable mission that does, in fact, become routine and boring. That way he doesn't have to "think about it all" *too much.* Seriously, with a mission that demands perfection every moment of every day, much is asked of these sailors. Just as much as has been asked of every one of America's Veterans since the Battles of Lexington and Concord at the dawn of the American Revolutionary War. No micro-aggression victim culture here.

While this all may sound *hokey* and *too puffed up* to the uninitiated, we ask simply that you "think about it all" for a few moments yourself. Think about the risk that these men took to even be on the ship, and then the awesome responsibility that they all accepted in the defense of the Nation. *Are you ready to sign up?* In any event, in action there is absolutely nothing *hokey* or *puffed up* about it.

There is a crew made up of a bunch of professionals from every corner of America, and it is a beautiful thing to see them bend the ship and the sea to their will. Like your favorite band making their best music.

It is, partly because of the awesome responsibilities involved and partly because of straight-up human nature, an intensely competitive career field. Excellence and success are expected; failure is *sometimes* tolerated. Tolerated, that is, if there is no negligence and if something can be learned from it so that "next time" we'll achieve even greater success having learned the lessons of this failure. So it was for GATO's Captain today.

The other reality is that, indeed, the other guy does get a vote in how this all goes. His mission, like the mission of all of America's own nuclear ballistic missile submarine Captains, is to always be ready and able to launch any or all of his missiles – and to not be harassed by some other guy while doing it. In other words, *part of their mission is to detect you and to harass you right back and to lose you if you are so audacious as to try and take up trail on him.*

There is an old saying that some "modern" folks think goes all the way back to General Colin Powell and the first Gulf War in the 1990s. It goes "No Plan Survives Initial Contact with the Enemy". It is operative here, too. The other guy got a vote, detected GATO and boogied on out of there.

But truth be told, this concept goes back long before Colin Powell. In <u>The Art of War</u>, back around 500 BC, Sun Tzu provided many key insights, two which are highlighted below:

"If you know the enemy and know yourself, you need not fear the results of a hundred battles. If you know yourself but not the enemy, for every victory gained you will also suffer a defeat. If you know neither the enemy nor yourself, you will succumb in every battle."

"The general who wins a battle makes many calculations in his temple ere the battle is fought. The general who loses a battle makes but few calculations beforehand. Thus do many calculations lead to victory, and few calculations to defeat. How much more no calculation at all! It is by attention to this point that I can foresee who is likely to win or lose."

These, and related concepts first expressed by Sun Tzu, then, have evolved over time. Plato, some two centuries later in his <u>Nomo</u> (Laws), developed one of these concepts from Sun Tzu to provide the insight that the successful preservation of peace requires readiness for war. Successfully preparing for war, of course, means many actions – but must be based upon the principles embodied in the specific insights quoted above (knowing both yourself and the enemy; making many calculations in advance – being prepared for all possible contingencies, etc.).

Later, in the late 4th century/early 5th century, Roman author Publius Flavius Vegetius Renatus published his treatise <u>De Re Militari</u> (Concerning Military Matters), which included the admonition "*Igitur qui desiderat pacem, praeparet bellum*" (Therefore let him who desires peace prepare for war). Nearly immediately this phrase was adapted to become "*Si vis pacem, para bellum*" (If you want peace prepare for war) – a phrase which continues as a guiding military principle to this very day.

One of the more effective late 20th century advocates of *Si vis pacem, para bellum,* who used a contemporized version of this (and, indeed, the other Sun Tzu principles noted above) as a personal philosophy was Admiral Hyman G. Rickover, the Father of the Nuclear Navy. Admiral Rickover created and drove Naval Reactors to reflect his personal philosophy, "*The more you sweat in peace, the less you bleed in war.*"

One aspect of "war" has changed in the last century, and this change must be noted here. Just what, exactly, constitutes "war" and "peace"? Before 1945 the absence of active combat was generally accepted as an appropriate definition of peace. With the advent and subsequent spread of nuclear weapons, however, it is now more widely understood that a "war" does not necessarily require active combat between the principals. Thus, we have the Cold War, the backdrop for GATO's operations here in 1985 – *a period, given the global strategic challenges of the 2020's, which is now more widely being recognized as the First Cold War.*

As this book is published, many characterize the current 2022 – 2023 period, with the ongoing Ukraine War, as analogous to the "Phoney War" period prior to World War II. Others openly refer to the current period as The Second Cold War. Regardless of terminology, however, it is inescapable that the truths of Sun Tzu, Plato, Publius Flavius Vegetius Renatus, Admiral Rickover and even Rick Hanson, in command of GATO in 1985, are as relevant in 2023 and beyond as they have ever before been.

For Rick Hanson the Lost Contact simply reinforced today's widely understood requirement to *plan for flexibility in battle – because you going to need it.* And, once again, *don't miss the point,* trailing a Soviet nuclear ballistic missile submarine is a very special form of high tension, high stakes battle – but it is battle within the context of a much larger global war, nonetheless.

Rick Hanson wasn't the first SSN Captain to lose a guy in trail, and he wouldn't be the last. He found his personal lessons to learn, and his operational control did not fire him for momentarily falling off the knife edge into that black, inky abyss known as mission failure. On the "plus" side, there was no collision – the guy hadn't rammed GATO – so GATO remained fully capable. On to the next mission.

At the end of the day, in fact, it may well be that it is because of this momentary failure – and the lessons learned from it – that GATO was able to excel in the mission that defined Hanson's – and, indeed, the entire crew's complete careers. *But more about that later...*

Finally, a thought about LT Clark – or, Clunk, as it were. We noted *"the old saw"* above about prior planning and performance (6P planning). This is from the same strategic point of view. Put simply, submarining – in particular, being an Officer (or even being a senior enlisted crew member) on a nuclear-powered attack submarine is like simultaneously playing multiple games of three-dimensional chess – *and not being able to see all the chess boards* – with your life, and your family's life, hanging in the balance.

Chapter 15

Halfway

Monday, November 18, 1985, Day 36, On Patrol, WESTLANT

Halfway night was a time-honored ritual on a run like this – particularly when there were no liberty port visits. Truth be told it was more of a boomer tradition than an SSN tradition, because most SSN deployments these days included at least one port visit. *But here we are.*

The best news in the whole world is that GATO did not get fired for losing her contact. GATO wasn't called home early to answer for her stupidity and sins. Instead, GATO was told that AUGUSTA had him in trail now and that a new job was coming up for the *Black Cat. A chance at redemption.*

It could not be said that the Captain was dancing on tables, but he wasn't slaughtering his Officers anymore, either. GATO *had gotten a second chance.* He was a little raw about AUGUSTA having that guy in trail now, but at least that guy was being trailed. GATO's unforced error wasn't as strategically important now, and there would be a second chance.

So, there was something to celebrate – however meager it was. Plus, baby, *it was all downhill from here.* They were one day closer to home with each passing day. That is called nuclear logic. Earth shattering, for sure.

For Halfway night celebrations each major group in the ship had to put on a short skit for the pleasure of the crew. The Chiefs and Officers were excluded from their respective Divisions – they had to represent for the Goat Locker and Wardroom, respectively.

The one good thing was that with nobody in-trail the patrol quiet status of the ship could be squeezed a bit. In other words, loud music was OK. Andre and Ike were nominated by the COB to represent the Chiefs. It was a tough call, but Andre and Ike were the most junior Chiefs onboard, *so it really wasn't tough for the COB at all.*

They decided to do a song and dance number to Phil Collins then-current hit <u>Easy Lover</u>.

Andre, slight of stature, played the beautiful chicky. The mop made for a good wig, along with the sheet for a skirt. Ike, bigger and taller, was Andre's date. The two of them, arms around each other, lip synched the song and did a dance, kicking away like Rockettes. It was a hoot.

The best act, universally proclaimed by everyone, was by the Sonar Crew. They had mixed Donna Summer's <u>Love to Love You</u> with some actual sounds that they had recorded of whales making babies. Their act raised the roof!

About the best thing that could be said about halfway night was that it served as an emotional cleansing event. The best you could say about the first half of the run was that it was a mixed bag. They had gotten good tape on that guy. Leave it at that, for he was history.

They were headed for another job, and in that job was the offer of redemption.

Chapter 16

The Cold War Peaks

Tuesday, November 19, 1985, Geneva, Switzerland
For GATO, Day 37, On Patrol, WESTLANT

The (First) Cold War started in the aftermath of the Second World War, as former allies became adversaries in a new strategic contest to "lead the world." Over this period, lasting from 1947 through 1991, there were a series of "ebbs" and "flows" in the conflict, but there is no denying the constant tension and high risk throughout. This tension and risk weighed heavily upon the whole world. ***Dr. Strangelove***, indeed.

While this new, never-before-seen type of war did not include direct armed fighting between the principals, there were several "proxy wars" and periods of very high tension. For example, the 1948-1949 Berlin Airlift and the 1962 Cuban Missile Crisis were two periods of extreme tension. On the other hand, the 1970's were generally a period of détente and included negotiation of the SALT arms limitation treaty.

Détente abruptly ended with the December 1979 invasion of Afghanistan by the Soviet Union. Starting with Ronald Reagan's election as President in November 1980, the United States then adopted a strategy of "Peace through Strength." This included a massive new US defense spending program. This accelerated US defense spending program featured, for instance, building a 600 ship Navy, as well as an advanced technology-based Strategic Defense Initiative.

The 600 ship Navy was the brainchild of now-legendary Secretary of the Navy John Lehman and was "achieved" in 1987, when the fleet peaked at 594 ships, including 139 submarines. For comparative purposes, on September 30, 2015, the US Navy only had 271 ships left in its Battle Force, the smallest Navy fleet size since 1921, although first generation American Ballistic Missile Defense systems were operational onboard select US Navy ships. *(Fleet size as of November 30, 2022, had grown back to 292 ships, including 68 submarines – a fleet which is broadly considered to be too small, particularly regarding the Submarine Force, to successfully deter the Nation's strategic threats in the 2020's.)*

For the Soviet Union to "keep up" with the United States during the Cold War, in particular with the US development of its Strategic Defense Initiative (colloquially known as "Star Wars") in the 1980's, it required a massive increase in their Defense spending. This was an outsized challenge for the Soviet Union. Even then the Soviet economy depended heavily upon oil and gas exports, but because the high petroleum prices of the 1970's had abated in the 1980's, the Soviet economy was having real hard currency problems.

It is with this backdrop that President Reagan and Soviet Premier Gorbachev had their first summit in Geneva on this date – right in the middle of GATO's patrol.

A careful review of history reveals a strong argument that it was on this day that the 45 year-long Cold War peaked, and definitively turned toward an end. Even though the only "real" outcome of this first summit was the start of a relationship between these two world leaders, from this moment forward the Cold War started to wind down.

Following this first summit in Geneva in November 1985 the two men met again in an infamous summit at Reykjavik, Iceland in October 1986. It was at this summit where the United States refused to "back down" on any of its positions. President Reagan, despite a strong desire to craft a peace deal, simply would not compromise his principles. This was then followed by meetings at the White House in December 1987, the Kremlin in May 1988 and then in New York where both President Reagan and President-elect Bush met with Premier Gorbachev in December 1988. Each meeting moved the world closer to peace.

Later, in November 1989, the Berlin Wall came down and then in December 1991 the Soviet Union collapsed, ending the Cold War for once and for all. Or so everyone thought then . . .

Meanwhile, here, now, in November 1985, GATO was headed to its second trail mission of the patrol. At the very peak of the Cold War, GATO was on the job, protecting America from a submarine nuclear missile launch.

Onboard the ship nobody knew much about anything going on in the outside world. Communication between GATO and the outside world was only through the official Navy communications systems.

GATO had two communications systems – and one was very, very slow. The Fleet Broadcast was there to be copied, with updated news inserted and then run in an uninterrupted loop on a conventional radio frequency. It was a crude version of what would later become the commercial "Headline News" channel. The trouble was that to get this broadcast a submarine had to sit at periscope depth for a _lo n g_ time with an antenna up. Not happening in this nuclear navy.

The other system on GATO in 1985 was the SATCOM system, where the ship could talk to a communications satellite and get specific operational news/information in quick burst transmissions that were later extracted after the ship went back deep.

Recall, though, that "burst" had a very different meaning in 1985 than it does today. Windows 1.0 (then-called MS DOS), the very first operating system from Microsoft, was first released for sale to the public on the second day of the Geneva summit. Computers in 1985, compared to the cell phone in your pocket today, were basically crude toys. There was no public internet and a "fast" modem was only a couple of thousand bytes per second, compared to today's typical modem/wi-fi speed of hundreds of millions of bytes per second. The bottom line is that SATCOM data rates were exceptionally slow by today's standards – meaning that the ship only got operational intel and information/ instruction. Further, the members of the crew each received only two 15-word "family gram" messages per run. In short, nobody knew what was happening in the outside world.

What the GATO crew did know was that the Cold War was at a peak and that they were on the front line. That is all they really needed to know to do their job.

Finally, a note about how wars are won and lost. Economists will tell you that war between rational actors is basically an economic negotiation, conducted by other means, with the sole objective of the negotiation being the achievement of a higher standard of living for your population. In other words, victory can be predicted by simply comparing the relative productive capacity of the two rational actors. Non-rational actors and/or terrorists are, of course, another story entirely.

In broad terms, the author agrees with this esoteric explanation. After all, the outcome of World War II was obvious when you consider only the production of war materiel during the conflict by the various parties. The United States, for instance, built more than 6,700 ships in less than four years during World War II.

Where the author disagrees with the esoteric economist argument about war, though, is in the implicit *a priori* assumption that actual execution of the physical war is irrelevant. Sticking primarily to World War II for this discussion, we offer three examples of how <u>execution is the definitive factor in determining the outcome of a war</u>, just as previously discussed in Chapter 14 above, <u>the demonstrated *readiness* to execute is the definitive factor in avoiding war.</u>

Because this is a submarine sea story, we would be remiss if we did not emphasize the outsized importance and role of submarines. *Remember, the most highly decorated ship in the more than 237 year history of the United States Navy is a Cold War Attack Submarine (USS PARCHE (SSN 683)).* Because we are open minded and fair, however, these examples and discussions are not exclusively limited to submarine examples. In that vein, while submarines were an import element of the Battle of Midway, as our first example this battle is primarily about carrier aviation. Additionally, the third discussion example concerns ground, not naval, execution.

- **The Battle of Midway.** Where would America have been without Commander Joseph J. Rochefort, Admiral Chester Nimitz,  Rear Admiral Raymond Spruance, Lieutenant Commander John S. "Jimmy" Thatch and the thousands of other heroes at the Battle of Midway, where the US Navy turned the tide of war in the Pacific? *They beat a larger, more powerful, more experienced force and, in doing so, halted Japan's eastward expansion in the Pacific. This gave America a chance to "let loose" its abundant productive capability and to build the Navy that was needed to, in the end, soundly beat Japan.*

- **The Submarine Force.** Similarly, what about the role of America's submarine force, which took the contest to Japan's doorstep while destroying Japan's own productive capability – and even actually invaded Japan's mainland with raiding parties – from the very start of the war?

Seven of the Medals of Honor which have been awarded to the Submarine Force are for combat operations during World War II. These Medals of Honor were awarded disproportionally to this small, exclusive, but exceptionally powerful element of the overall combat force.

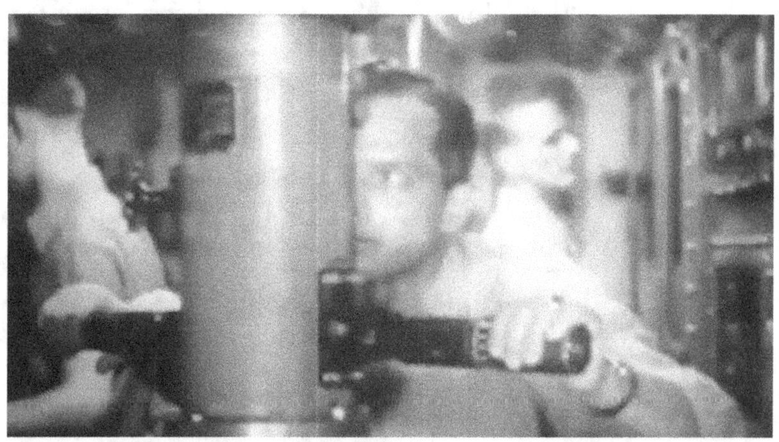

o **Commander Lawson P. "Red" Ramage, Captain of USS PARCHE (SS 384).** Navy Cross for heroism during the Battle of Midway in June 1942; first torpedo hit on an enemy aircraft carrier while Captain of USS TROUT (SS 202) in August 1942; Medal of Honor awarded for his daring surface attack on an enemy convoy while he commanded PARCHE in July 1944. Red Ramage sank 4 enemy ships, firing 19 torpedoes in the 48 minutes characterized as "the wildest of the submarine war." *As noted earlier, his wife, Barbara Ramage, was the ship sponsor for* GATO. USS RAMAGE (DDG 61), *a flight 1 Arleigh Burke Class Destroyer, honors VADM Ramage.*

o **Commander Eugene Fluckey, Captain of USS BARB (SS 220).** "Lucky Fluckey" Most tonnage sunk by a submariner; Medal of Honor. During BARB's twelfth War Patrol in July 1945 Fluckey sent a landing party ashore at Karafuto and destroyed a 16-car supply train. Previously, during BARB's eleventh War Patrol, Fluckey had invented a new tactical approach to surface convoy attacks, in the process setting a then-world speed record for submarines (23.5 knots). USS BARB (SSN 596), *a Thresher Class SSN, carried this name during the Cold War. On October 13, 2020 Secretary of the Navy Kenneth Braithwaite, a noted fan of Naval history, broke the then-current tradition of naming SSNs for States by naming future Virginia Class submarine SSN 804 as* USS BARB. *This will carry Lucky Fluckey's tradition of excellence in combat through much of the 21st century.*

o **Commander Richard "Dick" O'Kane, Captain of USS TANG (SS 306).** While in command of TANG, Dick O'Kane sank 33 ships, the greatest number of ships sunk by a submariner, resulting in him being awarded the Medal of Honor. Captured and survived as a POW after his ship was sunk by a circular run of his own torpedo, sinking TANG and resulting in the loss of all but 8 members of his crew. USS O'KANE (DDG 77), *a flight II Arleigh Burke Class Destroyer, is named in his honor*

o **Captain John Cromwell, Commander Submarine Divisions 203, 44, 43, embarked in USS SCULPIN (SS 191).** Posthumously awarded the Medal of Honor for preventing loss of critical intelligence information by electing to go down with SCULPIN rather than being rescued by the enemy, November 1943. *Cold War Destroyer Escort* USS CROMWELL (DE 1014) *was named in his honor. Cromwell Hall, at the Naval Submarine School at Subbase New London is also named in his honor.*

o **Commander Samuel Dealey, Captain of USS HARDER (SS 257).** On HARDER's fifth War Patrol in May & June 1944, Dealey was awarded the Medal of Honor after he sank 6 enemy Destroyers, precipitating enemy abandonment of a key anchorage and the decisive Battle of the Philippine Sea, a major American victory. *Dealey Center, the main auditorium at Submarine Base New London, was named in his honor.*

o **Commander Howard W. Gilmore, Captain of USS GROWLER (SS 215).** Posthumously awarded the Medal of Honor. During GROWLER's fourth War Patrol, in February 1943, while engaged in furious close-quarters surface action with an enemy escort, GROWLER's only escape was to quickly submerge. Wounded and on the bridge, Gilmore ordered his XO to "take her down!" sacrificing himself to save his ship. *Cold War Submarine Tender* USS HOW-ARD W GILMORE (AS 16) *was named in his honor.*

o **Commander George L. Street, Captain of USS TIRANTE (SS 420).** On TIRANTE's first War Patrol in April 1945, Street took TIRANTE into an enemy harbor, while surfaced, and using his last 7 torpedoes, sank a freighter and 2 escorts. Street was awarded the Medal of Honor for this daring action; the ship was awarded the Presidential Unit Citation and XO then-LCDR Edward L. Beach was awarded the Navy Cross. Notably, Beach later rose to individual fame as both the first Captain of the Navy's only dual-reactor nuclear powered Attack Submarine, USS TRITON (SSN 586) (and conducting the first completely submerged global transit in February – April 1960) and as an author (e.g., <u>Run Silent, Run Deep</u>).

o **Commander Dudley "Mush" Morton, Captain of USS WAHOO (SS 238).** While Mush Morton was not awarded the Medal of Honor, being awarded the Navy Cross 4 times instead, he, too, is a legendary submarine Captain. His 19 ships sunk typified America's World War II submarine force, as did his tutelage of his junior officers. Dick O'Kane, noted above for his own Medal of Honor, served as Mush Morton's XO.

At a time when America had no other way to deter Japan's militarily superior Navy, these heroes took the war to Japan's front door and gave America a chance, and time to catch up and build a modern Navy. Combined with victory at Midway, this was an effective 1-2 punch, without which ultimate victory over Japan was far less certain.

Rick Hanson, commanding GATO during this <u>69 Day Run</u> at the height of the Cold War, stood on the shoulders of and emulated the very best of these – and countless other – great submariners. *Just as today's submariners stand on the shoulders of and emulate Rick Hanson, Ike Barnes, Andre Perot, Barry Joseph, Willy Williams and every great submariner to have preceded them. While the characters in this book are, indeed, composite Sea Story characters, <u>the reader should make no mistake</u> – they each represent the real American heroes who tamed the Wild Beasts of the Thresher Class, as well as the other submarines which were victorious in the Cold War and in other operations before and since.*

"*We shall never forget that it was our submarines that held the line against the enemy.*" – Fleet Admiral Chester Nimitz.

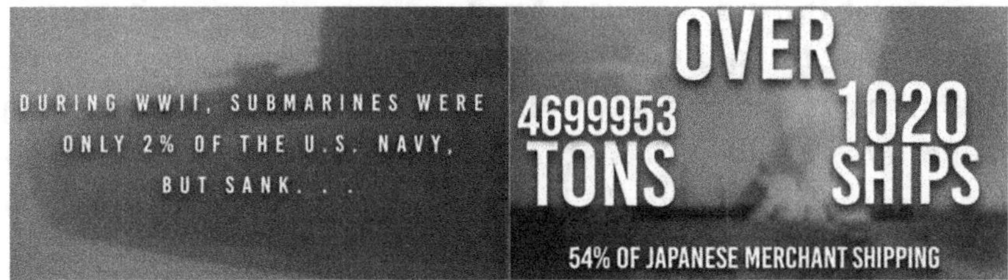

- **The Battle of the Bulge.** Finally, where would Europe be without America at the Battle of the Bulge? General George S. Patton, Brigadier General Anthony McAuliffe, Lieutenant Colonel Henry Cherry, Lieutenant Colonel James O'Hara, and Major William Desobry – along with the

thousands of other heroes involved in the key battle at Bastogne – ended what could well have been a late-stage reversal for the Nazis in Europe. *Germany had, by then, developed the ME 262, the world's first practical, fast jet fighter/bomber – and just needed time to build enough of them to change the course of the air war. The V-2 Rocket, the world's first long-range guided ballistic missile, was also causing great disruptions and many Allied casualties. Finally, Germany was very, very close to having their own atomic weapon. German victory at Bastogne – the decisive conflict point in the Battle of the Bulge – would have stopped the Allies' march to Berlin, perhaps giving Germany enough time to change the outcome of the whole war in Europe. This is not unlike how victory at Midway and the efforts of the Submarine Force had given America time to build back up its defenses in order to beat Japan.*

Execution matters. *This lesson is crystal clear.* **During the Cold War one of the most critical forms of execution was having an SSN –** *ready to "snapshot" a warshot at the first sign of an impending missile launch* **– on the ass of every Soviet Boomer at sea. Period. Full Stop.** So, as the Cold War finally turned decisively toward an end there was GATO. No more and no less than an everyday, run-of-the-mill Cold War SSN. Ready for its second major overhaul, but representative of the 98 other active SSNs at the time, and their 10,000 – odd heroic crew members at any given time. *All executing the mission with skill, passion, dedication and complete and absolute commitment.*

Execution is the *strength* in **Peace Through Strength**. Without it – who knows what would have happened? *Eh' Comrade?*

The Celtic Knot – A Symbol of Inner Strength

Chapter 17

Almost . . . Bluenose

*Thursday, November 21, 1985, Day 39, On
Patrol, WESTLANT, Northbound Approaching
66° North Latitude, Classified Longitude*

Sailors are creatures of habit and tradition. Crossing certain geographical milestones, such as the International Date Line, the Equator and the Arctic Circle are events to celebrate. Homage must be paid to King Neptune to ensure your safe passage in these sacred realms. It is an initiation rite to match all initiations.

The rites probably started years ago in the days of sail, when a sailing vessel could easily find itself in the doldrums – that is, without wind for the sails – in the equatorial region. Today, of course, we understand why the atmospheric patterns are as they are far better than we did in the 18th century. Nonetheless, paying homage to King Neptune is a sacred tradition to this day.

GATO was headed *Up North* to catch the next guy coming down. This was supposed to be a very special job, some kind of unusual guy. The anticipation was building; all necessary preparations for travel in cold, sub-freezing arctic waters on the ship were complete. Some tanks were vulnerable to freezing – they were taken care of – certain watchstanders started wearing sweaters (it gets cold in normally hot places within the ship whenever you are *way Up North*) and the Main Air Conditioner was adjusted and coddled a bit.

The air conditioner remained vital for directly cooling all of the Sonar Computers and other electronic equipment up forward, as well as for moisture control in the ship's internal atmosphere, but she was running at far less than half capacity – and she was a bit finicky with such a small load. But, no problem, even with the crazy patch job installed on day one of the trip, she ran fine with a little TLC – *even Up North*.

The emotion in the ship was once again on a positive track. And the farther *Up North* that they went, the more likely it became that they would cross the Arctic Circle (66° 34' North). Recall that each minute (') of latitude is only 1 nautical mile and you can realize that they were getting close.

The ship's Yeoman was checking everyone's official records to put together the initiation list. This was serious stuff. A sailor could decline to be initiated – but it would be *known* far and wide. Those who were certified Blue Noses were busy planning their event. By all accounts and estimates they would become *of the realm* on Friday, the next day.

Suddenly, late on Thursday night the ship talked to the satellite and got new orders. Instead of continuing North, they were now headed West. Hmmm.

For the next couple of days, the watch routine continued as normal, with GATO in the hunt but with no contacts bagged. The almost Blue Nose was like a perfect allegory for the trip so far – *frustrating and ultimately not at all satisfying.*

Then, suddenly, on Sunday (Day 42) it happened. This time the Navigation Department kept it a secret until it actually happened. They were all sworn to secrecy, and it worked.

Suddenly the lights went on in all the berthing areas – the first time since leaving New London – and everyone was rousted. All Pollywogs to the Crew's Mess. The preplanning from a couple of days earlier had paid off. There was no escape for the uninitiated.

Chief Barnes was among those standing for initiation, but he was pulled out of line.

"You are King Neptune's baby, and all pollywogs have to kiss your belly as they pass through the gauntlet," was the COB's pronouncement.

So it began. With the Pollywogs in their underwear, warming up for initiation by sitting in a tub of ice as they waited in line for the solemn ceremony, the fun began. What a mess! What a hoot! Chief Barnes' belly was coated in a mixture of peanut butter, olive oil, sardine juice and some other nasty concoctions. Great fun was had by all.

To top it off, the ship's hot water heaters had magically been tagged out for some phony maintenance. No hot water. The Nukes had no problem, though, sending lots of cold water forward for the showers that day.

Coming on top of the halfway night, the crew was completely cleansed and regained their confidence in themselves. They were ready for the job that would define many of their careers.

Chapter 18

New Guy

Tuesday, November 26, 1985, Day 44, On Patrol, WESTLANT

It started as usual, with Sonar identifying the contact to the OOD in Control. But from the start this one was just a bit different. Many in the crew thought that this guy was of no special significance. Just another trail job. A few knew differently, and it was their different attitude/approach to the job that revealed that this guy wasn't just another run-of-the-mill boomer but was, indeed, a boomer with something very special about it.

A couple of days later, Ike Barnes thought that he knew what was up with this guy, but he wasn't sure. He and Barry Joseph were shooting the bull in the Chief's Quarters after they had gotten off watch and had midrats. **_Doctor Detroit_** was on – *big surprise there.*

"Barry, I was wondering about this guy . . ." started Barnes.

"Ike, you know I can't say anything about him," replied Joseph.

"Yeah, but it seems to me that a new ZZZ might be involved here," continued Barnes.

"Who the hell told you? You can't repeat that to anybody. Christ, don't talk about it, man," an excited Joseph immediately replied.

"Well, relax. Now that I *know* I am not saying anything to anybody. I figured it all out by putting the pieces together," replied Barnes.

"Well, don't say anything, OK."

"About what"

Barnes had shrewdly been watching everything, and everyone's reaction to it all, and knew that this guy was not your average boomer trail job. A keen student of both Soviet and American Naval things, he had Nuked it out. Now he knew – but he wasn't going to tell anyone. And he
never did.

Chapter 19

Thanksgiving . . . Yeah, Sure

Thursday, November 28, 1985, Day 46, On Patrol, WESTLANT

Thanksgiving is that most unique American holiday. To many on GATO. missing Thanksgiving with the family was B – A – D, but had been accepted as part of the mission from the start. Then something *R – E – A – L – L- Y B – A – D* happened just before the Thanksgiving meal.

GATO got a message from its operational control to expect to stay with this guy and that their return to port would be extended if no other SSN became available to take over the mission.

Return on Christmas Eve was beginning to look like a pipe dream.

Word passed throughout the ship like a lightning bolt. Some claimed that the Engineroom Lower Level watch knew before the Captain did. Not likely, but not much of an exaggeration, either.

Can you spell *B-U-M-M-E-R?*

Despite sharing the bummer, Chief Williams and his cooks put on a feast that rivaled anything ashore. By this time in the trip the crew had eaten their way almost down to the decks throughout the ship – almost all of the food that had been stored in the two layers of cans in the passageways had been eaten and the cooks were almost back to occupying just their normal storerooms. No concern, yet, for running out of food, and the Thanksgiving feast had been fully planned well before they left New London. It was, as planned, a truly great meal. The crew was good company to be with – if you couldn't be with family. *But what a pervasive bummer about the extension.*

That afternoon the COB assembled all of the Chiefs in the Goat Locker.

"Guys, it is up to us to nip this bummer in the bud. The best part of this run is yet to come, and we owe it to the Captain and to the ship to step up and lead by example. OK, we had a bad Thanksgiving. It is over. Don't let us destroy the rest of the run, too."

They all knew he was right. They also knew that they needed the Wardroom to do the same thing. On a submarine the attitude of the Wardroom is a reflection of the attitude of the Captain. The attitude of the Chief's Quarters is a reflection of the attitude of the Wardroom. And the crew follows the Chiefs. In closing the COB told the Chiefs that the XO was in the Wardroom right now having the same talk with the Officers.

Slowly, over the next couple of days, it took hold. The focus turned positive, and things got better. Better still, this guy that they had was proving to be both predictable and a juicy contact. Good stuff. No, *great* stuff.

Chapter 20

Reactor SCRAM

Saturday, November 30, 1985, Day 48, On Patrol, WESTLANT

Small steam leaks never, ever, ever stay small for long. Like a fast running river eroding a landscape, steam cuts like a hot knife through butter and erodes even a steel pipe or seal as it leaks out. High pressure steam is dangerous stuff.

That little steam leak that Anderson had told Chief Barnes about as they had started up the propulsion plant for the trip was getting nasty. It was, in fact, becoming a personnel safety hazard. Worse, yet, it was shooting down and condensing on some sensitive electronics equipment. While it hadn't damaged anything or injured anyone – *yet* – it was getting ugly. It was time to start making a plan.

With this new guy in-trail it seemed clear to Chief Barnes that they were not going to get a port visit this trip so that they could shut the Reactor down and fix this thing in a convenient manner. *Christ*, he thought, *we'll probably be out here in January eating peanut butter crackers for dinner chasing this guy. No, there would be no convenient port call to do the maintenance. It had to be done underway.*

When he saw LT Clark, he told him that he thought that they should sit down with the Engineer and talk about the steam leak. LT Clark arranged for them to get together that morning in the Wardroom. Chief Barnes came prepared. The Captain was also there. The Engineer had already reached the same conclusion during his daily tour of the Engineroom and had been about to call the meeting himself when LT Clark approached him. It wasn't about *"if,"* it was about *"when"* and *"how."*

Recognize, now, that nobody would ever choose to do this job underway if there was any good alternative. Particularly when engaged in a hugely important tactical mission. *That they decided to proceed with this maintenance effort in the first place should tell you everything that you need to know about how dangerous the leak had become.*

"Eng, Captain, we have got to fix the steam leak on XXX valve. It has become a personnel hazard and it is now condensing on YYYY electronics. It is only going to get worse and nothing good is going to happen if we put it off any longer. The way that I see it, we are holding about steady speed on this guy, and we can do this speed with part of the Engineroom shut down. We won't be able to sprint, but it seems like this guy isn't racing around anywhere. We have laid out a plan, and I believe that it will take us 30 hours from start to finish until I can give you back the whole Engineroom and full speed capability. In the interim we will be limited . . .," started Barnes.

For the next two hours the ship's mechanical engineering brain trust reviewed the plan, looked at the operating manuals, considered the restrictions, talked about the procedures and the "what ifs" that could happen when they opened up the leaky valve. It was as detailed a review and plan briefing as you'd find at a shipyard with 30 engineers and 50 overseers involved. But it was the four of them.

They had all done repairs at sea before, but none of them had repaired this particular valve at sea before. Throughout the entire Fleet few, if any, people had ever done this repair at sea. Normally, because of where it was located in the steam system, it would have been a week long major job with tender and/or shipyard support. But at the end of the planning and review meeting they had developed the right plan and they were ready.

Shifting the Reactor and Engineroom lineups around would be a bit tricky, but there was a clear procedure in the operating manuals to get to the right configuration. While none of them had done it at sea with the Reactor still operating before, all of them had done it many times in the shipyard. They would go strictly by the book, and all would be well. They all had great, well deserved, faith in the operating manuals.

Chief Barnes left to assemble his maintenance team. Most likely they would be doing some repair machining on the inspection cover. They might have to do some weld repair on the valve body. He was ready with his welder and with his machinist. The lathe was set up and the welding equipment was broken out. From the maintenance side of the job, they were prepared. They even had the right spare gasket for the valve on hand.

The plan was to brief the oncoming watchsection before lunch and then to do the shift right after they got on watch. Chief Barnes conducted the briefing, with the Captain and the Engineer both in attendance and adding appropriate color comments. Each operator was quizzed by the briefing team and the oncoming EOOW about the procedure, what they should expect and then what limitations they would have to observe while in the reduced capability operating mode.

It was classic Nuclear Power 101. The fact that this submarine, far away from home, while still engaged in a huge tactical mission, was using exactly the same planning and execution process that they would have used in a shipyard or alongside the tender under the direct scrutiny of Rickover himself is evidence of a discipline that runs at the heart of how the US Navy has safely steamed well over 100 million miles on nuclear power – around the world under all sorts of conditions. Nukes are Nukes, and they follow the rules and do it *right,* whatever the situation.

Everything went well . . . that is, until they got to step two of the procedure.

The Captain was up in the Control Room. The Engineer and Chief Barnes were stationed in the Engineroom, watching the plant indications on the Plant Control Electronics Panels. It was too crowded to be in the Maneuvering Area, where they were double manned for the transition procedure.

Then they heard the Reactor SCRAM alarm. It had been drilled five million times, but it virtually never happened for real – unless it was a training drill. It should NOT be happening now.

With a sick feeling in the pits of their stomachs both Chief Barnes and the Engineer looked at the indications and saw that the Reactor was, indeed, now shutdown. *Holy shit, Batman.*

But there was no obvious reason why the protective system had tripped and SCRAMMED the Reactor . . .

As they looked up from the indicators the Captain flew through the watertight door and was almost instantly right there in front of them.

"What happened?"

"We did it exactly by the book . . . ," with a bit more amplification and detail on the sequence of events, replied the Engineer.

"Will the trips clear?" was the Captain's reply.

"Let me see," was Chief Barnes' reply as he hit the reset button on the protective system.

"All green," was his reply to the Captain and Engineer – who were looking at the same thing he was.

"I know why it SCRAMMED. Start this thing up RIGHT NOW," came the Captain's emphatic order.

"Yes, sir," replied the Engineer as he quickly headed off to the Maneuvering Area to give the order to the Engineering Officer of the Watch.

The Captain flew back through the watertight door and up toward the Control Room. With them right on this guy's ass he did not want anybody even dreaming about preparing to snorkel and starting the Diesel Engine. They would get the Reactor back online well within the capacity of the ship's Main Storage Battery and he did not want anyone doing anything ELSE that could lead to them being detected by this guy. It wasn't going to happen again . . . *not today, anyway.*

Later, after everyone's adrenalin overdose had been worked off, things were looking up. The Reactor and Engineroom were operating in the desired limited capability mode and the steam line had been cooled down, drained and they were about ready to start the actual maintenance procedure. Better, still, their guy had not detected them and was merrily off doing his thing and GATO was continuing to roll tape on him. They had passed through the *valley of the shadows* and had come out the other side intact and still *in the game.*

As the maintenance work started, the ship's trusty Main Storage Battery was also recharged. Like the ship's high pressure air banks, the Main Storage Battery provided essential reserve energy for use in emergencies – *like an unplanned Reactor shutdown when submerged at sea.* There were two types of battery charge – "normal" and the "equalizer". A normal charge simply replaced the energy which had been used, and "topped off" the battery, while the periodic equalizer was a deep charge designed to recondition both the battery plates and the electrolytic fluid. GATO met the requirements, this time, for doing an equalizer and that is what they were doing.

Because of the process involved, there is some minimal/manageable danger in doing an equalizer. Normally, because of this, you'd like everything else to be "routine" when doing this type of battery charge. At the same time, you also don't like to steam around submerged in an unusual propulsion plant lineup with a partially discharged Main Storage Battery. So, just like you don't want to be submerged with discharged air banks (recall the flooding during Hurricane Gloria), recharging the Main Storage Battery was immediately started once the Reactor and Propulsion Plant were restored to normal, if limited, operations. Like the several hundred equalizers done over GATO's life, prior planning, great training and sound, safe execution led to a trouble-free result.

Once all of this had started the Captain called for the Engineer, LT Clark and Chief Barnes to join him in the Wardroom. He was feeling like a redeemed man.

"Well, gentlemen, I could have done without the SCRAM, but nice job in getting this set up," started the Captain.

He had caught them all a bit off guard. They had arrived thinking that it was to be a critique and that, as a minimum, they were going to get their asses chewed out – *at least a little bit*, for something or another.

"When I was at Naval Reactors for my pre-command visit, they told me about something that had happened on one of the SSBNs that was very, very similar to what just happened to us. It had happened in a shipyard, and it had taken them over a week to troubleshoot and find the root cause of the problem. (he went on to explain the details of the problem and how it was eventually discovered, and how he knew that it was the same problem that GATO had just experienced).

So, as you can see, it is a byproduct of the conservative nature of our design and our equipment specifications. In fact, it was an unintended/unnecessary SCRAM that was not required to protect the Reactor. We did nothing wrong and Reactor safety was not ever jeopardized. Now, here we are, with 98 of these Reactors running around the world for more than 25 years now, and this is only the second time that this has ever happened. It could have happened for us at a more convenient time, though . . . That is why, once the trips immediately cleared, I knew the cause and that we could safely start it right back up."

He went on to direct that the Engineer prepare a written report for Naval Reactors about exactly what had happened and what they had done about it. This report, among lots of others to lots of different Navy groups, would be sent upon their return to port. Because the cause was known, was a benign overconservative design item, and it wasn't a safety issue, it became a more routine report that did not have to be immediately sent off by radio message.

Wow, thought Barnes. *The 1954 design logic got us right here in 1985. It could not have happened on a 688 Class ship . . .*

Twenty-nine hours after it had all started the repair was complete. While the cover plate had required machining repair, the valve body had fortunately not required any weld repair. With the pre-evolution briefings completed everyone took their stations and restarted the shutdown portion of the propulsion equipment.

This time there were no surprises and at exactly 30 hours after they had started, GATO had its full speed capability back. All the while, their guy was oblivious to them and what they had been doing. Tape had continued to roll in the Sonar Room. *Rock on, GATO!*

Meanwhile, Chief Barnes and his maintenance crew had not slept for this entire time. They were either standing their normal watches (6 hours on, 12 hours off), or working on the maintenance job nonstop. Let's face facts – you don't go to sea on a submarine with extra people onboard to do emergent maintenance underway. You go to sea with enough people to operate the ship and to execute its mission. Emergent maintenance crews come directly out of the watchstanding crew.

Bone tired and dirty/nasty/smelly, the Chief and his maintenance crew rewarded themselves with both Hollywood showers and equalizers. That is, they each took long showers where they let the hot, soothing water continuously run down their backs for a good 100 to 150 seconds, or so. *Normally verboten, but, heh, M Division makes the water and we have just worked our asses off fixing a B-I-G problem.* They weren't going to take any crap from anybody about it, and, wisely, nobody offered any. . . And then they each were rewarded with almost 12 hours of uninterrupted sleep, equalizing and refreshing their worn-out bodies. That done, all it took was a good meal and they were all G2G once again.

In marathon terms, referring specifically to the Boston Marathon, in their 26 mile run from way out in Hopkinton in to the City at Copley Square, they had just crested Heartbreak Hill at Mile 20, near Boston College in Newton. GATO's marathon continued, just like for the Boston Marathoners, but there was a renewed vigor and confidence in having bested their greatest challenges in getting this far.

Chapter 21

SKIPJACK Will Relieve Us!

Monday, December 9, 1985, Day 57, On Patrol, WESTLANT

Ever since the SCRAM, a little over a week ago, things on GATO had stayed on a very positive track. Their guy had kept doing his thing and tape had continued to roll in Sonar. While GATO had continued to suffer from routine aches and pains, she was, once again, "over the hump" in this marathon and it was all downhill to home from here. It was almost as if they had all – both the ship and her crew – passed though *the crucible of Hell, fire & brimstone* and were all *hardened* and *tempered* now. GATO's crew had proven themselves to be "good enough" for her, to be truly "worthy," and she had responded with approval.

Nothing very serious had broken or caused any trouble – even the damned Head Valve had worked fine when they had had to do their mandatory periodic ventilations of the ship. You could run only for so many days on the same air in the boat and then the medical rules required you to change it out with new air from up above. Even the ships with oxygen generators had to do this, so GATO was suffering no disadvantage. The electricians had had to shift over to #2 400 cycle set – the bad bearing on #1 had just gotten too bad to keep running it – but even that *bad boy* had come on-line with very minimal brush sparking. Chief Perrot was beaming from ear to ear. And Chief Barnes was proud of his boys and their little emergency patch job on the Main Air Conditioner. That *bad boy* was also still holding pretty and making plenty of cold water. It would be lots of maintenance when they got home – you could never get underway with a crazy patch job like that in place – but it didn't matter. They were good. No steam leaks. Controllable seawater leaks. Just wonderful.

Yesterday, on Sunday, they had even had an ecumenical Sunday service. Every week at sea the Catholic and Protestant Lay Leaders held services in the Crew's Mess. Chief Barnes was the Catholic Lay Leader and LT Wallace, the Weapons Officer, was the Protestant Lay Leader. With 110 people onboard and with about one third of them on watch at any given time, each service usually drew about 10 guys. Heh, it was a real effort to get out of the bunk and sacrifice sleep . . . On Sunday, with Christmas approaching (and with Sunday also having been a Catholic Holy Day – the Solemnity of the Immaculate Conception) the two Lay Leaders had agreed to go in together. They even had had the Captain come down and say a few words. About 25 men showed up – it had been a wonderful GATO family moment.

At this point in any run the crew would naturally have been counting down the days until their arrival home. GATO, however, had no idea when they were getting home. They knew that their families had been told that they were involved in an extremely important mission and that the ship might not be back until mid-January. So, there was no way to count down. In true GATO style, then, they were counting up the days. Today was day 57 – and everybody knew that they only had the promise of 33 more days of food onboard. No way that they would be out more than 35 or 40 more days. The crew had also taken an inventory of toilet paper, and that supply was holding out pretty well, too. As a lot of old salts would say, you do not want to be onboard a nuclear-powered submarine that has run out of toilet paper at sea . . .

Then the message came in. Once again it shot throughout the ship like a lightning bolt. SKIPJACK is going to relieve us on station, and we are going to be home either on or before our originally planned date!

USS SKIPJACK (SSN 585)

If the ship had not been right on this guy's ass, and if the ship had not been in *serious* patrol quiet mode you would have heard the loudest cheer in the universe. As it was, it was an incredibly lively silent cheer and imaginary jump for joy. Yes, dear, there is a Santa Claus. His name is SPOOK, and he works at Fort Meade, MD for the National Security Agency.

As it turned out, there were two drivers that had gotten them a relief on this job. First, it seemed that the spooks *really, really, really* wanted to get their hands on some of the tape of this guy as soon as possible. Maybe he had some new equipment onboard. Who knows what the interest was 😉 😉, but the spooks wanted the tape

ASAP and there were no convenient messenger buoys out here in the briny deep. The only way that the spooks were getting tape was if GATO was in port. Second, while SKIPJACK had been scheduled to deploy at that time in any event, the job assignments had shifted somewhat, and it had freed up SKIPJACK to continue this mission. Really, it was the spooks who had driven this bus. *Anybody want to kiss a spook for Christmas?*

Chapter 22

Rendezvous

Friday, December 13, 1985, Day 61, On Patrol, WESTLANT

Chief Barnes woke up in his bunk and he knew that the ship's Main Engines were wide open. He could feel it in the hull. *What the hell*, he thought, *what are we doing at FLANK speed?* Ever since they had picked up this guy, they had been very predictable at a relatively low speed. *Had they lost him? Oh, no . . . then he realized that it was Friday the 13th . . .*

When he got out to the Chief's Lounge, between the Berthing Area and their closet sized combo shower/bathroom, to start getting ready for his watch, he found out.

"Hey, Barry, did we lose this guy?" he asked his buddy, the Sonar Chief.

"No, Ike, nothing like that. Our operational control ordered us to break off and head for a rendezvous with another ship – and it is not even a US Navy ship! It turns out that the Father of one of your Nukes had a really bad heart attack and they are sending him off. Guy named Gibbs."

"Wow, he is one of our Reactor Operators. Good kid. Hope his Dad is going to be OK. Christmas is coming, and everything."

"Well, by tonight he will be back in his hometown. Makes you feel good about the Navy, trying, anyway, to be human. He has to leave the ship with nothing on him that gives the name of our ship, and until he gets back on US soil, he won't be allowed to discuss the name of his ship – but that isn't too bad. We'll be back on this guy later today. The P3 airplanes are covering him for us while we are away. They can't roll the same kind of tape that we can, but they carry torpedoes, and they will vector us back into the vicinity. We also have so many rolls of tape on him by now that I can't imagine why anybody would want any more... At this point I think that the objective is just to see where he goes and, of course, to have him in-trail with a ready weapon available at all times. We got the *hot intel* – too bad for SKIPJACK that they will just get a trail job out of it."

An hour later GATO was gently rocking on the surface. Gibbs was topside with a small support team in safety harnesses, and he was being transferred to a small boat for the first leg of his unplanned trip home to see his Dad. All of the Nukes, and many of the forward sailors had offered him their best wishes and had sent him off with their prayers.

Gibbs' father would later claim that the Navy sending his son home to him was one of the key things that helped him to pull through his crisis. Despite the shock of his Dad's heart attack, Gibbs and his family had a very merry, very thankful Christmas, indeed.

To cover the absence of one of GATO's three Reactor Operators, the other two ROs gladly stood Port and Starboard watches for the rest of the trip. This is when each man stands watch for 6 hours on, gets 6 hours off, and then goes back on watch. It was only for a week or so and they didn't mind it at all. Especially since they were doing it to support their shipmate's return home to his ill Father.

As soon as Gibbs was safely off and the topside support team was down below, GATO pulled the plug and got submerged again.

Not long and they were deep and back at FLANK speed. By the time that they had been vectored back and had slowed to hide their return to station, they had been away from their guy for about 14 hours.

No matter, nothing had changed. They took up trail and started to roll tape again. GATO was back on the job.

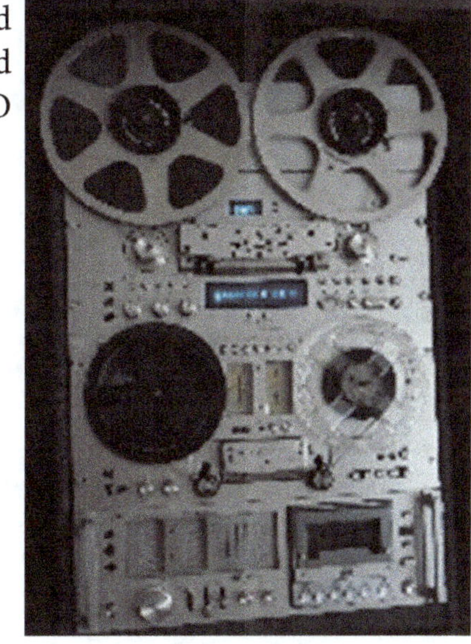

Chapter 23

Now Surface, Surface, Surface!

*Friday, December 20, 1985, Day 68, In
Transit to New London, CT*

It was Friday afternoon watch and GATO was headed home. They would arrive at 9 AM on Saturday morning. Chief Barnes was on watch back aft and was shooting the bull with Martin down in Engineroom Lower Level. The handoff to SKIPJACK had gone well a few days ago, and she had that guy as their own prey now. Sonar had already packed up the huge load of tapes for both of their trail jobs for the spooks. GATO was in transit home!

"So, Martin, name me two major components on this here wonderful ship that were designed and built within commuting distance of your hometown – that your Dad *could* have worked on."

"Chief, my Dad works for Ford at the Cleveland Engine Plant. He didn't work on anything for this ship. Hey, by the way, have you noticed that our 72-day run has turned into a <u>69</u>-day run?"

Martin was being playful, and the Chief was smiling, too.

"OK, you knucklehead, what things in the Reactor plant were made in northeast Ohio?"

"I'll know if you tell me."

"That is what I am trying to do – give you some oolies to take home for Christmas – if you will only cooperate."

Oolies are useless technical details that Nukes tend to accumulate as they read through volume after volume of the technical material about their equipment. Certain oolies were only good to impress other Nukes with. Others were good for the girlfriend set. Barnes was trying to give his guy one of those to take home to the world-famous Cleveland suburb of Parma, OH and to his girlfriend Andrea.

"OK, I give. What Reactor plant stuff was made near Cleveland?"

"Well, my friend, that little cutie Andrea might be impressed to know, before you pull out the ring, that not only were our Steam Generators (nuclear boilers) made in Barberton, OH by Babcock & Wilcox, but our Reactor Control Rod Mechanisms – the things that actually move the Reactor Control Rods – were made by TRW right there in Cleveland. Impressed by that and your other *dragon-slaying* tales of the *Black Cat*, she will certainly be under your spell and unable to resist your charms when you pull out that ring!"

"Man, I hope so . . ."

It must have worked as Chief Barnes had predicted. Maybe it wasn't the oolie, maybe it was just Martin and his own charm, but it worked. Twenty years later, in 2005, their first son, Midshipman William Martin, started at the Naval Academy in Annapolis. Like his Dad, who had retired as a Master Chief Petty Officer, he wanted to sail on SSNs as soon as he graduated. It is, after all, an honorable family business.

When they got off watch they went up forward for dinner. The lights were all on in the berthing areas. The ship had held field day that morning, cleaning everything up to prepare for their return home. All the lights went on and everyone got up for field day, but that did not explain the lights still being on now. The Chief knew, of course. *Channel Fever* was hitting the *Black Cat* <u>hard</u>.

Nobody *ever* slept the day before coming home from deployment. It is physically impossible. Nothing more than cat naps. Too much to think about. In the last 69 days the world had changed in so many ways – both on the ship and ashore. In 1985 – *pre-internet, remember* – the crew had no idea what the world had done over the last couple of months plus. There would be a lot of catching up to do, and a lot of decisions to make . . .

Three men would meet newly born children for the first time tomorrow. Chief Perrot would discover that his new car was still new, and that this girlfriend was a keeper – they would be married within six months. So, of course, would Martin and several other crew members. Hey, they were headed into overhaul next year – it was a great time to get married and start a family. All manner of things had happened in the world, and unfortunately not all of them were good. Two GATO sailors would discover to their horror and despair that their wives had been unable to handle the stress of separation and had taken up with other men. They would both sadly be divorced in a few months.

The Captain would get his fourth gold ring – be promoted – on the back of this phenomenal run. The loss of the first major contact was more than overcome by the intel value of the second one. Plus, while it was not *"officially recognized"* he got *"extra credit"* for having taken a ship that was a poster child for *really* needing an overhaul and having met (and perhaps exceeded) expectations by being able to stay deployed on *"on station"* for the whole run. GATO was something of an Admiral maker – her first Captain had retired as a Vice Admiral. This Captain eventually retired as a Rear Admiral.

When Chief Barnes had reported to GATO a few months earlier he had been honest with the Captain. He had completed his undergraduate degree in marine engineering while he had been assigned to FULTON and was actually a licensed Engineer Officer in the US Merchant Marine before he arrived onboard. He had wanted to complete the undergraduate degree and then go on to be an SSN Officer, but it had taken him too long – he was too old by the time that he had gotten there.

So, as he had told the Captain upon his arrival, he was only on GATO to have a good time. He was obligated to stay in the Navy for 13 months after arrival on GATO and he announced his intentions when he arrived. He was going to get out and go be an engineer in civilian life. He was clear about this so that there would be no surprises later. He had also promised to not make a big deal about his plans onboard and had told the Captain that part of the plan "to really enjoy" his last duty station was to make GATO the *best running* ship in the fleet. On day 68, as well as later the next year when he finally left the Navy, everyone agreed that they were glad that Chief Barnes was having such a good time – GATO was the better for his pleasure.

Barnes would leave GATO and the Navy and end up at Electric Boat, still in the submarine family. Some years later he would be an Engineering Manager at EB, leading the design team for the conceptual design process on what would become the USS VIRGINIA (SSN 774) Class twenty-first century nuclear attack submarine. While Barnes had really loved the LOS ANGELES (SSN 688) class design in 1985, by the time that USS VIRGINIA (SSN 774) was commissioned in 2004 he found himself to be partial to his own design handiwork, and to the handiwork of all of those who he had worked with at EB.

USS VIRGINIA (SSN 774)

That night, Day 68, Barnes made his ritual trek up to the bridge after they had surfaced to enjoy the wonderment, and the crisp clean air. It, of course, stung his lungs a bit – fresh air does that after having been deployed on a submarine for so long. Tonight nobody was sleeping down below, so why bother trying?

It would turn out be Chief Barnes' last trip to the bridge of a nuclear-powered submarine underway at the end of a trip to sea.

While GATO did a number of trips over the next few months before overhaul, including taking part in a major fleet exercise the following February, the Chief never felt like heading up again. This was it. Satisfaction, tinged with a bit of regret.

Chapter 24

Homecoming

Saturday, December 21, 1985, Day 69,
State Pier, New London, CT

The anticipation was building. Normally deployments don't end on a weekend, but this was GATO. It had taken them that long to get home from the classified location where SKIPJACK had relieved them. The navigation team brought the ship through the Slot (between Montauk Point, Long Island and Block Island) and into Long Island Sound early in the morning. Then they headed on past the Race, a tricky little current area by an obstruction known as Race Rock and on into Fisher's Island Sound. GATO knew the way home and tracked true to her course. Soon, Point Alpha was ahead.

As they headed up the river they spotted Electric Boat, another key landmark on the waterfront. EB had been the birthplace, of course, of GATO. As they passed, they could see a huge TRIDENT submarine up on the land level construction facility preparing for launch. Along the waterfront there was another TRIDENT floating at the dock, along with several SSN 688s, also under construction.

GATO's construction period at EB had been a long, long time ago. Her design came straight from the 1950's, before many of her crew had been born. But she was coming home today a winner in the submarine challenge of the Cold War.

It would only be twenty minutes now. As they moved North, with the tugs now tied up and with the Harbor Pilot onboard, they had the broom tied to a mast up on the bridge. GATO had swept the oceans clean for America!

They made the turn and on the pier the crowd *oohed* and *ahhhed*. It was a pretty good-sized crowd – particularly for a Saturday in December. Even a photographer from the New London Day, the local newspaper, was there to greet GATO. She was getting the red-carpet treatment – and rightly so!

As they got smartly and crisply tied up the first sailors off the ship were the three new fathers. The next one was the guy who had won the ship's raffle, held last weekend. It wasn't long before the others started to leave the ship.

The Nukes, of course, still had a Critical Nuclear Reactor on their hands. The shutdown would take about an hour – and was paced by getting hooked up to shore electricity. Chief Perrot was leading his guys in that task – but stopped to steal a hug and a kiss from his soon-to-be-wife.

http://americanhistory.si.edu/subs/ ashore/subfamily/index.html - #

Soon Chief Barnes was up on the pier – and his 4 kids came running toward him.

"Daddy, Daddy, you made it home for Christmas. Mommy told us that you might not make it, but then she said you would. Daddy, Daddy, it is so nice to have you home!"

On State Pier in New London, CT on a brisk December day, officially the last day of fall in 1985, many similar reunions were taking place.

GATO was home.

The Secretary of the Navy takes pleasure in presenting the

MERITORIOUS UNIT COMMENDATION

to

USS GATO (SSN 615)

for service as set forth in the following

CITATION:

For meritorious service from 1 October 1984 to 30 April 1986. The personnel of USS GATO (SSN 615) consistently demonstrated unparalleled success in providing regional presence, intelligence collection, and strategic defense in the Western Atlantic area. USS GATO (SSN 615) . . .

Epilogue

For Generations to Come . . .

Chapter 25

GATO Departure Ceremony

*Friday, April 7, 1995, Pier 32, Naval Submarine
Base New London, Groton, CT*

Ten years on and the peace dividend has claimed Submarine Squadron Ten and the State Pier installation. As the fleet has shrunk with the end of the Cold War and the collapse of the Soviet Union in 1991, the submarine force has consolidated up at the Submarine Base.

GATO, the last of the THRESHER Class to have been commissioned all those years ago and now the last one left, had just come home from her last official mission. Commander Rick Martinez, GATO's final Captain, had just taken her up to the THRESHER gravesite. There, they had surfaced the ship and held a solemn ceremony. They read the names of the 129 men who had been lost that fateful day, had fired a 21-gun salute to the lead ship of their class, and had tossed a wreath into the sea following prayers for those on eternal patrol.

It had been a fitting end to the THRESHER Class, and for GATO.

Now, alongside for her departure ceremony as she prepared to leave for her decommissioning and disposal site, where her nuclear Reactor would be removed and the rest of the ship will be dismantled and recycled, GATO stood proud and looked sharp.

Out of respect for the ship and for the shipmates who had sailed her, many of her former crew members had come to the ceremony. These included a half-dozen from the WESTLANT '85 deployment. Ten years, my how they have flown by.

As Ike Barnes, some of his old buddies and their former Captain gathered on the pier, they were, of course, delighted to see each other. They toured the ship and universally thought two things. First, *she was such a small girl. Very small.* And second, they all looked at GATO's crew and thought to themselves that *it was only just a bunch of kids. Even the Captain was a kid!* Then they remembered themselves ten years earlier and realized that they had all been just a bunch of kids, as well.

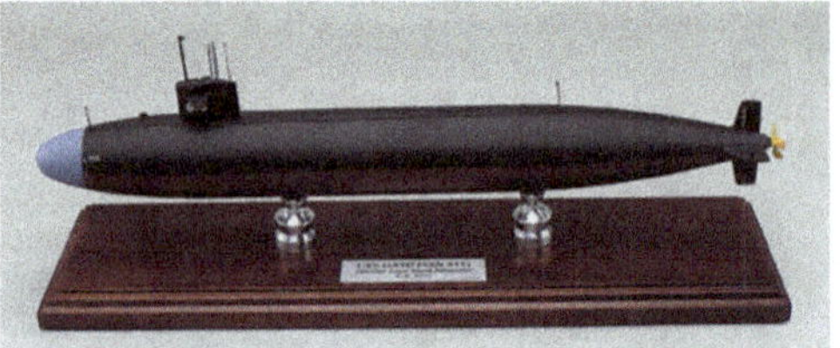

USS GATO
SSN 615
THE GOALKEEPER
DEPARTURE CEREMONY
UNITED STATES SHIP
GATO
(SSN 615)
07 APRIL 1995
NAVAL SUBMARINE BASE
GROTON, CONNECTICUT

Coat of Arms

The scarlet, yellow (gold) and blue of the shield are the colors of the Presidential Unit Citation. The five points in the shield, which simulate sharks teeth, symbolize the five World War II patrols for which the first USS GATO was awarded the Presidential Unit Citation. The yellow wavy area above the blue represents enemy vessels, naval, and civilian, against the red sky of war.

The shark "submerged" beneath the waves, alludes to the name of the ship. GATO is a small species of shark found on the west coast of Mexico. The opened jaws and the arrow, simulating a torpedo, depicts GATO's constant readiness and aggressiveness in the accomplishments of its mission in the world's oceans, symbolized by the blue background.

The Portcullis above the shield, a device to prevent access to or from a castle, is used as a symbol of the pertinacity with which the first USS GATO hunted the north entrance of Bouganville Sound. The unswerving determination with which this was carried out led Admiral Halsey to nickname the ship "THE GOALKEEPER," a sobriquet fittingly used as the ship's motto. The scallop shell, a symbol of pilgrimage, is used in this instance to symbolize "patrol," the 13 stars representing the 13 war patrols made by USS GATO (SS 212) in World War II, and the 13 Battle Stars subsequently awarded.

This Coat of Arms was designed by the U.S. Army Institute of Heraldry.

Chapter 26

Final Farewell

*Wednesday, October 9, 1996, Puget Sound
Naval Shipyard, Bremerton, WA*

Ike Barnes had left Electric Boat after the conceptual design of the VIRGINIA Class had been completed. It had been left to others to complete the detailed design and to actually build the ship. He had moved on to become General Manager at another defense contractor that designed and built naval shipboard controls equipment.

He had promised his customer at Naval Reactors that he would personally visit a jobsite at Puget Sound Naval Shipyard, where an aircraft carrier's entire maintenance period had the upgrade of Barnes' Reactor Control Equipment as the controlling path to completion. In other words, the job needed to go well or the aircraft carrier's departure from the shipyard could be delayed. Nobody wanted to be the controlling path job and delaying an aircraft carrier from leaving a shipyard period was a political football that nobody wanted to own. Barnes was there to ensure that his team had everything that they needed to get the job done on or ahead of schedule, and to make sure that they called him the moment something did not go per plan.

As he was escorted to the jobsite by the onsite Naval Reactors representative in Bremerton, he noticed something out of the corner of his eye. Could it be GATO? He asked. It was. He asked for a moment, and then realized that the submarine that was next in line to enter the dismantling area was the one on which he had earned his submarine qualification dolphins. It nearly overwhelmed him.

The picture of GATO above was taken at Bremerton, just before she entered the dismantling area. When Barnes saw her that day, she was nearly completely dismantled. GATO was stricken from the Naval Vessel Register on November 1, 1996. GATO no longer existed as a naval ship, but she will live on forever in the hearts and minds of those who had been privileged enough to have sailed in her.

Submarine Disassembly & Recycling – Puget Sound

Chapter 27

Homecoming – with a Twist

*Friday, October 24, 1997, Pier 32, Naval
Submarine Base New London, Groton. CT*

It is a family business, there can be no doubt about that. But today, instead of being on the ship, Ike Barnes is on the pier. His son Mike is returning from his first deployment to the North Atlantic in USS PHILADELPHIA (SSN 690). He has been gone for 3 months and now it is Ike's turn to stand on the pier.

PHILADELPHIA, Electric Boat's first 688 Class Ship, is a great looking ship today. And the circle of life continues today. Memories of 1985.

Author's Contextual Note

As discussed earlier in the book, GATO's WESTLANT '85 deployment occurred during the Fall of 1985, as the Cold War peaked and started to head toward a conclusion. In addition, the Cold War itself ended, for good, with the collapse of the Soviet Union in December 1991. Finally, GATO ceased to exist with the completion of its recycling program on November 1, 1996.

Given all of this, and the long passage of time – more than 35 years – since WESTLANT '85, one might conclude that the lessons discussed in this <u>sea story</u> version of that deployment are now simply an interesting story. <u>This conclusion could not be farther from the truth.</u>

In fact, these lessons are as vital today as they ever were. It has been said that the person who studies and learns from history can avoid being doomed to repeat it. So, too, with these lessons.

In the rest of this book, we will discuss two "modern" submarine catastrophes, demonstrating that this is all still quite relevant right now. In the first accident USS SAN FRANCISO (SSN 711) smashed into a sea mountain at maximum speed submerged. Yes, that's right – submarines still fly blind under water at full speed. That the ship was saved, and only one crew member perished, is nothing short of a miracle, and serves as validation of every lesson presented here. In the second catastrophe, USS CONNECTICUT (SSN 22), also grounded at relatively high speed during a Pacific transit. While CONNECTICUT was badly damaged and will be out of service for many months of repairs, fortunately nobody was lost in this tragedy. ***GATO's WESTLANT '85 story, then, is as relevant to the entire US Navy fleet and as timely today as it ever was in 1985.***

So, perhaps we have brought you to the realization that some lessons are eternal. Better, still, if you have come to realize that the Freedom virtually every American takes for granted is the gift of those special few who put on the uniform of our American military and take up a post, stand a watch or take command.

Modern Day

Times Change: the Risk is Eternal

The Greatest Danger to a Submarine Remains the Sea Itself

Chapter 28

Submarines – A Dangerous Business

Saturday, January 8, 2005, 360 miles Southeast of GUAM

As the world had changed, so had the submarine force. With a smaller fleet of attack submarines but still the same oceans to cover, the Navy had moved three SSNs to homeport in Guam, far out in the Pacific. These ships would have significantly reduced transit times to the western pacific region and would help make up for having fewer ships.

USS SAN FRANCISCO (SSN 711) was one of the early LOS ANGELES class submarines and had been one of the three SSNs assigned to Guam. She had just been overhauled and refueled and was ready for the second half of her career in the fleet.

The crew was looking forward to some liberty in Australia, a favorite submarine port since forever. And then tragedy struck. Fortunately she did not sink. Sadly, one man died, Machinist Mate Second Class (Submarines) Joseph A. Ashley, of Akron, OH.

Below are the unclassified messages sent by Rear Admiral Paul F. Sullivan, Commander, Submarine Force, US Pacific Fleet (COMSUBPAC) to inform the other flag Officers of the status as it developed.

"Subject: USS SAN FRANCISCO SITREP - 1500W/8 Jan 05

Fellow Flag Officers,

I wanted to provide an UNCLASS email on the status of the USS SAN FRANCISCO (SSN 711) in order for all of you to be conversant on what we presently know of the apparent grounding incident in WESTPAC:

USS SAN FRANCISCO (SFO) apparently grounded at 080142Z JAN 05, at approximately 360 NM Southeast of Guam, during submerged transit from Guam to Australia. At the time of the incident, the ship was transiting on an easterly track at high speed in a submerged moving haven. The ship sustained damage to equipment and injuries to personnel. The ship is currently on the surface and stable, transiting to Guam making eight knots.

Approximately 60 of the 137 personnel on board are injured. The primary personnel concern is one crew member who is in critical condition with head injuries. Another is in serious condition with head and back injuries. Twenty-two additional personnel are injured to an extent they are unable to stand watch. Most of the injuries consist of broken bones and lacerations. A medical doctor from a support vessel vectored to the SAN FRANCISCO was transferred aboard at approximately 081300W to provide medical attention to the injured crew members. Transfer of additional medical personnel and MEDEVAC of the critically injured crew member via HELO will occur when conditions permit.

CSS 15 held a notification briefing for families four hours after the incident and is providing regular updates and counseling. COMSUBPAC is responding directly to AMCROSS inquiries from concerned family members as they arrive.

The nuclear Reactor plant, propulsion train and electrical distribution systems were unaffected by the incident. The primary material concern is buoyancy. Main Ballast Tanks 1A/1B/2B and the sonar sphere are assessed to be partially flooded and compromised, resulting in a slight port list, increased draft and slight down angle. To maintain adequate buoyancy for normal surface transit, the low-pressure blower is operating continuously on the forward main Ballast Tanks. The ship is holding steady at a zero-degree trim angle with a port two-degree list. There is visible damage topside to the sonar dome.

An emergency procedure was developed by NAVSEA and provided to the ship to allow use of the Diesel as a blower for the forward Ballast Tanks in the event the LP blower fails. Diesel crank web deflections are satisfactory.

USS SAN FRANCISCO will return to port Guam for a damage assessment. Buoyancy assist devices, underwater assessment and welding equipment and technical experts are being sent to Guam for this purpose. The ship is making hourly position and status reports to CTF 74, and COMNAVMARIANAS has been designated as the On-Scene Commander. The focus remains on treating injured personnel and getting the ship to Guam safely. The situation will continue to be very fluid for several more days. Finally, the fantastic support we have received from the entire Joint and Navy Team has truly made a difference in this most difficult of circumstances. For those directly involved, I thank you for this support and assistance. I'll keep you updated as the situation continues to unfold.

Sent: Mon Jan 10 02:17:01 2005

Subject: USS SAN FRANCISCO SITREP - 2100W/9 Jan 05

Fellow Flag Officers this is my second unclas update on the SAN FRANCISCO incident for your situational awareness:

At 10 January 1634 local (100134 EST) the USS SAN FRANCISCO returned safely to Apra Harbor, Guam. The ship moored with her own line handlers in a normal submarine configured mooring (AFT draft is 27'-10" (normal AFT draft is 32') and FWD Draft is above the draft marks with the waterline at the point the towed array faring begins; 0.8 degree STBD list and 1 degree Down bubble indicating by naval architecture calculations that 1 A/B and 2A/B MBTs are most likely flooded). The severely injured Machinist Mate (Engineroom Upper Level Watch at time of grounding) was evacuated immediately and transferred by ambulance to Naval Hospital Guam where a fully staffed medical team was standing by. He is conscious and in stable condition. Approximately fifteen additional injured personnel requiring medical care subsequently departed the ship and were transported to the hospital after taking a moment to meet with family members.

Crewmembers from the USS CORPUS CHRISTI, HOUSTON and FRANK CABLE assisted in line handling and various return to port evolutions such as propulsion plant shutdown, shore power cables, and rig for surface. Standing by on the pier was a full complement of watchstanders from USS CITY OF CORPUS CHRISTI (and SAN FRANCISCO stay-behinds) to satisfy all watchstanding requirements for Reactor plant shutdown with follow-on inport forward and aft watchsections.

Following the grounding on 8 January, the ship transited on the surface at 8 kts with surface escort, USCGC GALVESTON ISLAND to Apra Harbor, Guam. Due to deteriorated weather conditions on the evening of 9 January, the Commanding Officer shifted bridge watchstations to Control and shut bridge access hatches to maximize watertight integrity in light of reserve buoyancy concerns. The ship maintained stability throughout the surface transit with continuous operation of the Low Pressure Blower on the Forward Main Ballast Tanks. SAN FRANCISCO has experienced no Reactor plant, propulsion train or electrical system degradations as a result of the grounding. The Commanding Officer shifted the Officer of the Deck's watch to the bridge on 10 January in preparation for piloting into Apra Harbor.

The critically injured Machinist Mate (Auxiliaryman) passed away yesterday afternoon as a result of his injuries. The MM2 was in Aft Main Seawater Bay at the time of the grounding and his body was thrown forward approximately 20 feet into Propulsion Lube Oil Bay. He suffered a severe blow to his forehead and never regained consciousness.

Emergency medical personnel, including a Naval Hospital Guam surgeon, Undersea Medical Officer and Independent Duty Corpsmen, arrived on the ship via helicopter transfer to provide immediate medical care and prepare the crew member for medical evacuation on the morning of 9 January. Unfortunately, the sailor's condition deteriorated and he died onboard while under the care of the embarked physicians. Just moments prior to the sailors death, I spoke with the Sailor's father in preparation for their pending travel from Ohio to the West Pacific to see their Son. Since then I have passed on to his Dad my condolences on their Son's death and reassured them their Son's remains would be treated with utmost respect and dignity. His father expressed great gratitude for the extraordinary efforts made by the Navy to save his Son's life. He told me his Son loved the Navy, having just reenlisting earlier this year and wanted to make it a career. That when he called home he always talked about the many friendships and the wonderful camaraderie the crew of SFO exhibited. Prior to sailing, he was really excited about the pending ship visit to Australia. The parents are considering traveling to Guam, with Navy support, at some point to meet the crew and partake in a memorial service for his Son.

For the remainder of the transit, the embarked medical trauma team administered medical care to the other injured personnel. Their careful attention and evaluation augments the ship's Independent Duty Corpsman's heroic efforts since the grounding.

Submarine Squadron Fifteen COMMODORE, Captain Brad Gerhke and Captain Paul Bushong, Commanding Officer of the Submarine Tender USS FRANK CABLE have mobilized their assets, staffs, crews and local Navy Community to provide comprehensive support to the SAN FRANCISCO. Professional counselors, medical personnel and Navy Chaplains are scheduled to meet with the entire crew to provide grief counseling and assistance throughout the next several days and as required over the long term. Brad has been meeting frequently with the SFO families and they are doing remarkable well. The entire Navy community in Guam has come to the SFO's families' assistance. I have talked to Kevin Mooney's (SFO Skipper) wife, Ariel. Her state of mind is positive and resolute, with a courageous and upbeat view of the trying days ahead.

The ship's Main Ballast Tank damage and deformation has degraded maneuverability and mandated the use of two tugs to moor in Apra Harbor. A Pearl Harbor Naval Shipyard/NAVSEA Material Assessment Team comprised of a structural engineer, MBT vent expert, air systems expert and naval architect arrived in Guam with special ship salvage and recovery equipment to stabilize the ship pierside as soon as possible. The team, led by Captain Charles Doty, commenced a seaworthiness and repair assessment upon the ship's arrival. Once additional buoyancy measures are in place and tested satisfactory, the Low Pressure Blower will be secured to allow divers to enter the water to conduct an inspection. While this grounding is a tragedy, with a thorough investigation led by Cecil Haney, we will find out all the facts and then ensure we learn from the mistakes. But, I too believe we have much to be thankful for today, and much to be confident in. An operational warship has returned to port on her own power with all but one of its crew after sustaining major hull damage. The survival of the ship after such an incredibly hard grounding (nearly instantaneous deacceleration from Flank Speed to 4 KTS) is a credit to the ship design engineers and our day-to-day engineering and watchstanding practices. The continuous operation of the propulsion plant, electrical systems and navigation demonstrates the reliability of our equipment and the operational readiness of our crews as a whole. The impressive Joint and Navy team effort which resulted in SFO returning to port safely says volumes about the ingenuity and resourcefulness of all our armed services. For all who participated in this effort, thank you and your people. We are all eternally grateful to each of you.

Very Respectfully - Paul Sullivan

USS SAN FRANCISCO (SSN 711) being repaired

Chapter 29

Grounding in the South China Sea

USS CONNECTICUT (SSN 22)
Saturday, October 2, 2021, in transit, South China Sea

USS CONNECTICUT (SSN 22) is in a faster-than-routine transit to Okinawa to allow a personnel transfer off the ship. At 0618Z the ship grounded on an uncharted bathymetric feature in international waters in the South China Sea.

USS CONNECTICUT (SSN 22) entering
San Diego December 15, 2021
with visible damage to the ship's bow

This submerged grounding unfortunately resulted from similar fundamental underlying causes as the SAN FRANCISCO submerged grounding nearly 17 years earlier. Fortunately, CONNECTICUT's crew, likely due, at least in part, to the lower transit speed at the time of the grounding, experienced only minor injuries. While crew leadership and navigation errors were the principal underlying causes, this grounding was also due, in part, to the crew's failure to effectively work around multiple equipment maintenance issues onboard this 23-year-old ship. SHIP MAINTENANCE MATTERS 24/7/265. The unclassified 76-page investigation report is available at: https://s3.documentcloud.org/documents/22035153/connecticut-investigation.pdf.

Finally, and most unfortunately, CONNECTICUT is one of only 2 SEAWOLF Class submarines available for routine operations (the third SEAWOLF Class submarine has been modified for special missions). With this grounding, half of the US Navy's *Apex Predators* (highest performance) submarines will be unavailable for an extended period of time.

DECLASSIFIED   UNCLASSIFIED   Declassified by: U.S. Pacific Fleet, N01SEC
                                                      Declassified on: 20 APR 2022
                            SECRET//NOFORN

                                                      5830
                                                      29 Oct 21

SECRET//NOT RELEASEABLE TO FOREIGN NATIONALS – Unclassified upon
removal of enclosure (1)

From: RDML Christopher J. Cavanaugh, USN
To: Commander, U.S. SEVENTH Fleet

Subj: COMMAND INVESTIGATION OF THE APPARENT STRIKING OF A
        SUBMERGED OBJECT BY USS CONNECTICUT (SSN 22) WHILE
        UNDERWAY IN THE U.S. SEVENTH FLEET AREA OF OPERATIONS ON
        2 OCTOBER 2021

Ref: (a) COMSEVENTHFLT 5800 Ser N013/080J ltr of 5 Oct 21
        (U/CUI)

Encl: (1) Final Investigation Report (S/NF)

1. (U) Reference (a) directed me to complete a command
investigation into the facts and circumstances surrounding the
apparent striking of a submerged object by USS CONNECTICUT
(SSN 22) while underway in the U.S. SEVENTH Fleet area of
operations on 2 October 2021.

2. (U) All reasonably available evidence was collected, and all
directives in reference (a) were satisfied.

3. (U) Enclosure (1) reports my findings of fact, opinions, and
recommendations.

                              J. CAVANAUGH

                            SECRET//NOFORN
DECLASSIFIED   UNCLASSIFIED

*USS SAN FRANCISCO (SSN 711) in
drydock, Guam, January 2005*

The price of Freedom has never been cheap. THRESHER and SCORPION paid with the ultimate sacrifice and SAN FRANCISCO and CONNECTICUT both dodged that bullet by the narrowest of margins, but not without SAN FRANCISCO's own horrible loss. Other nuclear-powered attack submarines, like GATO, have had illustrious careers and/or continue to serve. Always striving for perfection; always imperfect, but always learning from every single mistake. Focused, committed, striving to always be the "best of the best."

Sailor and ship. The challenge of the sea. It is an age-old tail of heroism and heroics, and it continues today. The Silent Service, all true American heroes.

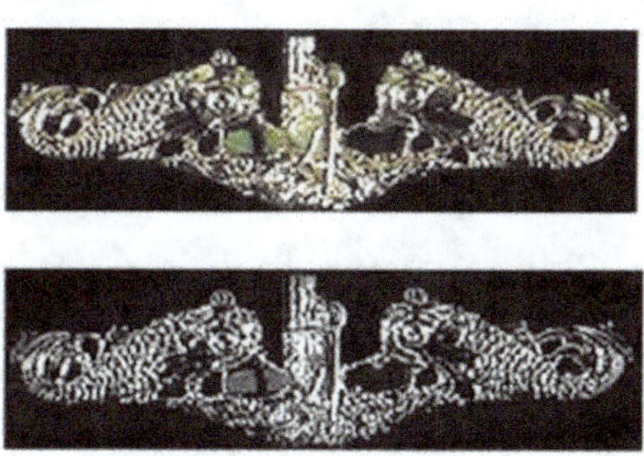

". . . without a Respectable Navy, Alas America!"

CAPT John Paul Jones, October 17, 1776

*"A good Navy is not a provocation to war.
It is the surest guaranty of peace."*

President Theodore Roosevelt, December 2, 1902

*"If we don't have the kind of military capability that we
need in the region to help delivery on a free and open
Indo-Pacific, then the People's Republic of China will
dictate the terms to the other nations in the region,"*

Admiral Philip S. Davidson, USN (Ret), Former
Commander, Indo-Pacific Command and Originator
of "The Davidson Window", June 8, 2022

Fact vs. Fiction; The Fictional Players

FACT: GATO existed in 1985 and had an outstanding Captain and crew. The ship did deploy in the Fall of 1985. As to where the ship went and what it did, <u>we don't talk about actual submarine operations</u>. Remember, we are the *Silent Service*. For all the reader may know, the ship spent the deployment in the Mediterranean Sea – or, perhaps, the Indian Ocean. *Or, GATO could have easily transited the Arctic and operated in the North Pacific.* <u>It's all speculation</u>. Further, while the ship did go through Pre-Overseas Movement Workup and Certification events, these did not include USS AUGUSTA (SSN 710), which was then a brand new ship and was at Electric Boat for her Post Shakedown Availability during GATO's deployment/preparations. Finally, GATO was awarded a Meritorious Unit Commendation, as indicated, for its highly successful missions during the indicated time period. The Mighty Mighty Warship GATO, *<u>Always a HOT Boat</u>*.

FICTION: The Fictional Players are all composite, fictional characters – inspired by real submariners with whom the Author served, but all are fictional nonetheless. **<u>No Fictional Player represents any single real submariner.</u>** The "story" is fiction. The Author has selected the classic, anodyne attack submarine mission of trailing Soviet ballistic missile submarine(s) as mission(s) for this deployment. In addition, the reason that GATO "lost" its first trail "assignment" in this story was to provide a hook to the discussion in Chapter 14.

The reason that AUGUSTA was included in the POM Cert exercise was to highlight that a mighty mighty THRESHER Class warship could, indeed, vanquish a much newer rival. These were exceptionally capable – *while exceptionally challenging* – little ships.

THE FICTIONAL PLAYERS:

CDR Rick Hanson, *USN*, *The Captain*	**MMC(SS) Isaac "Ike" B. Barnes, VI**, *Mechanical Division Chief*	**EMC(SS) Andre Perot**, *Electrical Division Chief*
XO, *The Executive Officer*	**ENG**, *The Engineer Officer*	**COB**, *The Chief of the Boat*
MM1(SS) Anderson, *Departing Crew Member*	**LT Clark**, *USN*, *Main Propulsion Assistant*	**LT Wallace**, *USN*, *Weapons Officer*
STC(SS) Barry Joseph, *Sonar Division Chief*	**SUBLANT Chief of Staff**, *SUBLANT COS*	**Squadron 10 Chief of Staff**, *Squadron 10 COS*
Squadron 10 Commodore, *The Commodore*	**MM3(SU) Martin**, *Engineroom Lower Level Watch*	**MM3(SU) Simpson**, *Engineroom Lower Level Watch*
MSC(SS) Walter Williams, *Chief Cook*	**LT Walsh**, *USN*, *Damage Control Assistant*	**Fleet Duty Officer**, *LT, USN*, *Atlantic Fleet Duty Officer*
Nav, *The Navigation Officer*	**Duty Ops**, *QMC(SS), SUBLANT Duty Operations Officer*	**Chief of the Watch**, *The Chief of the Watch*
Dive, *The Diving Officer*	**TM2(SS) Jones**, *Crew Member in the Bow Compartment*	**Jock**, *CDR, USN*, *SKIPJACK's Captain*
ET2(SS) Winston, Forward Electronics Technician	**ETC(SS) Nelson**, *Reactor Controls Division Chief*	**ET2(SS) Gibbs**, *Reactor Operator*
Andrea, *Future Mrs. Martin*	**MIDN William Martin**, *USNA*, *Future Submarine Captain*	**MM3(SU) Mike Barnes**, *PHILADELPHIA Crew Member*
	Doctor Detroit, *Chief's Quarters Mascot*	

Acknowledgements

1. The author wishes to acknowledge the friendship, review and constructive feedback provided on this project by an exceptional Cold Warrior, whose many battles won range from his time in command of a very successful nuclear powered attack submarine, to his service, at a pivotal moment in time, as the third successor to Admiral Rickover as the Director of the Navy's Nuclear Propulsion Program and on into private industry. As the  author has told him on many occasions, while the author has known and served under several great Commanding Officers – the author really wishes that he could have gone to sea with this Admiral on his *Hot Rod* 688 Class ship when the Admiral was its Commanding Officer. It would have been an absolutely great experience. **Thank you, Admiral Frank L. "Skip" Bowman, USN (Ret), a true American Hero and an example of a great life lived.**

2. The author wishes to acknowledge the contribution and input of the "Marine Engineer's *Engineer*" whose three decades of service in support of the US Navy's operations as a seagoing engineer in the Military Sealift Command, among other things, made possible the operations of America's entire fleet – *except submarines* – through underway replenishment. Without the Combat Logistics Force, for instance, America's 

vaunted nuclear-powered aircraft carriers would be militarily impotent after much less than 69 days of underway combat operations. Aside from the CLF, his service as First Assistant Engineer on USNS RANGE SENTINEL (T-AGM 22) – berthed in Port Canaveral to support ballistic missile submarine launch testing – enabled him to "fill in" some holes in the author's memory about the specific "delights" offered by PCAN back in the mid-1980's. **Thank you, Chief Engineer Jeffrey R. Bartlett, US Merchant Marine, former Regimental Commander at Maine Maritime Academy and a true American Patriot.**

3. The author wishes to acknowledge the friendship and encouragement of one of America's great submarine design engineers, who spent a career in service to the fleet at Electric Boat. Over the years when we worked together at EB, and throughout our long-lasting friendship until this very day, he has responded to the author's occasional _Sea Stories_ by suggesting a book. _Here it is, my friend._ Having perfected his craft during the design of America's  current ballistic missile submarines, the OHIO (SSBN 726) Class, his leadership and efforts in designing the VIRGINIA (SSN 774) Class were an essential element of some of the most radical design improvements debuted in this marvelous ship. Not only is this design much more capable than all predecessors, but his work also made this enhanced capability actually cost less than the "old way" would have cost. _Strength vs. Stiffness_, my friend. _Strength vs. Stiffness._ He is the embodiment of the reality that the heroes _"in the breach"_ at sea require heroes in port, from design concept through sustainment, to make it all possible. He is among the many thousands, at EB and throughout the Navy and the industrial base, who have devoted their careers to this reality. **Thank you, retired Engineering Manager John Alden, Jr., a true American Patriot.**

4. The author wishes to acknowledge the camaraderie, trust, confidence and friendship of all his shipmates, over the years, Officer and Enlisted. While none of you are reflected in this book as specific characters, you have each inspired elements of the characters that I used to tell this "Big story" about our collective experience in winning the Cold War under the sea. Hopefully you'll agree that – collectively – they fairly represent us, in all of our imperfection, as we enjoyed the privilege of service. Together, each and every one of us, along with many others like us, we changed the world for the better – a truly worthy endeavor. **Thank you, my fellow shipmates, you are all true American Heroes.**

In particular, Thank You, CDR Richard Severinghaus, USN (Ret), who I first knew as one of the many who I knew simply as "Eng", but who later had the distinct privilege of serving as the first Commanding Officer of a ship named for his alma mater – USS ANNAPOLIS (SSN 760). *Don't worry, Eng, we will get her ready for on-time underway. . .* **For everything that you have done and continue to do in support of the Naval Submarine League (you are both a great submariner and an excellent editor) you are a true American Hero.**

USS GATO (SSN 615) Crew,
Portsmouth Naval Shipyard, 1986
The real WESTLANT '85, 69 Day Run Heroes

USS GATO (SSN 615) sliding down the ways at launch,
May 14, 1964

*USS GATO (SSN 615), Initial Sea Trials, Atlantic Ocean,
with Admiral Rickover onboard. October 13, 1967*

*USS GATO (SSN 615)
All ahead Flank on the surface*

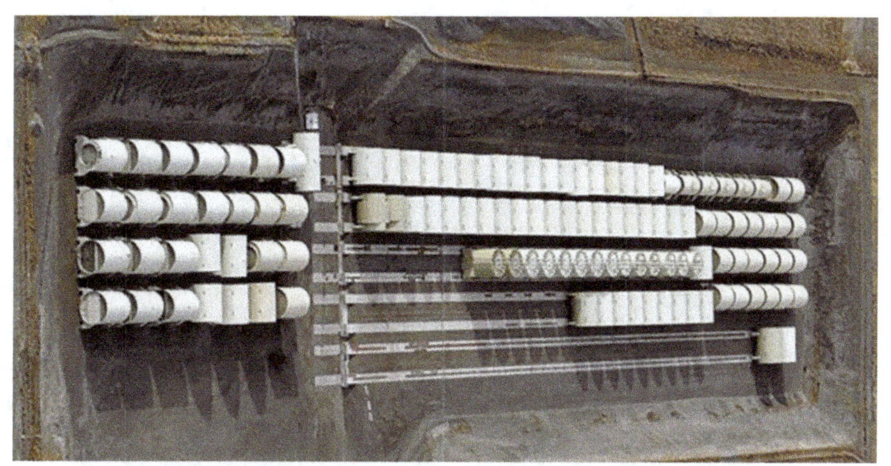

The final resting place for US Navy Submarine Reactor Compartments; Trench 94, Hanford Site, Benton County, WA.